KT-563-870

AUTHOR'S NOTE

ALL the characters in this story are fictitious and bear no relation to anyone living or dead. Although some actual place-names have been used, Filbert Terrace and the house Honeycroft are entirely imaginary. The story is set in South Shields, but the particulars relating to Corporation workers are those of another borough.

Catherine Cookson was born in East Jarrow and the place of her birth provides the background she so vividly creates in many of her novels. Although acclaimed as a regional writer – her novel THE ROUND TOWER won the Winifred Holtby Award for the best regional novel of 1968 – her readership spreads throughout the world. Her work has been translated into twelve languages and Corgi alone has 31,000,000 copies of her novels in print, including those written under the name of Catherine Marchant.

Mrs Cookson was born the illegitimate daughter of a poverty-stricken woman, Kate, whom she believed to be her older sister. Catherine began work in service but eventually moved south to Hastings where she met and married a local grammar school master. At the age of forty she began writing with great success about the lives of the working class people of the North-East with whom she had grown up, including her intriguing autobiography, OUR KATE. Her many bestselling novels have established her as one of the most popular of contemporary women novelists.

Mrs Cookson now lives in Northumberland.

and published by Corgi Books

Rooney

Catherine Cookson

CORGI BOOKS

ROONEY

A CORGI BOOK 0 552 08913 3

Originally published in Great Britain by
Macdonald & Co. (Publishers) Ltd

PRINTING HISTORY
Macdonald edition published 1957
Corgi edition published 1958
Corgi edition reissued 1972
Corgi edition reprinted 1972
Corgi edition reprinted 1974 (twice)
Corgi edition reprinted 1975
Corgi edition reprinted 1976
Corgi edition reprinted 1977
Corgi edition reprinted 1978
Corgi edition reprinted 1979 (twice)
Corgi edition reissued 1980   .
Corgi edition reprinted 1981
Corgi edition reprinted 1984
Corgi edition reprinted 1986

*This book is copyright. No portion of it may be
reproduced by any process without written permission.
All enquiries should be addressed to the publishers.*

Conditions of sale:
1. This book is sold subject to the condition that
it shall not, by way of trade *or otherwise*,
be lent, re-sold, hired out or otherwise
circulated without the publisher's prior consent in
any form of binding or cover other than that in
which it is published *and without a similar condition
including this condition being imposed on the
subsequent purchaser.*
2. This book is sold subject to the Standard Conditions
of Sale of Net Books and may not be re-sold in the U.K.
below the net price fixed by the publishers for the book.

This book is set in 9/9½pt. Baskerville

Corgi Books are published by Transworld Publishers Ltd.,
61-63 Uxbridge Road, Ealing, London W5 5SA,
in Australia by Transworld Publishers (Aust.) Pty. Ltd.,
26 Harley Crescent, Condell Park, NSW 2200, and in New
Zealand by Transworld Publishers (N.Z.) Ltd., Cnr. Moselle
and Waipareira Avenues, Henderson, Auckland.

Made and printed in Great Britain by
Hunt Barnard Printing Ltd., Aylesbury, Bucks.

CONTENTS

1. THE M.P.

Being Friday night The Anchor was busy, Saloon, Bottle and Jug, and Bar. In the M.P.s' corner, away from the piano and the dart-board, sat four men. Let us come into the open here; an M.P. in Shields did not stand for Member of Parliament, but Muck Pusher. In The Anchor, any man who lifted a dustbin, or pushed a broom, went under the pseudonym of an M.P., and the title often followed him up certain back lanes of the town.

Joseph Rooney Smith had been an M.P. for the Corporation for fifteen of his thirty-five years, and as time went on he had been more and more thankful that he was employed by such a body. The Corporation was no jumped-up business that could be affected by supply and demand, by slumps or wars; the Corporation went steadily on, and in Rooney's opinion gave a stamp of security to its employees.

But all of Rooney's fellow-workers were certainly not in agreement on this point, and the terms 'daft', 'dim', and 'loopey' had been attached to him when from time to time, in the face of strong opposition and demands of rights, Rooney had put forth temperate arguments, made up of short sentences such as 'Let's be satisfied, man,' 'Just compare us the day with afore the war,' 'If you get it in one way, man, they'll just take it off you in another.' One answer that was nearly always thrown back at him was, 'If you had a wife and bairns you'd be singing a different tune.'

Rooney happened to be the only unmarried member of his particular gang, and although he was not aware of it, the envy of three of them. Fred Hewitt, Bill Stubbly, and Albert Morton were apt to say, 'You don't know you're born, Rooney.' But Danny Macallistair, their ganger, never said this, for Danny was happily married.

At one time Rooney's pals had added, 'Wait till you get hooked, man.' But it was some years now since they had said that, for they were all agreed on one point concerning Rooney, he was too cute to be caught. With skill and surprising determination in so meek a young fellow they had seen him evade four widows and two spinsters during the past ten years.

But being untrammelled with the cares of matrimony did not mean that Rooney was without his troubles. Escaping the blessed state seemed to complicate his life to such an extent that at times like tonight he was weary of it.

Fred, nudging Bill, winked and said, 'She after your blood again, Rooney?'

Rooney pushed his coarse, fair hair back from his forehead and under his cap, and took a drink from his pint mug before answering, 'She's a proper tartar. I can't get in or out for her, man. All I want is peace and quiet and some place to sit of an evening. And can I get it? Why won't they let me have a house on me own?'

'You're hoping some,' put in Bill. 'And eight of us in three rooms! Don't be daft, man.'

'But I've had me name down for years, Bill.'

'Aye, you might have. So've I, an' hundreds of others. Just thank your stars all you've got to worry about is escaping women. The time to worry is when you can't escape.... Which reminds me, as if I wanted reminding'—Bill finished his beer in one gulp and then his sentence—'she'll be waitin' ... in a hell of a sweat. I'd better be making a move.'

'Where you goin' the night?' asked Fred.

'The usual, the Palace ... her mother's comin' in to see to the bairns. So long....' Bill rose, buttoned up his coat, adjusted his cap, then patted Rooney's shoulder, saying, 'Cheer up, man. Go and get bottled up and give her a hammering. That'll scare her off.'

Rooney smiled but made no comment. And Fred, rising and going to the counter, said, 'Just one more for me, an' then I'm off an' all. What about you, Albert? Comin' yet?'

'No,' said Albert dully, 'not yet.'

Fred did not return to the corner but, drinking up a quick half-pint, waved his hand towards them and followed Bill.

Rooney and Albert sat on, not speaking. Rooney's eyes moved over the room, past the line of men standing at the counter to the group around the dart-board, along the table under the window, and back to Albert again. Albert was in a mess. He was the youngest member of their gang, being only twenty-nine. He had been married a year and his wife was already playing fast and loose with him. Albert would stay on till closing time; he wouldn't go home because there'd be nobody there. And if you asked him where his missus was the night he'd say, as he invariably did, 'At her mother's.'

It was funny, Rooney thought, the things that kept people in the same place. There was Albert sitting here rather than go home and sit alone, whereas all he himself wanted was to go back to his room, have his meal, put his feet up, and have a bit read, all alone.

Whenever possible, Rooney worked his life to a pattern. Each dinner hour he brought his bait to The Anchor, in preference to going to the canteen, and, accompanied by a pint of beer, he ate his dinner. Monday night he called in and had two pints before going to the pictures. During the winter he generally spent the other evenings in his room, with the exception of Saturday night, when after having been to the match in the afternoon he might take a walk up to Horesly Hill and the dogs; afterwards calling in at The Anchor and adding to his usual two pints a double whisky, no more, no less. During the summer he had a leaning towards fishing. This was the pattern of his days when no one interfered. But when a landlady wanted to ... get thick, everything went wrong. If only he could bring himself to go into lodgings until he could come by a house of some sort, life, he knew, would become much simpler. But he couldn't ... because of his bits and pieces.

Rooney's furniture had a meaning for him which he found impossible to translate into thought, much less into words. It was part of his security, as was his job on the Corporation. His furniture was home, some place that belonged to him, no matter what its surrounds might be. The deep meaning that the furniture held for him went back into his past, to his early youth, in fact to the day his mother died. It was from that day of release that furniture began to have a meaning, for when his mother was carried from the house his father began to live again. The perpetual look of worry left his face, his rounded shoulders squared themselves, for no longer would he come home to find his wife sleeping off her drink, or be warned by a sympathetic policeman to collect her from outside some bar or other to save her from being taken into custody yet again.

They had been living in Hebburn at the time, and his father had sold the few remaining pieces of furniture that his mother had been unable to dispose of to supply her drink, and had moved to Shields. And there, in a furnished room, he had started, almost with the eagerness of a lad himself, to gather together a home for them both.

Rooney never looked back to those years spent with his father without pain for the happiness they had held, and in moments of deep loneliness he would ask himself why they had been brought to such an abrupt close. If there had been an illness leading up to it he could, in a way, have accepted it; but there had been nothing. One night, after having been for a walk, his father had sat down in his armchair, put his hand to his waistcoat, given a little gasp, and died.... Heart failure, they said it was. And it left Rooney without a relative in the world. He had nothing, only his job and his furniture.

The furniture had been bought piece by piece over the years until two rooms had been completely furnished, and the buying of each piece had been in the nature of an adventure, among second-hand shops tucked away in side streets, in stables, even in front rooms of houses. From among these troves of conglomeration they had acquired a bed, a fine brass one without a dent or mark on it, and an equally fine feather mattress, a Scotch chest of drawers of good quality, an odd tub-shaped dressing-table with swing mirrors, a drop-leaf table, two kitchen chairs and two armchairs, all of different styles, a Welsh dresser, plus various pictures, linoleum, and mats. He was a man of twenty when his father died, yet he grieved for him as a child would have done. He ached inside for the closeness that was no more. All he had missed in his mother's care his father had made up for. They had been like brothers, pals; they had comforted each other in a wordless way for the nightmare of life they had been forced to endure. And once deprived of this comfort the past had leaped back into Rooney' present. It was as if his mother had died but yesterday instead of seven years previously, and he saw all women as prototypes of her.

'Get yersel' married, man,' Danny Macallistair had said; 'there's nowt like it. There's plenty of lasses around, good lasses. You only have to look. Don't take no notice of them what's always on about their women, it's only talk half the time.' Danny was in his forties then and had been married only three years. The three years had since grown to eighteen, and Danny's attitude had not changed in the slightest.

But what, thought Rooney, was Danny's life to go on compared with all the others: Bill, with his six bairns and his periodical rows, Fred with a real sloven of a wife, and Albert, whose wife lived in dance halls. Even without the memory of his mother to deter him, Rooney's cautious nature would have found sufficient deterrence against marriage in the lives of his workmates. And it wasn't as though he had never been tried by the arch-temptress herself. He had, twice. First, in his great loneliness, and then again at the age of twenty-five. It was the lass who had backed out of the first effort, but in the second it was himself, for he had discovered in time that although the lass had thought quite a lot of him she had thought very little of his job and was determined to force a change once they were married. Rooney did not like change in any form, and the only thing he would have changed then and now in his life was the place that housed his furniture. His idea of heaven was a house with his own key to the front door. He might be called upon to share the back yard, but to have his own front door was the summit of his ambition. But as Bill had said, what chance had he?

'Rooney!'

Stoddard, the bar manager, was beckoning to him, and he rose and went to the counter.

'Hear you're on the hunt again, Rooney?' The manager spoke under his breath and smiled quizzically.

'Yes. That's about it,' said Rooney.

'Do you know Johnny Casson, him over there, near the dartboard, beside old Foley? He's a newcomer here.'

'No,' said Rooney. 'I've seen him about, that's all.'

'Well, as far as I can gather his mother-in-law's letting rooms. I heard him on about her last night.'

'Oh?'

'Will I call him over?'

'Aye, do.'

'Johnny!'

A small, dark man turned and looked towards them. Then handing his dart to the older man he made his way over.

'This is Joe Smith, better known as Rooney,' said the manager.

Rooney and the slight dark man nodded.

'He's lookin' for a room. Can you do anything for him?'

The manager drew a cloth over the counter before moving away to attend to his customers.

'Me name's Casson ... Johnny Casson,' said the little man. 'And aye, I know of a room. Me mother-in-law's startin' to let.

13

In Filbert Terrace.'

At the mention of the street name Rooney's eyes widened just a fraction. He knew every inch of the layout of the town, and Filbert Terrace, although not up to Westoe or the Harton end by a long chalk, was quite a way above the streets in which he usually sojourned. Yet this Johnny Casson looked a very ordinary type of bloke.

'It's a fair biggish house,' said Johnny. 'Seven rooms and an attic. The old girl's got to let, her youngest's gettin' married next month. And if she wants to keep the house on she's got to do something, you see.'

Rooney asked no further information about the room, but very quietly put forth two tentative questions.

'Will she be livin' alone? Is she a widow?'

Johnny's brows contracted a little. 'Aye, she's a widow, but she's not livin' alone. There's old man Howlett, her father-in-law, and Nellie, her niece. They'll still be there when the young one goes.... Why? Do you want a widow on her own?'

Rooney, jerking back his hair, exclaimed, 'No fear! No fear!'

'Oh, it's like that, is it?' Johnny's eyes twinkled. 'Well, you need have no fear of owt like that. She's had seven bairns, five lasses and two lads. The lads were killed in the war, and the last of the lasses, as I said, is gettin' married. The old girl's over sixty, although you wouldn't think it; she's still quick on her pins.'

'It's an unfurnished room I'm wanting.'

'Well, you could have that, I think. Doreen, that's the one what's gettin' married, she has her things stored in one and she's taking them next week. She's got part of a house up Westoe end.'

'It sounds all right,' said Rooney. 'But there's one thing. You know I'm on the Corporation ... collecting?'

'Oh, that. Well, beggars can't be choosers. I work in the docks meself. But between you and me the old girl fancies herself; she would like to be something. And so would the rest of her tribe. My Betty's about the only one who doesn't think she's the cat's pyjamas. And I can tell you she's gone through it because she married me. Old Ma Howlett wanted them all to have white-collar types. I can tell you I was a come-down.... Have a pint?'

'No. Thanks all the same,' said Rooney. 'I've got a pal over there.' He nodded towards Albert. 'When could I go and see Mrs. ... your mother-in-law?'

'Ma? Well, I suppose I should warn her first. I'm on me way round there now. Friday-night schedule ... all the gang of them except the eldest one, Queenie, call in on a Friday night.' Johnny paused and rubbed his hand over his mouth as if wiping froth away, then, with the twinkle in his eye deepening, he added, 'Take you round now, if you like.'

Rooney looked down at himself. He wasn't in his working clothes, but he wasn't wearing his good suit, just the odd coat and trousers he wore of an evening. But commenting to himself that if he went to live with these people they'd certainly see him worse than this, he said, 'All right. I'll just tell me pal.'

Going back to Albert, he said, 'I've got the chance of a room, I think, Albert.'

'Where?' asked Albert without much interest.

'Filbert Terrace.'

'Filbert Terrace? Goin' up, aren't you? They won't have your bits and pieces there, man.'

'Well, I can only go and see. So long.'

'So long,' said Albert.

Rooney joined Johnny at the door, and they walked out into the dimly-lit street and into the late November drizzle. Coming to the crossing at Laygate, they made their way to the Chichester, up Meldon Terrace towards the Infirmary, then turned off and walked through a number of short streets until they came to Filbert Terrace. And here even the darkness could not hide the difference of this terrace from its immediate neighbours, for jutting from the foot of each tall house was an iron railing encircling a square of ground inside of which could be sensed rather than seen patches of green, broken in some places by crazy paving, and even bird baths.

It was with definite trepidation that Rooney stood behind Johnny as he rang the bell; and had not Johnny's very ordinariness kept itself apparent in his chattering, Rooney would surely have beaten a stealthy retreat.

'This'll startle her for a start,' said Johnny over his shoulder. 'I usually come the back way.'

As Johnny rang the bell again, the front door was suddenly pulled open to reveal in the dim light from the hall the large bulky figure of a woman.

'Hallo, Ma. I've brought a fellow, a Mr. Smith. He's lookin'' for an unfurnished room. Come on in.' Johnny rattled on as he crossed the threshold. And Rooney, after a moment's pause, followed him, passing the woman with his head slightly bent.

As the door closed behind him he pulled off his cap.

The woman had not spoken, but she switched on another light, and Rooney, raising his eyes to her and on the point of bidding her the time of day, found his words hanging stupidly on his lips. His eyes became fixed on her head; he could not tear them from it, for it subdued into drabness every colour in its vicinity. Her hair was like a miniature busby, and its colour was that of a freshly scraped carrot. And to Rooney's startled eyes it looked almost afire.

Seemingly not at all unpleased by his scrutiny, Ma returned Rooney's gaze, but her eyes did not stay on his hair, they wandered over him, taking in his thick but well-set-up figure, his fresh complexion, and square blunt face. She smiled.

'Good evening,' she said formally.

'Evening,' said Rooney.

'Well.' She paused as if uncertain of her next move, then added, 'You'd better come in and sit down a minute. You see, my daughter's got her stuff in the room. She's getting married soon, and she's taking it next——'

'I've told him,' put in Johnny, moving towards the second door along the hallway. 'Come on——' He beckoned to Rooney and led the way into the room.

Anything but happy, Rooney went to follow him; then paused to let Ma precede him, which she did with a jauntiness that put him in mind of a young lass and made her appear slightly ludicrous.

The room into which he stepped seemed to him to be packed with people, and Ma, sweeping a plump, jumper-encased arm around it, said, 'This is my family.'

Rooney nodded once to include the three women and two men.

The men with different motions of the head returned the nod, as did one of the women, but the other two fixed on him expressionless stares that immediately put him, as he thought, on hot bricks.

'Sit down.' It was Johnny who pushed a chair towards him. Johnny seemed to be enjoying himself. 'This is me wife, Betty,' he said.

Rooney inclined his head to the young woman who had favoured him with a nod. He had somehow guessed that this one would be Johnny's wife. She wasn't got up so much as the other two—in fact she looked none too spruce, and it surprised him that she was a relation of the others at all.

'Mr. Smith has come to see the room,' said Ma. 'I'll just go up and see if I can get in.' Ma turned her eyes on Rooney again. 'My daughter's got her stuff in there, and——'

'I told you,' put in Johnny with irritating emphasis, 'I explained it to him.... He knows.'

Ma cast a look at her son-in-law that should have silenced him, or at least put him in his place. But what Johnny's place was, Rooney was finding it difficult to understand. If he had been in Johnny's shoes he would have been sitting with his mouth shut, among this lot.

Ma left the room, and Johnny, seating himself next to his wife, asked a question of her in two words, 'All right?'

'All right.' She smiled at him. Then, leaning forward to see past her husband, she looked at Rooney and remarked, 'It's been a nasty day.'

'Yes, it has,' said Rooney.

'Do you work inside?'

'No ... out,' said Rooney. 'I work on the Corporation.'

'Oh.'

Uneasily now, Rooney realized that he had the entire company's attention. But it was a polite attention. Working on the Corporation could mean anything from Parks and Gardens to ... dustbins.

Rooney swallowed. 'I'm on collectin' ... ashbin-man.'

'And likes it,' put in Johnny, thrusting out his lips and wagging his head. 'What do you think of that? Wouldn't change, would you?' Johnny was going on the conversation they had had on the way here, and although it was perfectly true that he wouldn't change his job, hearing it from Johnny made it sound something of a disgraceful admission.

One of the two men sitting by the fire, after looking at Rooney under lowered brows, slowly got to his feet. He was a tall man, thin, with a querulous expression and fast-growing baldness, and, as he made his way somewhat casually towards the door, Johnny looked at him and remarked quietly, 'If she doesn't let that room, Dennis, it'll be ten bob a week off each of us as soon as Doreen goes.'

'Really! You get worse. You're ... you're past bearing.'

The woman who had got sharply to her feet Rooney surmised to be the tall man's wife. She was glaring now across the

17

room at Johnny. But Johnny was in no way intimidated.

'It's true,' he said, 'isn't it?'

'Of course it is,' said Betty, his wife, 'and come off it, our Pauline. If Mr. Smith's going to live here he'll soon know how things stand. What d'you say, May? And you, Jimmy?' she appealed to the other couple.

The woman addressed as May made no comment, although her face showed displeasure, but Jimmy, her husband, in a deep bass voice, which was in sharp contrast to his delicate-looking face and slight figure, said, 'True. True. But there are ways of approaching these things, Betty. And Johnny always favours the bull-at-the-gap tactics. He delights in it. Makes you feel good, doesn't it, Johnny? Getting one over, sort of.'

'Would you come up now?'

All eyes were turned towards the door where Ma was standing, but Rooney did not rise immediately; he looked towards the bald man, giving him a chance to have his say. But when Dennis turned and sat down again Rooney got to his feet and left the room on the heels of Ma. And as he did so he determined definitely that this was no place for him. He would look at the room, and no matter what it was like he would say he would let her know, and that would be the end of it.

The stairs led up from the right of the hallway on to a large landing with a number of doors leading off, all brown-painted.

Ma walked briskly across the landing towards one of the doors.

'This is the room. It's a front room, and lovely in the mornings when the sun's on,' she said.

Rooney did not point out that that was the least of the attractions he looked for, as he wouldn't be in in the mornings.

The room was packed with a dining and bedroom suite and various oddments, but he could see it was a big room and had a fine fireplace.

'It's nice,' he said.

'Yes, it's a lovely room,' said Ma. 'And cheap.'

'Yes?'

'Seventeen and six a week.' Ma looked straight at him.

Rooney remained silent. He was only paying twelve and six where he was, but of course this was a much better room. Yet likely the rent of the whole house wasn't much more than what she was asking him.

'You'd want me to cook for you?'

'Er ... aye ... yes.'

'Well, I'll do that for ... shall we say seventeen and six? That would make thirty-five shillings a week. It's very cheap when you think...'

Ma did not go on to say what she thought, but she stared at Rooney with her round, doll-like, pale-blue eyes. Then, adjusting her skirt and smoothing down her jumper over her swelling breasts to fill in the pause that Rooney was creating, she added, 'I'm sure I'll do all in my power to see you are comfortable. Are you a widower, Mr. Smith?'

'No,' said Rooney. 'I've never been married.'

'And you've got your own furniture?' She gave a high-pitched laugh. 'Well, it's about time you were. When Doreen gets married in a fortnight's time she'll be the last of mine; I'll be lost for something to do. Well there it is, Mr. Smith. I'm sure you'd be comfortable.'

'Yes. Yes, I feel I would, but I think I'd better tell you I'm on the Corporation ... collectin' ... the bins.'

'Oh.' Ma's mouth, wide in a fixed smile, slid to a straight line and remained there for a second before stretching again. 'Well now, are your clothes very dirty? That wouldn't include your washing, not the thirty-five shillings.'

'No. My clothes aren't very bad at all. I change my top things at the depot. And I understand about the washing.'

She moved out on to the landing, and he gave one last look at the room. He could see all his bits here and himself sitting afore the fire of a night-time.... But that lot down there—he couldn't put up with them no more'n they could put up with him.

'There's the bathroom.' Ma pointed to the door opposite. 'You could have a bath when you wanted one. And that's something ... the fire's always on in the winter. It's a back boiler.'

'Thank you. Yes, that would be something.' And it would, too, he thought, to have a bath in a house without having to go to the public baths to get clean.

At the foot of the stairs he paused. He didn't want to go back into that room; but he had left his cap there, so he could do nothing but follow Ma again. Immediately, he noticed that the miserable-looking fellow and his wife had gone. But another woman had come into the room. She must have made her entry from the kitchen doorway almost at the same time as Ma and he had come in from the hall, for she was still holding on to the door handle when Ma said, 'Oh! It's you, Nellie. You're late, aren't you?'

The girl turned. At least Rooney thought she was a girl because of her height and the slightness of her figure, until he saw her face, and then he realized that she was a woman. But of what age he found difficult to place ... she could be anything from thirty to fifty.

'This is Nellie, my cousin,' said Ma.

Nellie inclined her head. And Rooney murmured, 'Good evening,' and found his gaze remaining on her as it had done on Ma. But it wasn't her hair that drew him, but her eyes, large, brown eyes in a small, dead-white face. He had never seen such large eyes in a woman, nor, he thought, such a tired face. He listened to the others greeting her.

'Hallo, Nellie,' said Betty. 'Tired?'

'Yes,' answered Nellie.

'That's put paid to my jumper then,' said May.

Nellie shook her head slowly. 'No, it hasn't. I'll finish it over the week-end.'

'Now, our May!' Ma's voice startled Rooney, for it suddenly matched her proportions, becoming large and forceful. 'You know she's got all Doreen's things to finish, and there's only a fortnight, so your jumper'll have to wait.'

'Most things have, for our Doreen,' said May under her breath. 'She's going to feel a draught when she's married.'

'They'll all be done in time.' Nellie had taken off her raincoat, and even to Rooney's uncritical eye she looked drab.

The same thought must have been prominent in the delicate-looking fellow's mind, for he said, 'It's about time you did a bit of sewing for yourself, isn't it, Nellie?'

'Well, are you takin' it?' Johnny's voice cut off Jimmy's, as he addressed Rooney. And Rooney, holding his cap once again in his hands and facing the battery of eyes, could only say, 'Yes. Yes, I'll be pleased to.'

2. MA

Rooney moved on a Saturday afternoon. Sep Tindall did the job, as always; and as he rolled up the lino at one side of the room he laughingly remarked to Rooney at the other, 'I know this little lot as well as me own bits. This is the ninth time I've moved you, isn't it?'

Rooney made no reply; all he wanted was to get the lino into the van and look on Mrs. Kate Sparks for the last time. That he was bound to look on her for just once more he knew only too well; she had planted herself in the passage, and she meant to . . . let him have it. He was well acquainted with the signs. She had cried several times during the past week in an effort to get him to stay. She had even said he had encouraged her to think she meant something. . . . My God! Women were awful. He sweated at the memory of last night, and he blushed for Kate's brazenness, for Mrs. Sparks had made it plain that he would be welcome to the fruits of matrimony even without a ring.

He had confided the whole business to Danny this morning. He could talk to Danny about these things whereas, as much as he liked his other mates, he could tell them nothing personal.

Danny had said some women were made like that and when they reached a certain age, round about the middle forties, they went man mad. Danny thought it was a good job he was moving to this new place, for if the woman had had a big family all the interest she would likely show in him would be of a motherly turn.

Rooney had pointed out to Danny that that was how most of them started, every woman he met seemed to think he wanted mothering. But Danny had insisted that by the sound of things this one was the safest bet yet. And on this point Rooney had agreed with him. Danny had ended their talk as always, 'You look out for a lass, Rooney. Why, man, you're wasting your life, and that of some good woman. Any young lass would jump at you . . . a fine-set-up fellow like you.'

It was all right for Danny to talk like that, Rooney thought, but where did he go looking for a lass? He couldn't dance, not a step, nor could he start from scratch and chat to a strange girl, like some of them did. The only women he could have spoken to were the ones that frequented the snugs and Bottle and Jugs, and he had sworn a solemn oath that never would he pick up with any woman he saw in a bar; he would rather remain alone to the end of his days than risk his father's life over again. It was about the only point on which he thought vehemently. As for being a well-set-up chap, he had no ideas about himself. He had a good strong body, admitted, but his face, he considered, was as plain as a dustbin.

When they moved into the passage it was to find Mrs. Sparks's matronly figure filling it.

Sep Tindall stood with the lino on his shoulder, and Rooney, standing at his side, murmured, 'Well, I'll be going, Mrs. Sparks.'

'You think you're doin' well for yourself, don't you,' said Mrs. Sparks. 'Filbert Terrace! Oh, I know where you're going.' She closed her eyes before resuming. 'And she won't do for you what I did, waitin' on you hand and foot.... Well'— her head was wagging now—'if you can afford to pay for Filbert Terrace you can pay me what you owe me.'

Rooney's eyes and mouth stretched, and it was a moment or two before he brought out, 'Why! I settled with you last night.'

'Yes, you did ... up to last night, Friday. This is Saturday, a new week, and I want a week's money in lee of notice.'

'But I gave you notice a week last night.' Rooney was looking completely mystified.

'Yes, I know fine well you did, aren't I telling you? And that week was up last night,' emphasized Mrs. Sparks. 'You've broken into another week, and I'm entitled to a week's money.'

Rooney cast a swift glance at Sep. And Sep, hitching the lino more firmly on to his shoulder, said very pointedly, 'I'd see her in hell first.'

'Would you?' cried Kate. 'Well, I'll take that lino with me, cos if he doesn't stump up I'm keeping that. And just you try to get it out.'

The two men looked at each other. Then Rooney, putting his hand in his pocket, drew out a handful of silver, and picking out five half-crowns he handed them to her.

'Thanks for nowt,' said Kate. Then very reluctantly standing aside she hissed one parting shot at Rooney, 'You big noodle, you!'

Safely in the van sitting next to Sep, Rooney wiped the

sweat from his face.

'You're well rid of that 'un,' said Sep. 'She's as bad as you've had 'em.'

He started the engine and as the van rumbled down the street he sent an amused, sidelong glance at Rooney and enquired, 'What's it about you, mate, that gets 'em?'

'Aw, shut up, man!' said Rooney with unusual tartness. 'I don't feel like chaff at this minute.'

'I wasn't chaffing, man, but all the old wives seem to make a set at you.'

'You've said it,' said Rooney. 'Old wives.'

'Well, not so old either. What was she ... forty-five or so? What's that these days? What's the one like where you're goin'?'

'Past it, I hope,' said Rooney. 'Seven of a family and six grandbairns. She's near sixty and her hair's dyed red.'

'Oh, my God!' Sep gave vent to a gale of laughter. 'A rejuvenated job! It might be the frying-pan into the fire....
You watch yersel'.'

'Oh, for the Lord's sake, man!'

'All right. All right.' Still laughing heartily, Sep swung the van in and out of the traffic; then through the quieter streets until he stopped at 71 Filbert Terrace. And there, jumping out and running to the back of the van, he had the lino on his shoulder almost before Rooney had time to ring the doorbell.

Rooney had not been near the house since his first visit, and in the daylight it seemed to have lost some of its pomp. The outside needed paint badly and the curtained windows weren't as spruce as many in the lower quarters of the town. But it still had the power to subdue him, for was it not a large terrace house with its own front garden and electric bell on the door, and the letter-box and number in brass?

Mrs. Howlett herself opened the door. She was wearing a green woollen dress, and from the lobes of her eyes dangled red ear-rings, the shade of which was at definite variance with the colour of her hair. Her lips were rouged and the powder was thick on her nose, making it stand out from her face. But her get-up did not disturb Rooney. If anything, it took away any dread Sep's merriment had aroused, for in the naked light of day Ma looked what she was, a fat old woman, done up.

'Well, here I am, Mrs. Howlett.'

'And welcome, Mr. Smith, I'm sure. Come in.'

'Do you mind calling me Rooney?' he said shyly as he

moved into the hall. 'Everybody does.'

Ma laughed. 'Rooney? It's an odd name, but all right, we'll call you Rooney. And I hope you're here for a long stay, Rooney. Well, you know where to go. Just lead the way now and show the man.'

Quite suddenly at his ease, Rooney went up the stairs. The door of the room was open, and he stood for a moment in pleased surprise. Being empty, it looked even larger than he had imagined it to be, and although all the paint-work was brown it appeared unusually light after the dullness of the stairs and landing. It struck him momentarily that everything in the house was brown.

Sep dumped down the lino, and together they laid it. But to Rooney's disappointment it did not cover one half of the floor.

Next followed the dresser; then the bed and mattress. And when they went down the stairs for the third time a young girl standing at the foot stared up at them. She could have been termed pretty had her face not been marred at the moment with temper.

'This is my youngest, Doreen,' said Ma, moving forward and taking a firm hold on her daughter's arm. 'Doreen, this is Mr. Smith. We are to call him Rooney.'

'How do you do?' Rooney, feeling almost gay, smiled widely. But his smile disappeared and his gaiety vanished when the girl, pulling herself from her mother's hold, flounced round and dashed into the living-room without even a nod.

'Tut! Tut!' Ma clicked her tongue.... 'Young and silly. She's in a bit of a stew today. She doesn't think she'll have her things ready for the wedding.'

Rooney could not really see the connection, and he felt dampened, but as he returned with a chair from the van Doreen's attitude was made perfectly clear to him, for her voice came in angry tones from behind the closed door, saying, 'Old rubbish! That awful bed. And the whole street watching. And my wedding so near. Doris Taylor and all the lot of them'll be laughing up their sleeves. If you had to let, why take him?'

'Be quiet! Else I'll ring your ear for you. Mind, I'm telling you.' Ma's voice was muted.

'I won't. A binman! What will Harold's mother say? You've bragged enough to——'

The voice was abruptly cut off, and Rooney continued his way slowly up the stairs. His spirits now at low ebb, he went into the room and put the chair down.

Old rubbish. He looked about him. His furniture might be all odd, but it wasn't rubbish, it was good substantial stuff. He felt hurt and experienced a rising feeling of ... not anger, that would have been too strong a term, but of annoyance. They all acted here as if they were ... the last word. And although he knew they were a cut above the usual people he lodged with they were still not the last word.

In his daily travels from door to door he had in his own way docketed the classes and, to his mind, they were many and various. There were those who were nothing and didn't care who knew it, and there were those who were nothing and tried to pull the wool over your eyes; then there were those who were something and went to a devil of a lot of trouble to make you recognize it; and then again there were those who were something and pretended they weren't and tried to be all pals together and made everybody uncomfortable; then there was a section you couldn't pinpoint, who dressed like one set and talked like another. Like old Mrs. Bailey-Crawford, or old Mrs. Double-Barrelled as they called her. She lived alone in a big ramshackle house in Westoe Village, and she ordered you about like a duchess, even though she looked like a tramp. There were all types, and Rooney was for giving them all their due, and the occupants of this house in particular. But to talk the way that 'un had done was to his mind getting too much above herself.

'Can I help you to fix anything?'

He turned to the doorway and there stood the little thing with the big eyes.

'Thanks. I'm managing all right.'

'What about your curtains? Will they fit?'

She looked to where his curtains, rolled into a bundle, were lying on the bed. 'These are long windows, six foot six.'

Rooney glanced at the two windows. 'Aye ... yes ... well, I hadn't thought. They're not that long. A foot out, likely.'

'Have they got a hem?' She walked to the bed and turned up the edges of the curtains; and after a cursory examination said, 'They'll let down top and bottom. I'll be able to fix them.'

She lifted the bundle up and, ignoring Rooney's protest, she went out saying, 'Grace says there's a cup of tea as soon as you're ready....'

'Thanks.' He stood in the middle of the room looking after her. She sounded off-hand, rather curt, but that might just be

25

her voice. It was husky as if she had a cold. But anyway, she was being helpful. He hadn't thought about the length of the curtains. Grace, he supposed, must be Ma's name.

Sep came in with the other chair, saying, 'If you'll give me a hand with the dressing-table and the chest I'll dump your case and the boxes in the hall, and then perhaps you'll manage. I've got another little job I'm going to and I want to finish afore dark.'

'All right,' said Rooney.

When the dressing-table and the Scotch chest had been installed, Sep looked about the room with approval.

'Your things look better here than they've done anywhere. You should be comfortable. And'—he leaned forward, pointing his thumb floorwards—'I don't think you need fear owt from old red-for-danger. My! there's hair, and your mother bald. Well, never say die. Huh! That's a good 'un, eh?' He nudged Rooney. 'Never say die.'

'Be quiet, man,' said Rooney.

'Okay, okay. That'll be fifteen bob. All right?'

'All right,' said Rooney, once more putting his hand into his pocket.

As the van rumbled away Rooney closed the front door. But during this short operation he noticed a definite movement of the curtains in the house opposite. It was as the lass had said, they were all on the watch. In Cartham Street, from where he had moved, they would have been at their doors and the kids swarming over the van, but there hadn't been a sign of a bairn in the street here and not a soul at a door, yet they were on the lookout all right. People were people the world over.

The last box up in the room, Rooney sat down on it and looked about him. It was as Sep had said: his bits looked good here. When the curtains were drawn and the fire on ... by lad! He smiled to himself. He'd be comfortable.

His spirits were rising again. What did it matter what the lass had said? She'd be gone soon. The old woman was all right, and the little one ... Nellie. Well, somehow he couldn't quite make her out. She was so quiet, like a mouse. Not shy as he knew shyness, but sort of closed up.

His china arranged on the dresser, his bed made and covered with a bright artificial silk bedspread, his clothes packed away in the drawers, the chairs one each side of the fireplace and his folding table placed under the window, he gave the room a last glance of appraisal before going downstairs and knocking at the living-room door.

'Come in. Come in.'

Diffidently he entered the room, and was relieved to find only Ma and the little one there.

'Don't knock,' said Ma. 'You must make yourself at home. Come and sit down and have a cup of tea. We don't have our meal till six. I hope that suits you. And will you be taking your meals with us, or do you insist on them in your room?'

He would have liked to say, 'In me room, please,' but the word insist put him off. So he said, 'Whatever suits you best. And six o'clock'll do me fine. I've got a little joint and things for the morrow, but after this I'd be obliged if you'd get my stuff in for me.'

'I'll do that,' said Ma, 'and it's arranged then that we'll all eat together. I won't say it won't be a big help, there's so much to do in a house this size. So you like your room now you've got your things in?'

'Very much, thanks.'

'Your curtains are nearly finished,' said Ma.

He looked to where the little one was sitting at a hand-sewing machine rapidly turning the handle. She didn't look up, not even when Ma placed a cup of tea on the corner of the table for her, but went steadily on, one hand pressing and easing the material under the needle like an automatic machine itself.

As he drank his tea Rooney glanced around the room, and the same impression struck him here as in the rest of the house … everything was brown. Brown-leather couch against the wall opposite the fireplace, brown table and chairs, brown sideboard, brown-painted woodwork, even a brown carpet, which, like the furniture, appeared very much the worse for wear. The room had a miserable look to him. Perhaps it was the fire; there was so very little in the grate. But then it was a close day. Looking at the fire reminded him to broach the subject of heating.

'Is there any place I could keep a bit of coal?' he asked.

'Well, yes, there's a shed in the yard. Doreen's bicycle's in it, but that'll be going soon.'

'Thanks!' he said.

The machine stopped whirring and Ma asked, 'Have you finished?'

'Yes,' said Nellie briefly, folding up the curtains.

Rooney looked at her in amazement. She had unpicked and

done those four curtains in much less than an hour.

'My! You've been quick,' he said.

Nellie made no reply, but in a tone that somehow robbed the words of praise Ma said, 'She does all our sewing.'

'Is it your job?' Rooney spoke to Nellie, but Ma again answered for her.

'No, she manages a drapery shop ... Bamford and Brummell's, off Green Street, you know.'

Bamford and Brummell's. Yes, he knew Bamford and Brummell's. And its name was the biggest thing about it—it was a little one-window place that sold mainly haberdashery; it was a cheap, poor sort of a shop, thirty years behind the times. As for a manageress, well, he couldn't see the place holding more than two assistants, if two would really be necessary. And as for custom, people had money these days and, he imagined, most of them went to Green Street proper, or down to King Street.

The sudden sound of a door opening in the hall caused Ma's relaxed body to stiffen in her chair and the smile to leave her face, and turning to Nellie she murmured, 'If he comes in here take him back.'

Perplexed, Rooney watched the little one squeeze out from between the chair and the table and make for the door. But before she reached it, it was pushed open and an old man shambled a step into the room. He looked a good age, about eighty, Rooney thought, and the most striking thing about him was the shaggy growth of white whiskers which sprouted from his face at all angles. He was small and slightly bent, but his eyes were bright and alert, and they fixed on Rooney with an almost tangible hold.

'What's goin' on here?' His voice was a thin squeak.

'Come on.' Nellie went towards him and took hold of his arm.

'Leave be, Nellie. Something's goin' on here. Who's he?'

Ma rose, and going to her father-in-law, cupped her mouth with her hands and yelled in his ear, 'Mr. Smith. He's come to stay.'

'What? Why can't you speak up? Who is he?'

Ignoring the old man, Ma turned to Nellie. And she, taking a pencil and a little pad from her overall pocket, wrote one word on it, then stubbing the paper twice with her pencil in a precise, definite movement she handed it to him.

Pushing his head back into his shoulders and holding the

pad at arm's length away from him, the old man read out the word 'Lodger'.

Rooney gave a conciliatory smile as the fierce old eyes came on him again. 'Don't want no lodgers. Whose house is this, anyway? It's my house.'

'Oh!' Indignation was now being expressed from every curve of Ma's body. She was rearing as she cried, 'Go on to your room!'

'What?'

She pointed.

'Don't order me about. I'm nigh frozen in there. What I want to know is, about this chap.' He pointed a quivering finger at Rooney.

Ma turned her back on the old man and in an aside to Rooney she whispered, 'I'm sorry. Don't take no notice.'

Rooney, not yet used to the technique, looked at Ma and answered reassuringly, 'That's all right.'

'Talkin'. I can hear you. Go on!' Grandpa glared at Ma's bulging back muscles, and on this she turned and yelled at him, miming as she did so by thrusting her finger into her ear, 'Well, where's your ear thing? Where is it if you want to hear?'

'That!' Grandpa's chin was thrust up aggressively at her. 'It's like you, no damned good. I can hear better without it.'

Nellie again took his arm, firmly this time. And his manner undergoing an immediate change, he said with almost childish pleading, 'No, Nellie, I don't want to go back yet, I want to sit here.'

Again Nellie took the pad and wrote one word, finishing it off with a double stab, and again at arm's length he read it. Then throwing the paper on to the table and lowering himself into a chair he muttered, 'Behave! Behave!'

No one spoke for a moment and, under the gimlet stare of Grandpa, Rooney began to shift uneasily, until he thought of his baccy. Taking his pouch from his waistcoat pocket he opened it and pushed it across the table. The old man continued to look at him steadily for a time before his eyes dropped to the tobacco. There were three short rolls in the pouch, and the old man, touching one, said, 'All this? Do you want me to have all this?'

Rooney nodded. And Grandpa, taking the roll, put it into the pocket of his woollen jacket.

The silence returned to the room, and during it Ma refilled

the teacups and also a large chipped cup that Nellie had brought in from the kitchen. It was Nellie who handed it to the old man.

'What's his name?' he asked of her.

Patiently Nellie again wrote on the pad, 'Mr. Joseph Smith. Call him Rooney.' And as she wrote Rooney visualized her in the shop continually writing out little bills—stab, stab—stab, stab.

After a long gulp of tea, Grandpa read the slip of paper, then asked pointedly of Rooney, 'Why Rooney if your name's Joe?'

Rooney held out his palms and shook his head and mouthed, 'Middle name ... mother's.'

'What's he say?' Grandpa turned to Nellie again. But she did not write any more explanations. Instead, taking up the *Shields Gazette* from a chair, she handed it to him, whereupon Ma, making the pretence of poking the fire, exclaimed angrily, 'Now what did you have to go and do that for? You know what he is when he gets the paper. Try to get him back.'

'He won't go yet. He's better with the paper than talking. He'll be all right,' said Nellie, and, lifting up the curtains from the table, she left the room.

Rooney knew that he too should rise and go upstairs, but it was always the way when he got sat down, he found it most difficult to get up again and had to wait for an opportune moment. And that moment, he somehow sensed, was not yet, for Ma was worried over the old boy. Well, she needn't be on his account, he had quite taken to the old fellow.

Somehow he made him feel more at home, sort of levelled things down a bit. He had seen a few like him in his time. The only really happy place he had lived in was with a Miss Cuthbert, and her father was just like this one. He had been a good old fellow really, and when he had died she got herself married to a bloke who objected to lodgers, and that had been that. So the old woman here need not get herself into a stew about what he might think of the old man. As far as he could see there was no doubt but that this one was an old tartar, and Ma had his sympathy in a way, for by the sound of him he'd take some putting up with.

'Damp-day pains are caused by rheumatism.
For speedy relief, take Thirty Days
Rheumatic Tablets.'

Grandpa read out the advert in a slow, high croak, then added, 'Tripe! Tripe! All adverts are tripe. And it's under Personal an' all. . . . It's false pretences.'

Ma groaned audibly, and attacked the fire with the poker.

'First Church of Christ Scientist.
Subject for Sunday: Adam and The Fallen Man.'

'They've got it wrong.' Grandpa looked at Rooney. 'Eve and the fallen man, it should be. There'd have been no fall without her.' His eyes flicked towards Ma, where she was now gathering up the cups. 'Women! They should be smothered at birth. . . . Are you saved?'

This question was addressed with startling pointedness to Rooney, and he again spread out his hands, smiled and shook his head.

'Well, you can thank God for that. And don't you be saved. And stop anybody from trying to do it. Women and religion, they drive you barmy. How old are you?'

Although Ma in an aside muttered, 'Take no notice,' she stopped and watched Rooney put up both his hands three times, then one hand with the fingers and thumb spread out.

'Thirty-five?' said Grandpa. 'You don't look it. No more'n thirty. Married?'

Rooney shook his head, and Grandpa stared at him fixedly.

At this point the front-door bell rang sharply, and Ma, after a moment's hesitation, left the room. The old man's eyes followed her; then leaning across towards Rooney, he whispered, 'You be careful, lad. I'm warning you. That scarlet menace'll have you singing hymns afore you know where you are. . . . And more'n that. . . . Ay, more'n that an' all. You look out. I've known her some years, and I'm tellin' you. . . . What brought you here?'

There was the sound of the front door closing, and Rooney indicated Ma's return to the old man with a movement of his head, whereupon Grandpa, taking up the paper again, stared at it, and as Ma came into his view, he read aloud,

'Regent Cinema.
Shields Operatic Society
Annie Get Your Gun
Full Chorus and Dances.'

He sniffed up both nostrils before going on,

'Palladium.
Sitting Bull.
Westoe.
Back to God's Country.
Savoy.
Mightiest Spectacle of the year on the screen.
The Prodigal.'

'Women with no clothes on. Look at them! That's the Bible for you. ... D'you go to the pictures?'

Rooney nodded and pointed to a picture of James Stewart in a Stetson under the heading of 'The Man from Laramie'. 'Cowboy,' he said.

The old man ignored this, and his eyes continued to roam over the paper. Then he exploded loudly, 'Birthday Greetings! Many Happy Returns! Lot of bunkum! Every week birthday greetings and congratulations to Tom, Dick, and Harry. What do they want to stick them in the paper for? Who wants to see them? Who does it matter to anyway, but among themselves, eh? Show off! Daft show off. That's what people do, they show off. Skint and save to show off. No coal. Look——' He pointed to the fire, and Ma, coming swiftly from the kitchen like a tugboat cleaving through the water, went to the room door and called sharply, 'Nellie! Nellie!'

There was a movement in the room above, and then a moment later Nellie came into the room, and without asking any questions she took Grandpa firmly by his arm and raised him to his feet.

'What's up? I don't want to go, Nellie. I'm all right. What am I saying? Nowt wrong.'

'Come on.'

Steadily she led him out of the room, and as the door closed on them Ma sank into a chair and covering the side of her face with one hand exclaimed, 'I'm so ashamed ... I wouldn't for the world ...'

As was often the case, Ma did not go on to explain what she wouldn't for the world, and Rooney said soothingly, 'There's no need to worry. I mean, about me. Why, there's nothing to worry about—he's only an old man.'

'An old man! A wicked old devil. Oh ...!' Ma checked her description, and her voice dropping she ended, 'If you only knew what my life's been like with him ... what I've gone through these past years ... I could write a book....'

The moment now seemed appropriate for rising, and Rooney rose. 'I'll have to be getting me foodstuff down,' he said. 'And then I'll be going out for the evening. It's time I was putting a move on.'

Ma said nothing, but she looked slightly taken aback, and with puckered brows she watched him depart.

On entering his own room Rooney was amazed to find his curtains up. How, he wondered, had the little one managed it? Even if she had stood on the window-sill he couldn't see her reaching the cornice pole. She wasn't more than five foot two, if she was that.

The curtains made all the difference to the room. Where they weren't faded they showed a soft pink and, being the remains of a good-quality pair, they hung nicely. They were lined and warm-looking. Now, he thought, if only he had a fire on he would have been inclined to stay put the night, but as he hadn't and no coal to make one—he hadn't dared remove the small amount of coal he still had left at Mrs. Sparks's—he would keep to his usual routine and go to the Dogs.

Ma cooked him the two rashers of bacon and the egg he took down for his tea, and set before it his half-pound of butter, a loaf and a pot of jam. But as he ate he did not feel entirely at ease, for Ma and Nellie were sitting down to small slices of what looked like cold potato pasty. Rooney liked to see a good table, and give Mrs. Sparks her due she had been a good cook and ate well herself and always saw that there was some tasty bit for him. Yet Ma here looked as if she could eat her share, for that bulk wasn't sustained, he imagined, on cold potato pasty.

'How,' he asked of Nellie after a long uncomfortable pause, 'did you manage to hang me curtains?'

'Oh, it was quite easy. I——'

'She's got a set of steps in her room,' put in Ma. 'It saves lugging them up and down stairs.'

'Well, thanks,' said Rooney.

Nellie did not acknowledge the thanks, but kept her attention on her plate. And Rooney, as he ate, glanced at her from time to time, and he thought that he had never seen anybody so white-looking. Perhaps it was the size and darkness of her eyes that made her face look paler than it really was. Her hair was the same colour as her eyes, dark brown, and could have

33

been nice hair if it had been cut properly. But it looked as if it had been cut round a pot pie basin. She was wearing a shapeless, grey woollen jumper, and, he mused, she could have done with a bit of Ma's bust, for it looked as if she had none of her own. Once, while Ma was refilling the tea-pot in the scullery, she raised her eyes to find his upon her, and hers did not drop shyly away but stared back at him with some defiance, and it was his head that went down and his colour that went up.

Later, dressed in his good brown suit and best cap and with his mac over his arm, he called in the living-room to ask if he could have a key.

Ma was sitting before the fire staring into it, her arms hugging her breasts, and she started and turned to him, surveying him a moment appraisingly before saying, 'Well now, we've only got the one key, but the back door's always open. You could come the back way.'

This to Rooney was a bit of a damper, for it meant that he couldn't go in or out without coming to the notice of whoever was in the kitchen and living-room, but, as usual, he couldn't press his point so just said, 'Well, if that'll be all right with you and I won't be intruding...?'

'No, no, not at all. Are you off to the pictures?'

'No, not tonight. I generally go to Horsely Hill on a Saturday night.'

'Oh!' Ma's expression became blank, and it was evident to Rooney that she was one of those people who weren't in favour of the Dogs.

'Well, I'll be off. So lo ... Goodbye.'

'Goodbye,' said Ma. 'And you can go out the back way if you like.'

From the sitting-room door he turned on his heel and with uneasy steps crossed the room and went into the kitchen.

It was a fair-sized kitchen but appeared small, for most of its space was taken up with a large table opposite the sink, and odd cupboards flanking the walls.

Nellie was standing at the sink, evidently finishing the washing up, and as he passed her he said, 'Good evening.'

She did not raise her head, but answered, 'Good evening.' And he went out thinking, I can't make her out at all. She's not uppish like that lot the other night, but she's more stiff somehow.

After half an hour at the Dogs, Rooney came to the conclusion that the new place had brought him luck, for he'd had two wins and was richer by three pounds fifteen. Now, as with living, Rooney had a method with his winnings. When he won, which wasn't often, he put two-thirds of it in the Post Office to swell the mounting store that his saving of a pound a week was making. The other third he would put on his favourite the following week. But tonight he felt a bit reckless, not quite himself at all, and in a sudden flash of devil-may-care he decided to risk the lot, and not on the favourite but on a bit of an outsider. That he had gone and done a real daft thing he was certain when he saw the dogs lined up; and even when they were off, bounding after the uncatchable hare with Tarantella lying third, he was bitterly regretting his impulsiveness. And then in one great, inspired spurt, Tarantella was home by a head.

He took off his cap and crushed it in his hands, breaking the peak, which showed how deeply he was stirred, for it was a new cap. Four pounds was the most he had ever won, and now to win thirty or over, just like that. What if he put the lot on the next race? No. No, that was a fool's game. He knew when to stop. And he wasn't going to put a third of this on next week either. He'd buy a suit with that third, and start in the usual way again, making ten bob his limit.

Pushing through the crowd, he collected his money and made his way outside the ground, carrying with him thirty-three pounds more than when he had entered.

On the bus from Westoe to Laygate he looked out on the shops, and he felt a little regretful that they were all closed for he had the desire to buy something for somebody ... but who? Ma and the little one? No, he mustn't start that. No, something for Bill's bairns. Toys, or sweets, or something.

From Laygate he made his way to The Anchor, and was a bit surprised to find only Bill occupying the M.P.s' corner.

'Fred not been in?' he asked. 'Nor Albert?'

'No, nor likely to,' said Bill. 'You missed somethin' the day, not comin' in.'

'Did I?' said Rooney. 'Well, I was moving me things, as you know. What's up?'

'What's up? What isn't up!' Bill threw off the remainder of his drink, drew his finger across his upper lip and began, 'It was like this. We called in as usual, and were sitting just here when a chap comes up and says he'd like a word with Albert. Well, they go to the door. And weren't there a minute when Albert comes back. White as a sheet, he was, and wouldn't say nowt for a minute. And then he ordered a glass of whisky. And then another as quick as lightning. And then he opens up. Apparently the fellow had tipped him off—his wife's goin' round with a coloured bloke.'

'A coloured bloke?' repeated Rooney in a slightly shocked tone.

'Aye, from across the water. And they usually cross over in the ferry about two o'clock,' the fellow said. 'By! lad, I've never seen anybody as mad as Albert. Although he knew fine well she was carrying on night after night at different dance halls he had done nowt about it, until he knew the bloke was coloured. "What's the bloody difference?" I said, trying to quieten him. "He's just another bloke. They're all the same under the skin." But it was no good trying to reason with him; it was as Danny said, "All black boys are oor brothers until they want to marry oor sisters or make a pass at oor wives, and then they're not even human beings." Well, off her went ... Albert. And we felt a bit uneasy. So the three of us decided to go home, have our dinner, and be at the ferry round about two. And it was as well we did. There he was, at the corner of the market place, in a doorway. We kept out of sight for a bit. And then they came, her done up like a doll, and this black bloke. Fine-looking chap, mind, I will say. Albert didn't wait, he went right in. Man, did that dark boy look surprised, but he would've knocked the daylights out of Albert if we hadn't interfered and pulled him clear. It was all over in a minute, and her and the bloke had cleared off afore the bobby showed up. We said there had just been an argument, and he told us to get moving.'

'What'll happen the night,' asked Rooney, 'if she comes back?'

'She won't. D'you know what he did when we got him back home?'

Rooney shook his head sadly.

'Took the poker and smashed everything he could hit. Look'—Bill pushed up his coat sleeve to reveal a great black-and-blue weal—'that's what you get when you try and stop a fellow with a poker. Danny got a welt on the shoulder. And he nearly knocked Fred out altogether. He's got a lump on his napper the size of a turnip.'

'Where's he now?' asked Rooney.

'Danny took him to his place. Best place he could be. Mrs.

D.'ll see to him. But boy, it's been a day! You've missed something.'

Without further comment Rooney went to the counter and ordered two pints. The glow of his winnings had dimmed somewhat. These four men with whom he worked were a sort of family to him. What happened to them affected him. He became filled with a sadness, and at the same time a strange feeling of relief and thankfulness that he wasn't in the heart-breaking, temper-trying, pocket-clearing state of matrimony, for being the kind of fellow he was, he felt sure that had he tried to pick a lass she would surely have turned out like either Bill's, Fred's, or Albert's wife, not Danny's.

When Rooney returned to the corner, Bill remarked, 'You looked pleased with life when you come in. Got some place to suit you at last?'

'It wasn't that, although the place is all right,' said Rooney, 'but I had a win the night.'

'Aye?'

'Aye. Over thirty pounds.'

'No!'

'Aye, I did.'

'Well, I'll be damned! ... By God, you're a lucky bloke, Rooney.' Bill leant across the table and pushed his pug face nearer to Rooney's. 'Do you know that? Do you ever realize just how lucky you are? Nowt ever happens to you, nowt bad.'

'I don't know so much. You try keeping clear of women who are out to get your blood.'

'Aw, that! If it was me I'd treat it as a pastime. But you are a lucky bloke. We all say it. And now thirty quid! Well'—Bill leant back and stuck his feet out—'you can pay for all the drinks the night.'

'I'll do nowt of the sort,' said Rooney. 'Things'll be as usual. But here'—he put his hand in his pocket—'here's a quid for the bairns. Give it to the missus to buy the bairns something. And mind, give it to her. I'll ask the bairns on Tuesday.'

Bill smiled slowly, then took up the note from the table.

'They'll get it. And thanks, man.... What do you say we go along to Danny's and see how things are?'

'Aye. Just as you like. It's dead here the night without the pair of them.'

Having finished their beer in one draught, they left The Anchor and walked to Eldon Street. Here the houses flanked

37

the main road which ran into Tyne Dock. It was broken here and there by long streets shooting off into drab sameness. Yet about most of the windows and doors of this main road was a sparkle that shone through the lamplight and defied the dust and muck from the docks beyond. If the painted window-sills, polished doors, bath-bricked steps were any indication of the interior of the houses, then most of them in this street would have been little palaces. And Rooney thought they were, for he judged every house with a bright exterior on Danny's. And yet he didn't often go to Danny's, for it unsettled him somehow. And now when Mrs. Danny opened the door and the cream-painted passage formed a setting to her neatness, the old feeling, that could have been envy, returned.

'Oh. Come in. Danny thought you might be round. Oh, hallo, Rooney.' Her greeting was full of sincerity. 'Where've you been all this time?'

'Dodging women, Mrs. D.,' put in Bill. 'That's all he does. He spends his time dodging women.'

'Go on with you.' She pushed them along the passage and into the kitchen. And here Danny rose from his chair.

'Hallo.'

'Hallo,' they both said.

'He's gone back home,' said Danny.

'No,' said Bill.

'Yes,' said Mrs. D. 'But he's comin' back ... he promised. Sit down.' She pushed chairs forward. 'He felt he must go and see if she turned up. But he'll be back. Now I know you've both been drinking beer, but would you like a cup of tea?'

'No thanks. No thanks, Mrs. D.,' they replied together.

The conversation centred around Albert and what line he should take. And as words repeated themselves and as the same thing was said over and over again with hardly a variation, Rooney's eye and mind wandered and took in the kitchen. This was the kind of place he would give his ears for. It was alive with colour and brightness. Not that the furniture was anything to crack on; there wasn't a piece as good as his dresser here—but it was the way Mrs. D. had things set out. And the light paint everywhere. And the bits of brass. And the hanging plant on the corner of the mantelpiece, with its green leaves flowing down the pink-ground wallpaper like a picture to be seen in some fashionable magazine.... She had everything lovely.... Then he put a rein on his thoughts. Even if he ever managed to get a house it might never look like this, for he was no hand at arranging things. He could put a bit of paint on, but it had taken more than paint to make this room look as it did.

'So you've moved again, Rooney, Danny tells me?'

'Aye. Again, Mrs. D.'

'When are you goin' to get married and move to a house of your own?'

'Aw!' Rooney moved his head from side to side. Then shyly he brought out, 'The truth is, Mrs. D., I'm waiting for somebody like you.'

There was a burst of laughter, and it included Rooney's, for he was amused and as surprised as any of them at his own gallantry.

'Ah! He's learnin'. What d'you think, Danny?' said Mrs. D.

'I think he's a damn fool,' said her husband. 'And I'm tired of telling him.'

'Oh, I don't know so much,' said Bill. 'Lucky, I would say. Do you know he won thirty quid the night?'

'No!' said Danny.

'Oh, I'm so glad,' said Mrs. D. 'And mind you look after it, Rooney.'

The conversation turned and turned again. And at ten-thirty, when Albert had not put in an appearance, Rooney and Bill rose to go. And as Mrs. D. led the way to the front door, Rooney stayed behind for a moment and stuck a note in the leaves of the hanging plant.

'Here! What you doin'?' said Danny.

'It's just a bit to get some flowers or something for herself,' said Rooney.

'You start doing that with everybody you meet,' said Danny, 'and your thirty quid'll soon go. You get dafter, you know. But thanks all the same. And she'll put it to good use and be as pleased as punch. But I wish you'd have some sense.'

Outside and having parted from Bill who lived near by, Rooney, making his way to Filbert Terrace, thought, Danny's right. I wouldn't have much left if I went on like that. Yet the pleasure he had got from making the two gifts stayed with him, and the desire also to buy something for somebody still lingered. The quicker he got the money into the Post Office the better, he told himself. He didn't know what was the matter with him the night. It was likely the result of a funny day, him moving, then winning that money, and Albert's do. It would be just as well when Monday came and he got back again into the old routine.

When he entered the living-room, Ma was sitting exactly where he had left her. It could have been that she had never moved since he went out. The little one was at the machine, her arm moving like a piston, her fingers pushing at a mass of grey material. She did not raise her eyes or give any greeting whatever. But Ma's greeting, covering a number of points in one breath, dispelled any feeling of awkwardness Nellie's attitude might have caused him.

'Ah, there you are. Have you had a nice night? Now do you want any supper, or have you had it? I was just saying I'd leave you something out in future so we wouldn't wait up And you could make yourself some tea.'

'I don't want anything the night,' said Rooney. 'I've been to a friend's house and had a bit supper. Thanks all the same.'

As he spoke he threaded his way across the room, quietly, as if he might disturb someone. And at the door he turned and said, 'Good night, all.'

'Good night,' said Ma. 'And I hope you sleep well.'

The little one said nothing. And if he hadn't remembered her gentle handling of Grandpa and the old man's evident liking for her he would have considered her at this moment the worst of the bunch.

He was just dropping off to sleep, his mind sinking into the layer where, to use his own term, daft thoughts struck him, where he sometimes heard himself reciting bits of poetry from his schooldays and where he sometimes saw himself doing the most extraordinary things, such as leading a lass down a fine staircase and on to a ballroom floor, or walking down a road dressed up to the nines in a trilby and wearing gloves, and a lass on his arm . . . or even kissing a woman on the palm of the hand—that was the daftest bit of all and the one he experienced most often. It was just starting, this one. There was the hand, palm upwards. He could see the lines on it; and it was lying in his big fist. And there he was, getting nearer and nearer to it, when the most odd thing happened . . . somebody swore. It seemed to be the owner of the hand. 'Hell!' it said. 'Damn and blast! Damn! Damn!' The hand leapt from his palm and made a thumping noise.

Rooney was wide awake, staring into the darkness. From behind his head came the sound of a soft thump! thump! as if someone was beating their fists into a mattress. He raised himself on his elbow and looked towards the wall. That was funny. He'd been dreaming. Yet that thump, thump, that wasn't in his dream.

Then to his amazement he heard the sound of sobbing, low, smothered sobbing. It did not last for long, yet he waited, wondering what he'd hear next. But there was no further noise. And when his elbow got the cramp he lay down again.

Who was next door? He couldn't imagine Ma lowering herself to use such words, or yet her daughter, who fancied herself. That only left the little one.... He must have been dreaming. Yes, of course he was dreaming. Who could she have been swearing at? But he hadn't dreamed that he heard someone crying—no, he hadn't dreamed that.

It was some time before he went to sleep, and when he did he dreamed he ran off with Albert's wife, and she was a coloured woman with white hands, which just showed you, he told himself the next morning.

3. THE BEADS

On Monday morning, Bannister, the foreman, came up to them in the depot and, addressing Danny, said, 'You're to take number four rear-loader the day and hook on a trailer for the waste paper. And by the way, there's been a complaint sent to the office that some bloke from your district refused to pick up a box of paper and a bag of rags.'

Danny looked round at them, and they looked back at him blankly, almost stupidly. 'Hardly makes sense,' said Danny. ' 'Twould be cutting off wor nose to spite wor face.'

'I'm glad you see it that way,' said the foreman.

'There was that iron bedstead and flock mattress. But I told you about that,' said Danny. 'We couldn't get them on at the time and I told her to contact the office.'

'No, this wasn't beds or mattresses. But what you blokes have got to remember is it's all salvage.'

He turned away and Fred, looking around the great open

sorting room, said, 'Salvage! Salvage! You get sick of the bloody sight of it.'

Rooney's gaze followed Fred's, but the conglomeration of stuff did not disturb him one way or the other; he was so used to seeing old John Crawley on the paper press that the surprising thing would have been if he had not seen him there. Sometimes they would return with the loader five times in one day to drop the salvage before going on to the controlled tip to dump the refuse, and each time Old John would be stuffing the paper into the press, switching on the machine and adding another two-hundredweight bale to his stock. Ned Harvey would be doing the same with the rags; Jack Llewellyn would be sorting metals, aluminium kettles and pans, lead from iron; Tom Paisley would be stacking mattresses or bundling up the threadbare remains of mats and carpets, or doing the brain-softening job of packing feathers; Con Rainton would be sorting the woollen rags from the cotton and spreading anything wet out to dry; while a number of young lads would incessantly be tearing up cardboard boxes to feed old John's press; and all working in a through draught that almost wiped the lugs off you.

It was all part of the pattern of the job, and it did not affect Rooney, only sometimes to make him think, By! who'd think there was money in this muck? For he, like every other man dealing with the collecting and sorting of the refuse, knew just what money there was in the salvage part of it ... they received quite a bonus from the Corporation after their wages had been paid, the maintenance of the lorries seen to, and other expenses connected with the work were paid. So naturally they made themselves conversant with the prices. Every man Jack of them knew the current price of each material, at times discussing the rise and fall of these prices in the manner of stock-brokers. For instance, it was to be regretted that wool was at the moment only bringing a hundred and fifty pounds a ton, compared with three hundred just after the war; rags were fetching thirty pounds today; paper eight; where copper would bring two hundred and seventy-five pounds, brass bed-steads and bicycle frames brought the handsome sum of two pounds ten. There was seldom much copper kicking around, so, as Danny said, if you didn't pick up paper and rags it was cutting off your nose to spite your face. Besides, there were so many blokes rag-, bottle-, and paper-collecting in the town to sell to the private firms that they'd run miles to get the stuff.

More than once Rooney himself had been approached by chaps to see if he'd drop stuff, particularly wool, on to their barrow for a back-hander. But that he considered would have been a mug's game, although Bill argued till he was blue in the face with Danny that material thrown into the dustbin was classed as abandoned material and was therefore nobody's property because the dustbin belonged to the householder, who had thrown away the stuff that was in it. Danny would always come back and say the lorry was the property of the Corporation, and once the stuff was in it the Corporation was responsible for it, so if it cut one way it also cut the other. If the Corporation were to be held responsible for the refuse then it should be classed as theirs.

The top and the bottom of it was, Rooney thought, there was more in muck than met the eye.

In the garage, they all made for number four, and Fred, pulling himself up into the driver's cab, sang softly in a ragman's call, 'Any rags, bottles, or bones? Any rags the day? Any rags for ruddy rubbystone?'

Climbing up beside him, Danny chided, 'It's not funny, Fred. I don't want any complaints about our lot.'

Rooney, Bill, and Albert got into the loader's cab immediately behind, and Bill, tugging his cap farther on to his head, muttered, 'Salvage! You'd think wor lives depended on salvage.'

'It pays wor wage,' said Danny.

'Who paid wor wages when it all went in the incinerator? We had to be paid then. They've got to have us.'

Danny, speaking over his shoulder through the let in the dividing partition, said, 'You'd grumble in heaven, Bill. You're young yet. You should have been on in the days when we were known as scavengers and classed below the muck we moved. They don't think much of us now, but they thought a damn sight less of us then. Long shovels and open carts it was in them days, and the stink would knock the devil down. No dustbins. You don't know you're born, lad.'

'I wouldn't have worked on the job in them days, Danny,' said Bill in a somewhat quieter tone.

'No, perhaps you wouldn't, Bill, but there was no pick and choose then ... we had to eat.'

There was a strong reprimand in Danny's voice, and Bill became silent. But Rooney thought, Nor would I; I wouldn't have worked like that, not even for to eat. The job now was still dirty and unpleasant, and you were often soaked to the skin, and in the frosty weather your hands almost froze to the bins, but if you were strong and liked outdoor work the job was bearable; if you weren't so strong but stuck it like some did, it broke your health and heart.

The lorry swung out of the yard, across the town, and up to Westoe Fountain; then into Westoe Village itself, which was but another section of Shields, the good-class section. Once the place of residence of shipbuilders and big business men of the town, now many of the big houses were turned into offices. Still, Westoe Village managed to retain its superiority.

The first two hours went by without a word from Albert, and Rooney, who was paired off with him, found the time a little trying. He felt that if Albert would let off steam in some way he would feel a lot better. He was saying as much to Bill as they tipped their respective bins into the container when Albert's voice was heard from the end of a long sidewalk that served as the tradesmen's entrance to Honeycroft, the home of Mrs. Bailey-Crawford.

'He's talking all right now,' said Bill; 'you'd better go and see what's up. Likely having a row with the maid. Anything female will do for him to get his teeth into at present.'

'Can't be a maid,' said Rooney. 'That's old Double-Barrel's place. She's got no maid now.'

'So it is,' said Bill. 'By lad! Don't say he's goin' for her.'

Rooney, leaving his empty bin by the grass verge, hurried down the tree-lined sidewalk, past stables as big as a house, and across the brick and grass-strewn yard to a glassed-in covered way, where stood Albert, pointing to the bin. His face was red and his voice high with anger.

'You report me? It's me that'll do the reportin'!'

'How dare you speak to me like that! Go away this minute, and take that bin with you. And I promise you you'll pay for your insolence.'

The old lady was standing in the kitchen doorway, and as usual she looked like a bundle of rags tied together. Her white hair was hanging loose from a couple of pins, and her face looked as if it hadn't been washed for a week. Yet she held her tall, lean body as straight as a ramrod.

'What's up?' asked Rooney.

'Look at that,' said Albert, pointing to the bin. 'Full of wet muck. Wet tea-leaves on top of all that stuff, and it's running out of the bottom.'

'Get away this minute! And take that bin with you,' ordered the old lady.

'I can refuse to lift it in that state.'

The old lady's face darkened even further. 'Get out of here at once!'

'Aye. I will an' all. And you can do what the hell you like with your bin.'

Albert, turning away, cried to Rooney, 'Come on.'

But Rooney did not immediately come on. He looked at the bin which was certainly in a mess, and he looked at the old lady, and quietly he said, 'Don't worry, I'll see to it. But, you know, you shouldn't put wet stuff in.'

'It's a bin, and I'll put what I like in it. And I'll report that man immediately.'

Looking at her, Rooney thought, She will an' all. He didn't like any trouble among the gang; there was enough in the yard at times, and if Bannister got any more complaints from this end he could become unpleasant and Danny'd be the first to get it in the neck. He pushed his hair back before replying, 'I wouldn't do that, mum. He's not usually like that. You see, he's in a bit of trouble.'

'Trouble? What trouble?' demanded the old lady.

'Well——' Rooney looked at his boots and said under his breath, 'It's his wife ... she's left him.'

'And a very sensible thing to do. Who'd put up with a man like that? Daring to speak to me in such a fashion! Because I'm alone they think they can do what they like. But they can't.... You'll take that bin.'

It was an order, and Rooney said, soothingly, 'Yes, mum, I'll take the bin.'

With a jerk from his wrist on the handle and a lift from his hand at the bottom he swung the dustbin on to his shoulder as if it was a pail, and as he did so he was thankful for his leather jerkin.

At the van, Albert challenged him. 'What you go and do it for? The likes of her! Who does she think she is? Her day's past, and a damned good job, too.'

'Aye,' said Rooney. 'But it'll save a lot of trouble, man.'

'Trouble be damned! There should be more trouble,' cried Albert, stamping away.

Rooney returned down the walk and put the bin under the covered way. The old lady was in the yard now and she watched him in silence. And as he passed her on his way back

45

he suggested again, 'I wouldn't put no more wet stuff in, mum.'

'I'll put in what I please. You only call when it suits you; weeks go by before you collect.'

'Oh, mum.' Rooney smiled, as if at an irritated child. 'We come if we can get in. But sometimes your gate's locked.'

She made no comment on this. So saying, 'Good day, mum,' Rooney departed, thinking: Poor old wife, living in that great place alone. He did not voice the opinion of the gang as to why she should be allowed to live there when the place would house four families comfortably—to him, old Double-Barrel was of a class that had always lived in big houses. Nor did he envy her any part of Honeycroft, for it did not fit in with his idea of a home. What he wanted was a little house, something he could manage. That place would be a headache to anybody, even the Council, he thought, for the whole roof needed retiling and the bricks pointing, for a start.

At the bottom of the road they stopped, and Fred and Bill, together with Rooney, gathered on the kerb. This was the spot where they usually had their break, after which Fred would wind up the van end to make way for more dirt.

Rooney had taken up a pole and was distributing the refuse more evenly, so that Albert could get his last binful on, when Bill said softly, 'Hold your hand a minute. What was that?'

Leaning over, he pulled from among the indescribable mess a battered cardboard box, in which a galaxy of colours was dimmed by ashes and clots of what could have been porridge.

'Beads, and bairns' things ... look.' He picked up some little bricks in one hand. 'They're bonny, they're painted with real little pictures, look——' He rubbed at them. 'They'll do for the bairns.'

'Better watch out,' said Fred. 'Remember Hughie Foggarty.'

'What's that got to do with it?' said Bill. 'I'm not going to sell the damned things, these are only bairns' bits. I'm havin' them, and to hell!'

Rooney himself could not see the harm in it. As Bill said, he wasn't going to sell the stuff, or anything like that. If a chap took stuff for that purpose he deserved all he got. But these were just beads and things; and well, after all, they'd been thrown away.

As Bill pocketed a rubber doll, a little monkey on a stick, and the bricks and beads, Rooney pushed the rubbish still farther back, exclaiming, 'I think there's some more here, Bill.

Red beads. Look!' He raked them forward towards Bill, and it was at this point that Fred warned them in a whisper, 'Look out. Here's Danny.'

Danny had always been dead nuts on them picking up anything. Long before Foggarty got pulled up, Danny would say, 'Now none of that, it's not worth the candle.' And so Bill abruptly finished his scrambling and turned away.

Rooney had the beads under his hand. They looked nice beads in spite of them being all messed up. They were on a chain of some sort, and it seemed a shame to push them back among all the muck, when they'd please some bairn. With a quiet movement he covered them with his fist and unobtrusively pocketed them.

Now that Albert's tongue had been released, it seemed impossible for him to control it. Walking half a dozen paces each way in front of the lorry, he stormed against his wife and the world that dared to give foot-room to Negroes, and women in general.

Danny motioned to the rest of them to let him carry on, and the fact that Albert carried on for the rest of the day contributed to Rooney's forgetting to hand over the beads to Bill. That, and one or two other things he had on his mind, the main one being that before he went home he had to make a purchase.

At four-thirty he left his mates at the depot, and making his way to King Street he started to look round. And it was before a high-class gentlemen's outfitters that he finally stopped and saw in the window what he wanted. It took him some time to enter the shop, for to his mind his working togs were not in line with what he was after, but had he gone home and changed the shops would all have been closed, and he would have had to wait until the week-end. And he couldn't wait till then to go to the bathroom. And he wasn't going to risk another look like he got yesterday when he met that madam on the landing, with just his trousers on and his galasses hanging down. He'd been having a bath when he ran into her, and she'd looked as shocked as if he had been naked. She was in a dressing-gown, they all wore them. The old woman made the breakfast in hers. And this morning he had seen the little one draped in a thing that made her look worse, if anything, than she really was.

In the shop, an assistant stepped forward and said, 'Can I help you?'

'I want a dressing-gown.'

There was a moment's pause while the assistant took in Rooney from head to toe.

'Yes, sir. Have you any particular colour in mind? How about this?' He went to a stand, where a red-patterned, artificial-silk dressing-gown draped a headless man.

'No, not like that,' said Rooney. He didn't want to look like a Chinese mandarin. 'Like the one in the middle of the window.'

'The mushroom-coloured one? Yes, sir.'

There had been no price on the dressing-gown, and when the assistant laid it on the counter and Rooney saw its thick, tartan-lined interior, he thought, I've done it now. I should have asked him what it was first.

'How much?' he said.

'Eight pounds nineteen and eleven. It's a lovely gown, beautiful quality.'

Eight pounds nineteen and eleven. Nine quid! It would have to be beautiful quality ... why, he could get a suit for eight pounds nineteen and eleven. He looked towards the headless man, and the assistant said, 'That's a very good value at seventy shillings, And we have others, thicker, a mixture of wool and cotton. But I think this will be more your size, sir. It allows for breadth, where the cheaper ones don't, and your shoulders are'—he smiled congratulatorily—'pretty broad.'

Rooney remained dumb, staring at the dressing-gown. He couldn't have a suit and this an' all and put twenty pounds in the bank. But did he need to put twenty pounds in the bank? If he hadn't had the win he couldn't have done it. 'I'll take it,' he said.

'And anything else, sir? Pyjamas? Shirts?'

Pyjamas. If you had a dressing-gown you'd have to have pyjamas, he supposed. He never wore anything in bed; winter and summer he slept ... blank.

He bought two sets of pyjamas.

'Slippers, sir?'

Lord! He groaned inwardly. He had slippers, but they were felt ones, and they certainly couldn't stand up to this rig-out. He bought slippers, leather ones with lamb's-wool lining, and left the shop fifteen pounds lighter, telling himself he was barmy, but accompanied by a feeling of recklessness touched with excitement. If his coal had come—he had asked Harry Baker on his way to work to be sure and drop him a couple of bags in—then he would get dressed up and sit in expensive comfort afore the fire.... By! lad, eh? He shook his head and laughed at himself. What would the chaps say if they knew? Phew! He grew hot at the thought.

As he opened the kitchen door of No. 75 he was immediately aware that there was company, for from beyond the closed door of the living-room there came the sound of voices, and the high-pitched note of a child squealing, 'Just let me have one more look. Just one more. Yes! Yes! Mummy.'

He took off his coat and his boots, and put on his slippers which he had left in the corner, and with the parcel under his arm, he entered the room.

'Oh! I didn't hear you come in. You're late. I thought you weren't coming.'

Ma was seated at the table, and across from her was the wife of the miserable-looking fellow Dennis, and the young, stuck-up piece, Doreen. And by Ma's side was a thin, pert-faced child of about six, who stopped her chattering to stare at Rooney.

'Good evening.'

Pauline had the grace to answer, but Doreen continued her meal in silence.

'I've got your pie all ready,' said Ma. 'Will you ...?' She paused as her grand-daughter cried, 'I'm going up to look just once more.' The child had slipped from the chair and was now at the door.

'You're not! Come here. Be quiet. We're going home in a minute,' said Pauline, with calm preciseness.

The child, ignoring her mother, appealed to Ma, 'Oh, Gran, can I? Just a peep. Say yes.'

'Go on then,' said Ma. 'And don't be a minute, mind. Now as I was saying——' She turned to Rooney. 'Oh, she's a chatterbox, I don't know where I was. Oh yes. Will you have your tea now or get washed first?'

Although he would, in any case, have said, 'I'll have a wash first,' he felt that Ma had a way of placing her words so as to make you do what she wanted. And she evidently didn't want him to sit down with her two daughters. Well, she needn't have worried.

'I'll be down later,' he said.

'Very well.'

As he mounted the stairs, Doreen's voice came up to him as it had done on Saturday, and he heard her say quite plainly,

'How can you be so smarmy with him! He's like a big gorilla.'

He stopped dead, and the heat from a wave of unaccustomed anger covered his face. Gorilla! By! lad, he'd like to take his hand and smack that one's face.

It was such an unusual thought for him that he was upset as much by it as by the remark that had caused it.

A light streaming from the room next to his own lit the dark landing, and as he passed the open door he saw the child standing beside a single bed, and on the bed, propped up by a pillow, was a doll. The room was small, but even its size could not take away the impression of bareness, for all he could see in it was a corner hanging wardrobe, a small chest of drawers, and a bed. As he went into his own room his anger was lifted a little, for the fire was on and his curtains drawn, and his chair arranged before the hearth. The picture it made eased the hurt of the stinging words, yet as soon as he had put down the parcel he went to the dressing-table and surveyed himself. His shoulders admittedly were big, and his body perhaps over-thick, but his face wasn't even dark, it was fair-skinned, and he had a good skin, if nothing else. His sandy-brown hair was a bit unruly and wouldn't stay put for five minutes, but he had seen worse. He had no false ideas about himself, but ... gorilla!

Before opening the parcel he went across to the bathroom and had a good wash. Then, once again in his room, he gently lifted the dressing-gown from its wrapping and tried it on.

Standing again before the mirror he stared for a long while at his reflection. Then his grey eyes gave himself an appreciative twinkle. By! lad, who would have believed he could have looked like this. It was the colour—mushroom, the fellow had said. Or was it the cut; easy, but fitting snugly like an old boot? ... And that one saying 'gorilla!' Oh! he'd like to show her....

A scream, suddenly rising through the floor from the living-room, startled him out of the rare act of self-approval, and he stared downwards.

It came again. And then again, but now through a confused babble of voices. And when it continued, he went swiftly to the door, and opening it, listened. It was the child, and it sounded as though she had been scalded or something. He heard a door open and the voice of the old man muttering, 'What's all this? What's goin' on?' Then the muted voices from the living-room seemed to explode into the hall, and he made out Ma's above the rest, crying to the old man, 'You get yourself back! ... As for you, you'll end up in the asylum.'

'And who'll put me there? She's not having it, it's mine.'

He was surprised to hear the little one speaking.

'Kathie ... leave go! Do you hear? All this fuss about a bit of a doll.' It was the mother's voice. 'Really, Nellie; you're beyond me.'

Then Ma's voice came again, outdoing them all, barking with finality, 'The child's goin' to keep it! What is it, anyway, but a clouty doll? You can make another. You're going bats ... you and your dolls!'

There followed a quick, odd silence, during which even the old man's tongue was still. Rooney moved forward to the top of the stairs, impelled by more than mere curiosity. Then very distinctly he heard the little one say, with quiet yet piercing emphasis, 'If I don't get it, I don't put in another stitch ... not one.'

The silence took hold again, until it was broken by Doreen's pseudo-refined tone: 'Give it back to Aunt Nellie, Kathie.' Another silence—then, 'If you don't, I won't have you for my bridesmaid, mind ... I'll get Aunt Betty's Doris. That's who I'll get.'

No more words, but the sounds of movement, and before he knew what had taken place, Nellie was on the stairs below him, and there was nothing for him to do but to pretend to be on his way down.

He stood on the top stair to let her pass, and as she came abreast of him he stared at her, fascinated. In the dim light she looked like a young girl of seventeen or eighteen hugging a child. The doll was dressed up in a white lacey thing, like a christening gown, and her hand was covering its head, pressing its face into her chest.

She was not aware of him until she was close upon him, and then she lifted her head for one brief moment, and the pain he saw in her face caused a feeling of pain in himself as if he were witnessing the baiting of an animal or small child, and he wanted to cry out to her, 'Don't be hurt like that, whatever it is.'

He watched her run across the landing and into her room, and after her door banged he waited a moment before softly returning to his own room. He felt bewildered ... he couldn't make it out. He didn't know what to think. She must set some store by that doll. Perhaps she'd had it since she was a bairn.... The picture of her face came back to him. He'd never seen anybody in his life with such sad eyes. And they could be lovely eyes, he thought, if she was happy.

He took off the dressing-gown and hung it on the back of the door, put the pyjamas away and the new slippers on; then sat down and waited until he heard Doreen come upstairs. When her door closed, he went down to the living-room. The mother and child were gone, the old man was not to be seen, and Ma was clearing part of the table. She went into the kitchen and returned with his meal before she spoke.

'I'm so ashamed. I'm sure you couldn't help but overhear that terrible carry-on.' She put the dish on the table, then threw out her arms. 'And all for nothing, absolutely nothing! It makes me so ashamed. We never have rows in the house, I can't stand rows.'

'Oh, it's all right,' said Rooney. 'Families always have dust-ups. It's all right.'

'It's not all right, Rooney. Not at all.' Ma placed her two plump hands flat on the table and leaned towards him. 'Can you imagine a grown woman making herself a doll? And just because a child takes a fancy to it, going on like she did? Between you and me she's a trial ... a great trial. What with her and him'—she motioned with her index finger towards the right-hand-side wall—'life isn't worth living at times.'

Rooney was never very curious about people, but there were a number of questions he would have liked to ask Ma, but all he could say was, 'It's better to have a family to quarrel with than no family at all.'

Ma looked at him hard for a moment, and after straightening and adjusting the back of her hair, she said, 'I suppose there is something in that.' She allowed a pause to follow before going on, 'But when you try to make people feel one of the family and you get nothing but ingratitude it hurts. Do you know I've had her here since she was ten? After her mother died I took her in—her father had died years before. My Queenie was nine at the time, and I had a boy ten and one eight, and three younger girls. But I didn't hesitate. She was one of the family—I treated them all alike—I didn't make flesh of one and fish of the other. And this is what I get. And'—she drew in her chins as she stared at him—'you've seen her, the sight of her. She gets worse. She doesn't trouble. Now, there are my girls—you've seen three of them. Do they look like her? And my Queenie ... no one would believe there's only a year between Queenie and her. You haven't met Queenie yet. She lives in Roker. I go over there once a month. She's got a beautiful place, modern house, everything really up to date. And a lovely garden.... They keep a gardener. Her husband's manager for a large wholesale firm.'

Ma delivered this information in short staccato gasps, then sat down. And there was another pause. She had folded her hands on her lap, and was staring into the fire. She seemed to be thinking of her eldest daughter and her grand house, and Rooney did nothing to disturb her reverie but went on quietly eating.

He was telling himself it was a good shepherd's pie, as good as any he'd tasted, when Ma suddenly exclaimed, apropos neither of rows, nor of Nellie, Queenie, or beautiful houses, 'Do you go to church at all, Rooney?'

It was such an unexpected question that Rooney swallowed, almost gulped. 'No, I'm afraid I don't.'

'You're no denomination?'

'No.'

'Have you ever thought about it?'

'Well, I can't say I have.... No, to be honest, I haven't.'

'Well, it's never too late. I'm Low Church myself, and I find it such a help. I've been sustained all my life through the Church. I've sung in the choir since I was a young woman, at the same church, St. Jude's, Francis Street.'

'Oh.'

'You must come in some night to one of the fellowship meetings, they'd be pleased to welcome you, they're all so friendly and chummy.'

Rooney ate hurriedly. 'It's very kind of you. Thanks all the same.' He began to sweat. If it wasn't marriage or money they were after, it was to get you to God. You were never safe.

'Well'—Ma rose—'I'll have to be making a move. We're starting tonight, practising for the carols. There's just over three weeks to Christmas. Doesn't time fly? I'll have to get ready, not that I feel like going out tonight. Are you going out, Rooney?'

'Yes. Yes, I'm meeting a friend.'

He'd had no intention of going out, but he wasn't going to leave any loopholes that might lead to him being roped in for a meeting. With a certain amount of irritation he thought there was always something to spoil an enjoyable evening.

53

He'd got a good book to finish, a good cowboy yarn. Moreover, he was feeling tired ... he'd done some humping in one way and another during the day.

The room door was pushed slightly open, and Doreen's voice came from behind it, saying, 'I'm off, Ma.'

'All right, dear. Give my love to Harry.'

There was no response to this, only the banging of the front door.

With an apology for leaving him, Ma left the room. And Rooney, having finished his meal, took the dishes into the kitchen and washed them up. He was in the process of drying them when Ma appeared again, dressed, as he termed it, up to the eyes. She was wearing a fashionable, heavy grey tweed coat with a deep roll collar and a close-fitting brown felt hat. He was set wondering how she had managed to get all her hair underneath the hat, but she had, and the result was, in his opinion, a turn for the better. And as he watched her preening herself before the little mirror to the side of the sink, he thought, The old girl fancies herself, and no mistake.

'I'll be in before you, I suppose, about half-past nine.' She spoke to him through the mirror; then turning towards him, she smiled. 'Is your fire all right?'

'Oh! ... Yes. I forgot to thank you for lighting it. It looked grand when I came in ... homely.'

'I'm so glad. It's nice to have a man in the house to do things for—you know, Rooney, you put me in mind of my eldest son.' Ma looked down. 'He was killed in the war.'

'I'm sorry,' said Rooney.

'It was the second cross God laid on me—but He also gave me the strength to bear it. Well——' Ma managed to smile brightly. 'Well, I must be going. I'll be seeing you. Ta-ta.'

His reply would have been 'Ta-ra,' but it would have sounded a bit too familiar by half, so very politely he said, 'Goodbye.' His only reaction to having been placed in the exalted position of resembling Ma's son was to make him think, She makes me hot under the collar.

He went upstairs and reluctantly changed all his clothes. The fire was burning brightly, the room was warm, and the chair was calling to him.... Damn! Why must he go out? There was no must, he could just say he had changed his mind. But he was supposed to be meeting a fellow.

'Nellie! Nellie! Open the door.' For the second time that evening he was startled by a voice, the old man's this time, and coming from the landing.

There followed a series of raps, and his voice again: 'It's me. It's only me, Nellie. Can you hear me?'

The rapping became louder, and for a moment a disturbing thought crossed Rooney's mind. Of course she could hear him, if she could hear at all. He recalled her face again, and as he did so he went out on to the landing.

The old man turned to him. 'Oh, it's you. She won't answer. Push the door open and see if she's all right.'

'She might be asleep,' said Rooney softly.

'What?'

Rooney shook his head.

'One of these days she'll do something. She'll drive her to it. Come on, push the door.'

Rooney was relieved of the trying necessity of coming to a decision by the opening of the door and Nellie appearing, her face no longer white but red from crying.

'You all right, Nellie?' The old man spoke tenderly.

'Yes.' She nodded her head and then catching sight of Rooney she pulled the door closed behind her. Then, taking Grandpa gently by the arm, she said under her breath, 'Come on.'

But Grandpa did not move under her guidance; instead he put his hand to his left side, then reached out and supported himself against the wall. Now that he was relieved of anxiety his strength seemed to have failed him, and he muttered, 'Let me get me breath, Nellie.'

Her back to Rooney, Nellie waited a moment. But the old man made no effort to relinquish the support of the wall, and his breathing became even more laboured. 'I'll ... I'll have to sit down, Nellie.'

'Bring him in here,' said Rooney, pointing to his door.

Nellie seemed to hesitate. She glanced towards the stairs: then easing the old man from the wall, she gently propelled him past Rooney into the room.

Rooney pushed the big chair forward, and with a sigh the old man sank into it. Then bringing the other chair up to the fire, he said to Nellie, 'Sit down.'

Without a word she sat down and took hold of Grandpa's hand, and after a moment the old man smiled at her. 'Long time since I did them stairs, Nellie.'

She nodded.

He looked at the grate full of glowing coals; then his head

moved slowly about, taking in the room. 'You're comfortable,' he said. 'Lovely fire.' He held out a hand to the grate. 'I used to have a fire like this when my missus was alive. But not for years now. Nellie'—he turned to her, seeming to forget Rooney's presence—'why don't you do it, like you were going to? Get some place, and take me.'

She shook her head.

'In the right place I'm good for a few years yet. Me breath going is only because of the stairs—why! look at a week gone—I went out, didn't I? By!' he laughed, 'that put her into a stew, to find me been out.' His voice became quivering eager. 'We could do fine, Nellie, on our own.'

Again she shook her head, and Rooney realized she hadn't her pad with her and knew it was no good answering.

'Then why don't you go off yourself?—don't mind me. I've told you time and again.' He looked up at Rooney. 'They've used her all these years, workin' for the lot of them. And that one will drive her off her head yet. Look what she did over Queenie.'

As if she had been shot to her feet, Nellie was standing. 'Come on.'

'No, Nellie. Let me stay a minute,' he pleaded. 'All right. I won't say no more. Just'—he disengaged her hand from his arm—'just let me sit here a minute, near this fire.'

Nellie turned her back on the old man and looked at Rooney. 'I'm sorry,' she said.

'That's all right. What's there to be sorry for? He can stay as long as he likes. It's nice having him—he's company. Sit down.' He touched the back of the chair, then added softly, 'There's nobody in. Doesn't matter where you sit, does it?'

She looked up into his eyes, staring into them. And he did not drop his gaze from hers when she said, 'Do you think I'm odd ... mad?'

'That's daft talk,' he said emphatically.

'Is it? ... No ... I know what I would think if someone went on as I do ... not speaking. You mustn't mind me not speaking when ... when Grace is there. You see ... Oh!' Her head drooped, and she swung it from side to side. 'It's no use trying to explain, it would all sound so silly.'

'There's no need to explain anything.'

She raised her head again, but turned her eyes sideways, looking towards the dresser as she spoke. 'About the doll. I must have seemed like someone demented to you. But you see,

you can't keep anything. I know it was only a doll, but——'
She brought her teeth sharply down on to her lip and stopped.
And he, affected by her embarrassment, rubbed his hand over
his chin. 'It's all right, I understand,' he said.

He didn't understand; he understood nothing; he couldn't
understand the people in this house, nor the things they did.
Why Ma could be religious and treat the old man, there, as she
did. For there was another side to the old boy, he could see,
and he was beginning to think that Ma had asked for all she
had got from him. Nor did he understand about the doll. Not
for anyone to get into such a stew as the little one here had
done.

He was surprised to realize that he had not yet been in this
house three days.

'I'll go down now, Nellie. I'd better get to bed.'

Together they went to him and helped him to his feet, and
as they walked him to the door he began to tremble. He was
going to have a worse job getting down the stairs than he had
up, Rooney thought. And so, on the landing, when the old
man paused again, he said, looking at Nellie, 'I'll carry him.'

'Can you?'

He smiled quizzically and added, 'He's no heavier than a
dustbin.'

It wasn't a smile that came on her face in answer to this
comparison but a soft, relieving light that was closely akin to
it. It was the first time, as he put it, that he had seen her let
up.

After a 'Here! Here! what you up to?' the old man relaxed
against Rooney, and in a matter of seconds was sitting in his
own room.

The sharp contrast from the bright warmth of the room up
above with this one struck Rooney immediately. But nothing
could be done, he saw at once, about arranging the furniture
into comfort, for there was too much of it. It lined the walls,
piece touching piece. Sideboard touching wardrobe; wardrobe
touching dressing-table, and that close-pressed against a large
dining-table. Chairs in a double row, and the bed, full-sized,
sticking out into the room.

'I'll get him a drink,' said Nellie, and when she had gone the
old man beckoned Rooney's head close to his.

'Here!'

'Yes?' said Rooney.

'Do you go in a pub?'

Rooney nodded. And Grandpa, pushing two trembling fingers into his waistcoat pocket, brought out half a crown. 'Could you get me a drop of hard?'

Rooney nodded again and took the half-crown.

'On the quiet, mind. Don't let her know ... the other one. Nellie gets me a drop at the week-end, but I'm all of a dither the night and need a glass. The other one would see me dead first. And she collars me pension. Half-crown, that's all I get, and me baccy coupon. Bad 'un, that. Hypocrite. She would have had me in the workhouse ... Harton. Aye, she would, but for Nellie. And she's treated her cruel. You don't know, lad.' The old man shook his head. 'I could tell you some things, but Nellie gets vexed. But she's gonna get a shock one of these days, that 'un is. And this is my house, the rent book's in my name. I came here when I was first married. Fine house I had. Happy an' all. I had the best wife in the world. And then my only son had to go and take her! Of all the women he could have had he had to go and take *her*. And she led him a life. Pushing him from one job to another, trying to live big. An upstart, that's all she was. D'you know something? I was glad when he died. Aye, I was. It's an awful thing to say, but I was. For he was at peace. He was a quiet lad, and if it hadn't been for Nellie, I'd have been with him long since. You'll get me that drop, will you?'

Rooney mouthed, 'Aye, yes,' nodding the while. And when Nellie came into the room, he went upstairs, put on his mac and cap, and went out. It must, he thought, be many a long day since the old man had bought any whisky himself ... four-and-six a glass, it was now. He paid nine-and-a-penny for a quarter-bottle, and when he was once again in the house he waited in the living-room until Nellie should come in.

She must have heard him, for she came out of the front room immediately and said, 'He shouldn't have asked you; I'd have gone.'

When he handed her the bottle, she looked at it. 'He only gave you half a crown, didn't he? You mustn't do this. Once you start he might expect it to go on ... he's old.'

'That's all right,' said Rooney.

'I'll give you the rest of the money.'

'No, it's on me. I had a win on Saturday, I'm flush.'

'It's very kind of you.' She looked up into his face, and repeated, 'Very kind,' before turning away and going out.

He stood in the room feeling at a loss. He didn't know

whether he should go out again or go upstairs. He could go upstairs and say truthfully, should the old girl ask him, that he had been out. He decided on this course, and in the room he donned his new dressing-gown, took up his *Dawn Came to Benders Creek*, and sat down before the fire.

But the combination of the fire, the dressing-gown, and the book had not the soothing effect they would have had an hour earlier. For one thing, he thought he'd been a damn fool over the dressing-gown. What did he want to go and pay all that money for? The three-pound one would have done just the same, and suited him better because he wouldn't have minded messing it up a bit at that price, but with this one he'd have to watch out how he used it. Anyway, why had he let himself be driven to buy a damned dressing-gown at all? Dressing-gowns weren't for the likes of him.

It had been a funny night. All this to-do starting from a doll. But the little one appeared different altogether when she got talking to you; the stiffness went and she didn't look so lost and sort of alone like. It was a funny house this and no mistake. He didn't think he'd been in a funnier. Why had she wanted so much to keep that doll? He couldn't work it out. Unless she wanted it because she hadn't got a ... He checked his thoughts and moved uneasily; but his mind had touched on bairns and refused to be jolted away from the subject in any rush, so he wondered how Bill's bairns had received all the junk their da had stuffed into his pockets. Which immediately reminded him of the beads. They were still in the inner pocket of his coat, and that was hanging up in the kitchen.

He was out on the landing before he realized he was about to go downstairs in the dressing-gown. Well, that's what it was for, wasn't it?

Almost defiantly he went into the room. Nellie was at the machine, and she looked up as he came in and her eyes stayed on him, and the surprise showing in them made him feel hot.

He pulled the cord tighter about him as he crossed the room, and when he was abreast of her he stopped and asked, 'Do you never leave that machine alone?'

'Hardly ever.' She smiled wistfully. And he said with sudden daring, 'Why don't you leave here, as the old man says?'

Her eyes dropped to her hands, and it was a long moment before she said, 'It's too late now.'

He could find nothing to say to this, but stood looking at

her. After an awkward pause, she said softly, 'Twice I was ready to go. The first time just before the end of the war. I had got a house and everything. And then Wallace, her eldest son, was killed. That was two, in just over a year. She was ill ... I couldn't go.'

'Was her man alive then?'

'No. He died in nineteen-forty. There was no money from any of them—her husband died of T.B., and the boys were married. If we had gone, Grandpa and I, it would have gone hard with her. And then later, when things were better, I was going to leave again.' Her head moved downwards now, and she shook it. 'Things hold you and you find you can't. You hate to stay and you're frightened to go.... It's too late.'

He was quite at a loss for any suitable reply. The only thing he could think of was the old tag, 'You know what they say, it's never too late.'

She did not take this up but started the machine again, and self-consciously he moved away into the kitchen, and going to his coat he took out the beads.

Now that he could look at them, he saw to his disappointment that they weren't really beads, not beads a bairn would like. There were only six of them, and each was hanging by a little chain from a main chain. And it didn't look like a chain either. The whole thing was stuck up and it would be impossible to make out what it was until he washed it.

Taking it to the sink, he ran the tap on it, and finally had to use the nail-brush to get the dirt out of the crevices. Then, having dried it on a towel, he laid it on the table.

Well, it didn't look much, although the stones shone nice and red. The chain affair looked like pieces of roughly battered tin with holes punched in them; it certainly wasn't of much value. It wasn't gold, and it didn't even look like silver ... tin, he thought, probably Woolworths. And yet not Woolworths, it was too old-fashioned for them. Anyway, he decided, he'd give it to Bill the morrow. Yet as he held it in the palm of his hand he thought, It isn't a bairn's piece. The stones were bonny and it would likely show up on a jumper. His head turned slowly towards the kitchen door—it might cheer her up.

No, by gum!—the necklace was thrust into his dressing-gown pocket—he was starting none of that. Although he was sure she would be the last person in the world to get wrong ideas, being so sensible like, he wasn't going to take any

60

chances.

As he entered the room again, she stopped the machine and asked quietly, 'You won't say anything, will you, about Grandpa and tonight?'

He looked a trifle hurt as he replied, 'As if I would.'

'I know. I didn't think I need ask.... But I'm always a little afraid.'

Always a little afraid. That was the main thing about her. He hadn't been able to pinpoint it before, but the impression she gave off behind that tightness was of being afraid.

'Well, you needn't be afraid of anything I'll say.'

The machine started again, and awkwardly he went out and up the stairs, and as he went he thought, I wish I'd never come to this place. And he asked himself why should he think that at this particular time, for this evening he had talked to a woman more freely than he could ever remember doing before.

4. THE WORM WITH THE ELEPHANT'S HOOF

During the next two weeks Rooney became well acquainted with the routine of the house. For instance, he knew that Ma's nights out were Mondays, Tuesdays, Thursdays, and Sundays. In fact, Sunday she classed as her day off. She went to church in the morning and again in the evening. Friday nights were given over to the family. He would have supposed that the little one's nights off would have been Wednesday, Friday, and Saturday, but, apart from Wednesday night, she stayed in the house. It would have been more correct to say she stayed at the sewing machine. And the time she spent there didn't seem to satisfy Ma, for there had been a shindy last Wednesday before she had gone out.

He had wondered where she went on this one evening, and Ma, expounding on the selfishness of people, had told him. She went to the Literary Society. Knowing there was piles of sewing yet to be done for the wedding, she had gone to the Literary Society. Could he understand it?

61

No, he couldn't. But not in the way Ma meant. He had thought she would have gone to the pictures to get away from the drabness of her days. But a Literary Society—it sounded dull and stuffy to him. And he never saw her reading. Well, as far as he could see she never had any time.

But her taste in pleasure had somehow put a new slant on her; and furthermore, what he couldn't understand was that he himself no more than Ma took to the idea of the Literary Society. Yet in the little one's defence, he said to himself, She's not uppish. But this Literary Society seemed to have suddenly swung her away out of his orbit, out of the category in which he had placed her.

Doreen's wedding was to take place on Saturday morning. There was to be a wedding breakfast held in an hotel in King Street; then the couple would leave for Edinburgh for two days. Because of this wedding Rooney had done more thinking around the term 'class' than he had done in his life before. Doreen had never spoken to him, but she had shown him plainly and in no tactful way that she considered him an unsuitable appendage to the family, and that the house had certainly lost caste in harbouring him. He knew she was nowt but an upstart, but just how much he didn't know until he'd had a talk with Johnny in The Anchor last Friday night. He had thought the bloke she was going to marry must be somebody well off, but when he learned he was a tally man, a door-to-doorer, he had thought, By hat! she's got something to stick her neb up about. And he was surprised that he should feel angry about this; and his reactions further surprised him when scorn was added to his anger on hearing that the actual wedding garments were being hired ... satin gown, trailing veil, morning suit an' all.... By hat! he had thought again, she's an upstart, all right. To his mind the hiring of clothes was equivalent to wearing second-hand things, and because every day he saw so much rubbish he had never been able to bear the thought of second-hand clothes; even though he knew that half the clothes he saw in the shops were the finished product of rags, it made no difference. And on this point Johnny heartily agreed with him. But he had added, 'It's fashionable now, man. Ye don't wear somebody else's cloes until ye're somebody, or trying to be.'

On Friday nights, when the gang, as Rooney called Ma's family, were assembled as usual in the kitchen, he would make his way out of the front door, avoiding them en masse, and so the only other members of the family he had encountered since that first evening were Pauline, on the night of the doll rumpus, and on one occasion, Jimmy, the fellow with the deep voice. He had seen him coming out of the Town Hall, where he worked, and although there had been quite some distance between them, and Jimmy could have gone on his way without acknowledging him and it wouldn't have seemed like a cut, he had raised his hand in salute and smiled across the distance, and Rooney had gone on his way, thinking, Well, he's human, anyway.

And now it was Monday and the wedding was almost upon the house. Ma was in a dither, worked to a standstill, as she put it. Even the choir practice had to be forgone tonight so she could go with Doreen and help her fix the curtains and fittings in the new flat, for, as she said to Rooney earlier, if she didn't go, Harry's mother would be along, and as much as she liked her she had no taste, yet was adamant in having her own way.

On this remark Rooney had resisted looking around the room, for he could see little evidence of taste here; not that he knew a lot about such things, he admitted to himself, but this room was so drab it even affected his stable spirits after he had been in it for any length of time.

After the door banged behind Ma there was quiet in the house except for the whirring of the sewing machine, which could only be distinguished by its faint irritation on the silence. Rooney had two fresh books. He had come across a new avenue of supply. It was in a shop in Eldon Street. Danny had put him on to it. 'Why don't you try for your books there,' he had said, ' 'stead of trailing right up to Boldon Lane? She only charges twopence a time.'

'Why pay twopence,' said Fred, 'when you can get them for nowt at the public library? Isn't that what we pay rates for?'

'Do you get your books there, Fred?' Danny had asked with a twinkle.

'I've no bloody time for reading,' said Fred. 'He's so lucky, he doesn't know he's born.'

Rooney thought of what Fred had said as, with his feet on the fender and a book on his lap, he stared into the fire. Aye, he supposed he was lucky. At least, he knew what he was coming home to. Fred or Albert didn't; and Bill knew a little too well. Yes, he had a lot to be thankful for.

The book promised to be a good one, but somehow he

couldn't get into it, for his thoughts kept straying—the posses and the shooting could not hold his interest tonight and he found himself thinking, She'll go on turning that machine until she's an old woman. He could see her down the years becoming like a little, shrivelled brown moth, but still turning the handle, sewing for another generation and its weddings.

He had been staring into the fire for some time before he realized the machine had stopped; and he found himself waiting for it to start again. When it didn't, he tried to read. But his concentration wavered, and quite suddenly he took up the coal scuttle and went downstairs.

Nellie was sitting in the armchair, her head back and her eyes closed. Her face was not its usual white but a grey mottled hue and he stared down on her for a moment before asking, 'Is there anything the matter? Are you bad?'

She opened her eyes but did not look at him.

'Are you all right?' he asked.

'I've ... I've been a little sick.'

'Sick?' he repeated. 'Can I get you something?'

'No. I'm all right now.'

'You don't look it.' He put down the scuttle. 'Let me get you something. I always keep a drop of whisky in, in case of a cold.'

'No. No, thanks.' She checked his departure by sitting up.

'It would do you good.'

She shook her head. 'I never take anything.'

'Well, I'll make you a cup of tea.'

He did not wait for her consent or refusal but went into the kitchen and put the kettle on the gas stove. When he returned she had her elbows on her knees and was supporting her head on her hands.

'You should go to bed.' He stood some distance from her. 'Why don't you?' he asked. 'Look. Go on—I'll pop the drink outside your door.'

When she did not reply, he glanced at the machine, and his voice rising, he said, 'It's all that sewing—you're never done. Can nobody else work that thing?'

The sight of the machine annoyed him, more than annoyed him. He had a swift, startling, almost overpowering desire to chuck it out of the window. The desire itself disturbed him, even frightened him a little, and he rubbed his hand over his face.

Nellie raised her head and said slowly, 'I'm all right now.'

64

'You don't look it.'

He went into the kitchen again, and after a few moments returned with the tea.

'If you'd let me put a drop of whisky in it....'

'Thank you, no,' she said hastily.

He stood on the hearth-rug watching her as she sipped the tea, and when the colour of her face did not change, he said, 'It's nothing to do with me, but I think you've about had enough. You're never done.'

She sighed, and shivered; then, turning slowly sideways, she looked into the fire. 'I had enough a long time ago.'

The few words were like a long, revealing confidence, bringing them together. Suddenly he felt he wanted to help her, that he must help her, and he found himself for the first time in his life offering someone else advice: 'I'd make a break if I were you. Why don't you? You've got a steady job, haven't you?'

'Steady job!' She made a harsh sound in her throat. 'You don't have to be told what Bamford and Brummell's looks like. And it's worse in than out.'

'But couldn't you leave there?'

'No. No more than I could leave here. There comes a time when you get frightened to move.'

He wanted to say, 'Oh, that for a tale!' but he suddenly looked at himself. Why had he not tried to make a move? Away from the bins, anyway. Why? Because he felt at home in his job, of course. No, it wasn't really that. It was because, in the back of his mind, he was uncertain of being able to tackle another job. He could have been charge-hand by now or even foreman if he had done a bit of pushing. He knew more about the work than most of them, but he had never been able to see himself giving other fellows orders.

'Thanks. I feel better.' She handed him the cup. Then, looking again into the fire, she said, 'Sometimes I wonder what we're here for, what it all means. Just living.' She brought her eyes up to his, and as he had no immediate answer to such a question he turned slowly red.

'You're happy, aren't you? I mean in what you do.'

'Well——' He moved his feet and rubbed his hand up the side of his cheek. 'I wouldn't say I'm happy about it, but I don't grumble. There's thousands worse.'

'Yes, I suppose that's a way of looking at it. There are thousands worse off than me, too.'

He wanted to say immediately, 'Not much, these days,' for, as far as he could see, lasses and women had gone mad—with dancing, drinking, and clothes. Drinking among the young folk in the town was so bad they were writing about it in the papers. He would put a stop to women drinking altogether, if he had his way—forbid them the bars, especially the young ones. It put years on them. Yet it wasn't drink that had put years on this one. He had a strong curiosity to know how old she really was. He would have liked to say, 'How old are you, anyway?' but he checked this, yet could not stop himself probing with, 'Why don't you get out more? You're young yet.'

Her eyes seemed to leap up to his. 'Young! ... Do I look young?' It was a challenge.

'Well,' he said, 'you're ... you're not old.'

'No, I'm not old. But you're frightened to say how old. I know. I won't ask you to guess how old I am ... I'll tell you. I'm thirty-four.'

'Thirty-four!' He was quite unable to keep the surprise from his voice. But then, he had thought she could be anything between thirty and fifty. Yet now, looking down into her face, into those great brown eyes, he could well imagine he was looking at a young lass. Her face had that odd effect on you. Sometimes it looked so young that the rest of her appeared incongruous, for about her body was the straight shapelessness of an old sack.

Suddenly, to his deep concern and embarrassment, she began to cry. The brown of her eyes was blotted out, and in a moment her whole face was hidden from him as she turned it into the corner of the chair.

'Aw,' he said. 'Aw, don't ... don't take on. What have I said? ... You don't look thirty-four, more like twenty-four. If you ...' He was about to add, 'got yourself done up,' but, again, tactfully changed it and said, 'If you had a mind you could be younger than any of them.' And thinking back to the four women of the family he had already seen, he thought, And there might be some truth in that an' all.

His hand went out, and for a moment hovered over her arm, but just in time he withdrew it, halted by two distinct views of such an action as a comforting pat. She might imagine he was taking a liberty, and he, off his own bat, didn't want to start anything. Remembering Kate Sparks, he thought, By lad! no.

Thinking he heard the back-yard door click he turned and

looked towards the kitchen door. If that was Ma coming in he'd make himself scarce. It wouldn't, he felt, do this one any good if he was found talking to her, and her crying. But when there was no corresponding click to the outside kitchen door, he sat down, pulling his chair opposite to Nellie's.

'Look,' he said, bending towards her and nodding to her hidden face, 'if I was you, you know what I would do?' He never remembered afterwards what it was he was going to advise her to do, for when Ma's voice struck him from the doorway, crying, 'Well!' he left the chair in one guilty spring, which brought him round to her and Nellie bolt upright.

'Well!' said Ma again, giving to the word so much meaning that guilt weighed Rooney down, and he stuttered, 'She's ... she's been ... been bad.'

'Bad!' Ma glared from one to the other.

'She was sick,' said Rooney. 'I was just passing through for some coal.' Why, he wondered, should he have to explain his movements, and why should he feel like this, guilty? It was as if he had been caught in an act of some kind. He had been doing nothing. It was the way she had yelled that 'Well!'

He looked into her flaming eyes—the blue had deepened until it was almost black. He watched her tear off her hat, her eyes still on him, and saw her hair spring from her head as if it was alive, like a picture he had once seen of a woman with snakes for hair.

Lad! she was wild. But why?

Nellie was on her feet now. She had stopped crying and had dried her swimming face, and in a flat unemotional voice she addressed Ma without looking at her. 'I had a bilious attack. I don't feel well, I'm going to bed.'

Ma made no response but watched her leave the room. Then turning to Rooney, she said for the third time, 'Well!'

'Well,' he answered, pulling the cord of his dressing-gown so tight that it caught his breath, 'it's as she said, she was sick. And she did look bad. I thought she was going to pass out.'

Ma seemed to be making an effort to get hold of herself. She tugged her jumper down viciously all round her; then with her back turned to him, she said, 'She plays for sympathy, she's always sorry for herself—she's eaten up with self-pity. I'm just warning you. She had what she calls a love affair years ago, and she's never let herself get over it. The man never intended anything, but she made a lot out of it ... I'm just warning you.'

67

'Warning me?' he repeated. 'Well, I can tell you straight, you've no need to do that.' And picking up the empty scuttle, he went hastily out of the room, ignoring Ma's rapid and conciliatory comments.

In his own room, he stood rasping his hand across his chin. Lord above! What was the matter with him anyway? Why did he always run into these situations?

The evening was spoilt. He couldn't read or settle down. He couldn't even sit staring peaceably into the fire. So he went to bed.

It was around half-past twelve when he heard the thumping sound again. And as he listened, he thought, The best thing for me to do is to get out of here, and quick. And if she doesn't get out an' all, she'll snap.

It was on the Wednesday morning that the letter came. The previous morning, Tuesday, no one had spoken to anyone else, and he had gone to work thinking, There's nothing for it but to get moving again; I couldn't live there in that atmosphere anyway. But on his return home last night Ma had been her usual gay self, and with one exception everything had been the same. Ma hadn't gone out, but he had. He had gone to Danny's and had talked the whole thing over with him and Mrs. D.

When he said the little one worked in Bamford and Brummell's Mrs. D. had exclaimed, 'Why! I know her—she's worked there for years. And a nice little thing. I remember her when she was just a young lass. Bonny she was, as light as a fairy. She's not the size of six-pennorth of copper, is she?'

'No,' said Rooney. 'Five foot two, I should say.'

'That's the one,' said Mrs. D. 'I haven't been in the shop for years though. And she's still there? Fancy.'

After two hours of chatting and various cups of tea Danny had offered his advice, which was to stay put for a while, and to take everything the old 'un said about the little 'un with a pinch of salt.

And then the letter had come. It was part of the morning routine that Nellie did the step and the front-door brass, and it was generally while she was doing this that the postman came. As a rule she brought the letters through when she was taking the pail to empty. She would drop them on the corner of the table where Ma or Doreen could flick through them should there happen to be more than one. This morning, the procedure was as usual. There were four letters, and Doreen, coming out of the kitchen, made straight for them. She picked out two; then with no small surprise she exclaimed, 'Why! This one's for you, Nellie.'

'Me?' Nellie put down the pail and came back to the table; then taking up the letter she turned it slowly over then back again. Doreen and Ma were watching her, and Rooney, just at the end of his breakfast, felt his interest to be as keen as theirs. It was evident to him that her letters, like those he received, were very few and far between.

'Aren't you going to see who it's from?' asked Doreen, her curiosity making her more civil than usual.

Nellie looked towards her before taking a knife from the table and slitting open the envelope. The letter, whatever it contained, was short, and, as she read, her neck took on a pink tinge, which spread to her face and over her eyes. It was the first time Rooney had seen colour in her face other than when she had been crying.

Ma went to the table and began to gather up the plates, and from there she asked casually, 'Who's it from?'

'That's my business.'

For all Ma's size her movements could be swift, and she swung round now with the agility of a young woman. 'Don't you speak to me like that!'

'Then don't ask questions.'

Rooney watched Nellie walk to the bucket and pick it up; then stand stock still with it in one hand and the letter in the other, looking towards the kitchen door. Then as quickly as she had picked the bucket up she put it down again, and turning slowly about she looked straight at Ma. But what her eyes said only Ma could read. But Ma did not say a word until the sound of Nellie's door banged overhead. And then, addressing a mystified Rooney, she exclaimed, 'Now I ask you! Was there any call for that? It's likely just an advert.'

'It wasn't an advert,' said Doreen under her breath.

'How do you know?' asked her mother.

'I don't. But didn't you see her face? I've never seen her look like that. It wasn't an advert.'

'What else could it be? She hasn't had a letter for years, eight or more.'

Ma's face looked pained as she said to Rooney, 'Every now and again I have this business. Look at the other night about that doll.... Oh! you don't know.'

69

'Ma!' Doreen checked her mother, making Rooney conscious of his presence. 'There's no need to go into that.'

But Ma had no intention of being silenced, and she exclaimed to her daughter, 'Why should I keep my mouth shut? Rooney should know all there is to know, else she'll play on his good nature. She's odd. Her mother was the same, although she was my own sister. She went to the devil with pride ... men and money, that's all she thought about. She married a waster. She thought he had money, but she was sucked in.... Oh, I could tell you some...'

'Ma!' The syllable was significant of Doreen's total disapproval of her mother lowering herself to take the lodger, and such a lodger, into her confidence.

Rooney relieved her of any further anxiety on this point by rising, but he looked her full in the face before saying, 'It's all right, I'm going.' He wished that he was a different kind of chap, ready with his tongue. He would have, at this moment, liked to level half a dozen words at her which would floor her.

That Doreen was now getting it he could hear as he went upstairs. He had just reached the landing when Nellie came running out of the bathroom, actually running, and more so than ever now she looked like a young lass.

At the sight of him she stopped, and, pushing the wet hair back from her brow, she came towards him, so close as almost to touch him, and straining her face up to his she whispered softly, 'It may not be too late after all.' Then darting away she went into her room. And he went into his, to stand blinking down at the dead fire and untidy hearth.

What did she mean, it might not be too late? Did she mean that she was contradicting what she had said last night, that it was too late to make a move? It was that letter. There was, as that 'un downstairs had said, there was something in that letter.

He left the house in a thoughtful mood, and he found himself wishing it was half-past five and he was coming in again, for he had a mounting curiosity to know about the letter. He gave himself a few guesses. Perhaps the fellow who had given her the go-by had come back again. Or perhaps she had won the pools. No, it couldn't be the pools—the chap would have come to the door. And yet not if she had stated she wanted to keep her name secret. But there were no pools done in that house. Perhaps she had been left some money by a rich relative. But she had no relatives, nobody in the world, Ma had said. No, the most likely guess was that the fellow had turned up again—that look on her face seemed to point to it being a fellow ... it had wiped the years off her in one go.

It had rained all morning. Fred had the toothache; Bill couldn't open his mouth unless he swore; Albert did not open his mouth at all; and Rooney, never the one to lead the conversation, remained mute. So it lay with Danny as usual to ease the situation. They were finishing their bait in The Anchor, and Danny, taking up last night's evening paper from the table, remarked to Rooney, 'See that about old Double-Barrel?'

'No,' said Rooney. 'Is she dead?'

'Dead? No. Her place has been robbed.'

'Go on.'

'Aye, it says so here. I saw it last night.'

'When?'

'Monday. They broke a window and got off with quite a bit of stuff, silver mostly. It says here'—Danny read—'some George the Third silver, cruets, a canteen of cutlery, a complete tea-service, two gold watches, and some jewellery.'

'Good luck to them. Why the hell should she have all that stuff!'

'A collection of snuffboxes,' continued Danny, ignoring Bill's remark, 'Nankin China and twenty pieces of ... Severs.'

'What's Severs?' asked Rooney.

'Damned if I know,' said Danny. 'Probably the name of the china.'

'They should have cleared the bloody hoose oot.'

'You'd have run the paper van round to help them if you'd known, wouldn't you, Bill?' put in Danny, laughing.

'Aye, I would an' all. There's the old bitch with twelve rooms, if she's got one, an' all to hersel'.'

'Well,' said Danny, with patient toleration, 'I don't suppose she's very happy in them, not on her own.'

'Then why doesn't she move to some place smaller? There's too many like her.'

Danny swallowed the last two mouthfuls of his dinner before saying, 'If you was born in a house, Bill, and married out of that house, and if you lived nearly all your married life in it, and your son was born in it and your man buried out of it, well, I suppose you'd want to die in it yersel'.'

71

'Is that a fact?' asked Rooney. 'Has she lived there all that time?'

'Aye, she has,' said Danny. 'And I'll tell you something else ... me mother was kitchen-maid there when she was a lass. And the old girl then was a bright spark, riding, dancing, and all the rest.'

Rooney had last seen Mrs. Bailey-Crawford on the Monday morning. Albert had said, 'You go down to that 'un. I'm not goin' in there, for if I do I'll give her a mouthful.'

The bin had been in the same condition as it had been the week previous, and he was standing looking down at it when she put her head out of the scullery window and barked, 'If you don't take it I'll report you.' Then she had screwed up her eyes and exclaimed, 'You're not the other one.'

'Mam,' he had said, 'I told you last week you must keep the bin dry, ashes and stuff.'

'I'm not putting the tea-leaves down the sink.'

He wanted to suggest that she should drain them, but looking at her old face, the flesh wrinkled, sagging and half washed, he had summed up her condition to himself with, She's past it, poor old soul. And as he emptied the bin and saw the quantity of tea-leaves he thought that she must have been bathing herself with tea. Now recalling the sight of her at the window, there was nothing left to suggest that she had ever ridden or danced, or even that she had ever been young.

'Has she no family left, no one?' he asked of Danny.

'Aye. She has a son. I don't know whether she has two or not, but I know she has one. He was something in the war, and he married a Frenchwoman. And as far as I know, he lives over there.'

'That's the moneyed lot for you,' said Bill. 'Let their old folk rot. I wouldn't see me mother in a mess that one's in. Something should be done. It's months since she had any help there.'

Danny let out a roar. 'For an ordinary puzzle-headed mule, let me have you, Bill! I bet the next thing I hear, you'll have taken the side-loader up there and have carted her down to your house.'

'To hell with you, Danny!'

'Same section to you, Bill.... Come on.'

With the exception of Albert, whose face these days wore a perpetual scowl, they all got to their feet laughing, and as they made their way out into the road and towards the depot three young lads on their way to school passed them, kicking a small football from one to the other along the gutter. The tallest of them, putting all his weight behind his foot with the intention of lifting the ball high over the heads of his chums, drove it straight on to the side of Albert's head. Had this incident happened a few weeks ago, Albert would have cried, 'Aye! aye! Is that your game?' and would have kicked the ball sky-high himself. But now, his face contorted with fury, he dived at the young lad and having seized him by the collar was raising his hand to cuff him when Rooney grabbed him by the arm.

'Steady on, Albert, man. He didn't mean it.'

'Leave go of him,' said Danny, pulling at the other arm. 'What's got into you? Leave go!'

The boy, once released from Albert's grip and recovering a little from his fright, backed away from the men and joined his pals. Then running to the end of the street, they turned and in a concerted shout yelled, 'Hit one of your own size, you dirty muck pusher, you! ... M.P.! Muck pushers! M.P.s! Mucky muck pushers!'

The men walked on, silent now. Albert was wiping the clarts from his cheek, but the look of fury still remained.

Inside Rooney was a sore feeling, as if some part of him were aching. Albert would have struck that lad, and hard; and he solid and sober. He didn't seem to be in his right senses ... he wasn't. And all through a woman, and her no good. Why did he bother his head? ... The soreness became touched with a slight feeling of humiliation. Those kids calling them muck pushers! Whenever kids shouted after them it always brought on this feeling. Not that he was ashamed of his job, he wasn't; yet, on the other hand he knew it was nothing to be proud of. Then why didn't he get out? He could, nobody was stopping him. There were the pits, the shipyards, the factories, all calling out for more men. He stuck, he supposed, because he liked working outside. And somebody had to do this job, hadn't they? Bill had a theory that in a hundred years' time the people who would be drawing the highest pay would be those who did the dirtiest work. And so the bin men would come into their own then. But it wouldn't do them much good then, would it?

He glanced at Albert. He was a nice bloke, really, not like he looked now. But this business made him feel a bit ashamed for him. That's what being married did to you. It was as they

73

all said, he himself had a lot to be thankful for.

Then, sitting in the loaders' cab, as the van swung into Fowler Street, Rooney saw the little one. She had just stepped out from a doorway, and with her was a man. The question of whether he was 'the man' did not arise, for he was an old fellow. But what struck Rooney as being strange was not that she was in the centre of the town when she should be either in the shop or at home for her dinner, but that she was laughing, with her head back and her mouth stretched wide. And why the sight of her laughing with an old fellow should make him feel more depressed he was unable to answer. And he thought, What's up with me? I've got the hump these days meself, without being married.

It wasn't until he almost reached Filbert Terrace that evening that he remembered it was Wednesday. Wednesday was half-closing day. That could account for the little one being in the town, but it still didn't account for her being merry. Merriment and the little one didn't seem to go together somehow.

As soon as he entered the back door, the kitchen door was pulled open and Doreen, after ascertaining who it was, withdrew sharply. And as he was taking his boots off, Ma came in saying, 'It's been a dreadful day, hasn't it? Are you very wet? You'll be glad to get in.'

'Yes, I am,' he said. 'But I'm not wet, I changed me things at the depot.'

'I got a neck of mutton for you today and made some broth with it. Is that all right?'

'Yes ... fine, thanks. Nothing could be better the night.'

'Is it still raining?'

'Yes. Worse than ever.'

Ma was going back into the living-room when she paused, closed the door, and came over to him, and under her breath said, 'You get about the town, Rooney. Have you seen anything of Nellie on your travels?'

She did not await his answer, and he had time to think as she continued, 'She went out as usual, but came back at ten. Ten, mind you. And wouldn't say what she wanted. She went upstairs for a minute. And we haven't seen her since. And it's Wednesday. She's always in by ten past one.'

He wanted to keep clear of this, whatever was in the wind, so he said, 'No, I haven't seen her.'

Ma drew in a deep breath which expanded her already large

74

chest to alarming dimensions before muttering between her teeth, 'And so much to do.'

She flounced out of the kitchen, and Rooney followed her into the living-room. Doreen was sitting by the fire sewing. She looked anything but happy, and as he passed her on his way upstairs he thought, Well, it's a change, anyway, to see somebody else with a needle.

After washing and changing he went downstairs again, and he had hardly entered the room before Doreen gathered up her sewing and made to leave. She was on the point of making some remark to her mother who was seated at the table when the back door clicked, and she turned and stood waiting for the door to open. Ma had risen quickly from the table, but she didn't wait for the door to open. Pulling it wide, she cried, 'Where d'you think you've been?'

There was no answer from the kitchen, and Rooney, although he was facing the door, could not see past Ma, but he could imagine the little one slowly taking off her wet things.

'Do you hear me! Where've you been? Everybody worried to death.'

'I've been to the pictures.'

There followed a silence, during which Ma turned and with popping eyes looked at Doreen, and as Nellie came into the room she stood back and surveyed her as if she wasn't sure she had heard aright.

'That's a dirty trick!' said Doreen.

'What?' Nellie said this word softly, with a sort of quiet enquiry as she turned towards Doreen.

'All my things to be finished; and only three nights left. And you going to the pictures! You've never gone to the pictures before on a Wednesday.'

'No,' said Nellie, still quietly, 'I haven't. But I've turned over a new leaf.'

'What's up with you?' cried Ma, who was evidently finding it impossible to understand this attitude. 'What you should do, as I've said before, is to see a doctor.'

'Very likely,' said Nellie, still quietly.

'It's spite ... spite!' cried Doreen, her voice breaking on tears.

'Spite?' Now Nellie swung round on her, no longer calm. 'Spite? You dare say it's spite! I've sewn nearly every stitch you've worn for the past ten years, and every night for weeks past I've sat at that machine and sewn and sewn and sewn.

Spite! How dare you say it's spite?'

Her face had lost its new serenity, and the old white tight look was back. 'Have you ever asked yourself why I should sit there and sew for you? Do you pay me for it, with even a kind word? No, you've been led to expect that I am here just to serve you all, to make whatever you want. It wasn't your fault in the beginning, but you've been old enough for years now to think for yourself.... Well, now you can sew for yourself. Your dresses are finished, and if you want to disport yourself in lace house-coats and fine lingerie you can sew them, and if you're too busy that's just too bad. You should have married a man more fitted to your ideas of luxury.'

'You're possessed, that's what you are. You've become possessed!' cried Ma.

'Yes,' said Nellie, now turning on her. 'Yes, I'm possessed. Possessed of courage, and it's a wonderful feeling.' She stared at Ma, and Ma stared back at her, but this time she did not speak. Her lips were moving, forming words, but no sound came.

When Ma did not voice her thoughts, Nellie gave her a look that could have held scorn before turning from her and leaving the room.

'The little cat!' cried Doreen. 'The old cat! Would you believe it! Her!'

Ma, still temporarily speechless, sank into a chair; then slowly she lifted her eyes to Rooney and with her face crumpling, she said, 'I ask you.'

Rooney tried to keep a level expression, but what he really wanted to do was to cheer. By lad! it had been an experience to see the little one standing on her feet. He wouldn't have missed this for worlds. Talk about a worm turning—she had turned all right.

'Stop it, Ma!' Doreen was no longer in tears, and as she chided her mother for hers, saying, 'Instead of crying you want to find out what it's all about,' Rooney too thought, Aye. There was something behind this courage, something big, big enough to make the little one into a new creature, or at least to make her brave enough to resurrect her old self. Whichever it was, he felt it was something unusual.

'Will I help meself to me tea?' he asked.

Ma, deep in her troubled thinking, replied absent-mindedly, 'Yes. Yes.' Then rising hastily, she exclaimed, 'No, no, I'll see to it—you've been out in this all day.'

As her mother went into the kitchen, Doreen sent a furious glance after her, and grabbing up her sewing and muttering something under her breath that Rooney could not catch, she left the room.

To Rooney's surprise, Ma was strangely quiet all during the meal, and he guessed that she was more than a little disturbed. It was not until he was finished and leaving the table that she spoke, and then her voice was tearful again.

'All this upset and the wedding so near. I don't know what I'm going to do.'

Her talking did not seem to require an answer, and Rooney went upstairs, glad to have escaped so easily.

He had not been in his room more than ten minutes before he heard Nellie come out of hers and go downstairs. Then came the sound of Grandpa's enquiring croak; and after a few minutes Ma's voice penetrated up to him. And when at one point it rose to the pitch of a scream he heard the front door bang, and he knew that the little one had gone out again. And for the moment he felt as frustrated as Ma. Somehow he had hoped that he would have had a word with her, and she would have cleared the mystery up, for had she not almost confided in him this morning? There would be no further chance the night ... perhaps in the morning he would know.

But in the morning, Nellie was not to be seen. She did not get up and take the pail and do the front, and it looked when Rooney left the house that she wasn't going to work either, for she hadn't yet put in an appearance. It also looked to him as if Ma was going to have a seizure.

It was not until eight o'clock that evening that he saw the little one. She had not come in at tea-time, and this had caused Ma's bulges to become filled with volcanic fury. She was no longer tearful, but ready to burst with frustrated curiosity, ascribing Nellie's attitude to madness, badness, frustration, complexes, and spite. But becoming calm for a moment, she had enquired if Rooney were intending to stay in this evening. When he answered yes she said she wanted to slip out to Betty's and couldn't leave the old man alone in the house in case he went out on his own, as he had done a few weeks ago and brought himself back in a taxi, for which she'd had to pay; or set the house on fire, which he had nearly done last year. But she wouldn't be long, she assured him; she didn't really want to go out at all, but she just had to, for it had been arranged that she—whom he took to mean the little one—was to take Saturday off to see to Grandpa while they were at the wedding. Somebody had to stay behind, and so she must go and try to persuade Betty to come now. There was the tea to be laid and things seen to, as Harry's people were coming back here in the afternoon. Oh, the trouble that one had caused! Nellie, he had been given to understand, had upset the whole blooming apple-cart, and it seemed a bit odd to him that it should be the one in the house who was of the least importance who was having the greatest effect.

Grandpa seemed to sense when Ma was out, for shortly after she had gone Rooney heard his door open and him going into the living-room. Fearing lest the old fellow did get up to anything, he went downstairs.

The old man was turning up the cushions of the big chair, and when Rooney's legs came into his view he glanced up and exclaimed, 'Where's the paper? ... Where's Nellie got to? She always brings me the paper. That one's gone out. Good riddance! Did you see what she gave me for me tea? Wouldn't feed a rabbit.' He straightened up and his bright old eyes darted from side to side before he beckoned Rooney to him with a quick wag of his finger; then in a gleeful whisper he said, 'Summat's up here, eh? Nellie's turned at last. She didn't go to work the day. By! I'm glad I've lived to see it.... I nursed Nellie as a bairn ... I know her and she knows me. She's good, is Nellie. She's a cut above any of God-forsaken Grace's lot, and I say it although they're me own grandbairns. Do you think they come in and see me? No. And never slip me a penny. Except Jimmy. Jimmy's all right—May's man. He's the only one who has ever let on I was alive. Jimmy's all right; I like Jimmy. Too damn good for May.... Now where's Nellie got to? She said she'd be in.'

Rooney shook his head, and the old man asked, 'You going out? Will you get me a drop? I've got the money. Quarter-bottle, like you did afore.'

Going to the sideboard Rooney took a pencil and paper from a coloured-glass fruit dish and wrote, 'Not the night. Get you one tomorrow.'

'Tomorrow?' said Grandpa dolefully. 'Could be dead by then. I'm so cold and she won't give me no coal but what hardly dirties the bucket.... Oh, where's Nellie got to?'

As if in answer to his plea the back door clicked, and a second later Nellie came into the room. She was dressed as usual, but she didn't look as usual—she was almost gay. She was carrying a parcel and some magazines.

'Hallo,' she said.

'There you are,' said Grandpa. 'I've hardly seen you the day. You're looking bonnie, Nellie.' He went up to her smiling, all querulousness gone, and patted her cheek. 'Aye, you're looking bonnie.'

She smiled back at him and pointed to the parcel, then turning to Rooney, she said again, 'Hallo. Everybody out?'

'Yes,' he said. 'Been enjoying yourself?'

She drew in her breath; and as she let it out again, she said, 'Yes. Just that.'

She put the parcel on the table and opened it, drawing the old man near her to observe the process. And the wrappings undone, she revealed to his delighted gaze two sets of woollen underwear.

'My!' Grandpa's eyes glittered as he fingered the vests. Then lifting up the long pants, he said, 'Them's wool, Nellie.'

She nodded, smiling.

'By lad!' He danced the pants up and down. 'Heavy.'

She nodded again, laughing happily.

Rooney looked at the garments. They were wool all right, real wool. He knew wool when he saw it. He often wished he could afford a couple of sets like these for the winter. But each of these pieces would cost about three pounds, if not more.

'Come on.' Nellie lifted up the things from the table and beckoned the old man with her head. And as they went out Rooney asked, 'Have you had your tea?'

'Yes,' she called back from the hall. 'But I could do with another cup.'

His brow puckered as he went slowly into the kitchen. She was different somehow ... there was an airiness about her that was strange and not a little disconcerting.

The tea made, he took it into the living-room, but it was some time before she came out of the old man's room, and he said, 'It'll be cold by now.'

'It doesn't matter ... I had to get him settled.'

She poured herself out a cup, then sat down at the table, sipping it in silence. After a moment she pulled one of the magazines towards her and flicked over its pages.

Rooney stood, uncertain what to do. His legs would not carry him to the door, nor could he sit down. Suddenly she looked up at him.

'You're wondering what it's all about, aren't you?'

'No,' he lied. 'It's your business. The only thing is I'm glad you're looking happier.'

'It's odd.' She turned and looked at the magazine again. 'You think you're dead and then a miracle happens, a miracle all to yourself, and you suddenly become alive. It's a frightening experience at first, when you know you're capable of feeling other things besides sadness ... and ... and resentment, and to know that you are no longer afraid.' She looked up at him again. 'You don't know how I hate this house'—her voice was deep in her throat now, husky, almost harsh—'the brown, dampening deadness of it. When I have a house it will be like this——' She flung the pages quickly forward, then back, and said, 'Like that.'

She twisted the magazine round towards him, and he bent over the table and looked at a picture of a room out of some swell house, all shining with period furniture and glowing chintz.

'Colour ... I'll have piles of colour. No old stuff, unless it's good—I like the modern stuff.' She was talking like an excited girl—a girl who had just become engaged, a girl who was going to build a home—and as she went on he became strongly aware of his bits in the room upstairs. If she was going in for this kind of furniture she must take a very poor view of his stuff. He was sharply affected by this and found himself rearing in defence of his possessions. They would do him, they were good solid pieces.

'Do you like it?' She was still looking at the picture, and he was bold enough to say, 'Not for meself, I don't. That room doesn't look used somehow. But,' he added, 'for some folks it'd be all right.'

'Home is where the heart is.'

'What?'

'Nothing.... Do you know'—she gazed up into his face, now quite close above hers—'I've talked to you like I haven't talked to anyone for years ... years and years. It's all right'—she quickly straightened up, putting out her hand in a defensive but reassuring movement—'you needn't be nervous. I'm—not after anything.'

'I'm not nervous. What makes you think that? And who said I thought you were after anything?' He was finding himself to be quite indignant.

Nellie smiled, a small tight smile. 'Grace would leave no doubt in your mind about that. Grace is the eternal mother and the eternal girl, and she imagines everyone else is the same.' She took a deep breath again. 'But now things have changed she's going to have something to think about.' She turned her face from his, saying, 'Oh, so much ... as much as I can possibly give her.'

Again she flicked over the leaves of the magazine and he went and sat down slowly at the other side of the table. He knew for a number of reasons that he should go upstairs, the main one being that if Ma found him here there'd be fireworks. But there'd be fireworks in any case ... he could see that.

'Do you like that?' She had pushed the magazine round and towards him again, and he looked down now upon the full-page picture of a fashionably dressed woman. She was wearing a blue tweed suit and holding open with artful effectiveness a top coat, the colour of his dressing-gown. But that which immediately drew his eye was the necklace the woman was wearing on top of the matching-coloured jersey. It was almost identical with the one he had upstairs.

He did not answer her question but said eagerly, 'See that necklace she's wearing? I've got one exactly like it.'

Nellie, leaning over the table, looked at the necklace. 'Have you? It's nice. It's costume jewellery. And you've got one like it?'

He sat back and laughed. 'Aye, yes. And it's funny seeing one like this. Look, I'll get it and show you.' He rose quickly and went out, and was back within a few minutes. 'There.' He put it on the table on top of the book. Then with some disappointment he added, 'Well, would you believe it, it isn't really like it, except the red beads hanging down and the colour of the tin.'

Nellie picked the necklace up and after looking at it for some time she said, 'It's a lovely thing.... It's old.'

'Do you think so?'

'Yes. It's silver filigree work.'

'Oh, I shouldn't say it's silver.'

'I think it is. There should be a stamp somewhere. And it is like this one'—she pointed to the magazine—'only prettier.'

'You have it.'

'What!' Her eyes darted up to his.

'It's no use to me ... I can't wear it.'

She dropped her gaze to the necklace lying over her hands, and when she raised it to his again her eyes were soft with gratitude. 'Thank you, Rooney.' It was the first time she had spoken his name, and it added to his feelings of excitement and awkwardness.

'That's all right,' he said. But having said it, he felt at a loss what to do, so he sat down again. No sooner was he seated, however, than the yard door clicked, and he was on his feet in an instant. Then looking at her in embarrassment for a second he made for the door, saying, 'I'd better...'

He did not finish, but she took it up and said, 'Yes, you'd better ... And thanks, Rooney.'

He was hot as he went up the stairs, not so much for having done such a foolish thing as to give a woman a necklace but far more for his ignominious retreat at the sound of Ma. And in his room, he thought. I hate this scurrying, as if I'd done something or other.

His eyes moved over his furniture. The lot, he supposed, wasn't up to much if you were comparing it with the stuff in that magazine. But who was comparing it? It was good stuff, and suited him. He sat down. She must have come into a bit somehow or other to be thinking of furniture like that, but he was no wiser than was Ma as to where she had got it.

Suddenly Ma's voice filled the house. He could not make out what she was saying, but the fury of her feelings came up through the boards. The living-room door must have been pulled open, for now he heard her crying, 'Don't think you'll hoodwink me, I'll find out.'

There came the sound of Grandpa's door being opened, then closed, then silence.

Rooney continued to gaze into the fire. He hoped that the little one would give Ma 'a good run for her money' and keep her guessing. But it disturbed him somewhat to find that he hoped she would not keep him guessing.

On Friday evening, the wedding eve, Rooney was greeted by Ma almost on the back-door step. Would he have his meal up in his room as the living-room was full? Queenie and her man had arrived earlier than expected, Pauline had brought the children round, and Doreen was in a state.

Yes, that was all right, he assured her with relief.

Very well then, she would bring it up to him.

He wanted to suggest that he came down for it, but that would mean coming among them again, so he refrained.

The living-room was full of people and chatter, and the chatter, to Rooney's painful embarrassment, died away on his entry.

Ma came in behind him, then pushed round him to the fore, and, with the attitude of a collector showing off a treasured piece and with the accompanying emotion in her voice, she presented her daughter Queenie.

Queenie inclined her head, which was but a younger edition of Ma's, and in an ultra-'refeened' voice said, 'How do you do?'

'How d'you do?' said Rooney, unconsciously giving the correct reply.

'And this is my son-in-law Tim.'

Rooney looked at the big fellow and nodded; and the big fellow nodded back. And, thought Rooney with some comfort, he looks about as happy as I do when among them. His impression of these two was that they were dressed to kill ... he was wearing a pepper-and-salt tweed suit and spanking great brogues, while she was decked out in a blue corded velvet suit. The man, although well over six feet, was flabby, running to fat, with more than a suggestion of a paunch, which was all out of place, Rooney considered, in a fellow who didn't look forty. He had straight black hair and a heavy blue jowl, and was handsome in a way. But for all his largeness there was something about him that seemed to belie it—he looked ... cowed. Aye, that was the word.

As Rooney, with feet that seemed to have doubled in size, picked his way out of the room, he met May coming in. She smiled at him and said, 'Hallo.'

In his surprise he almost let her pass without answering, but managed to say, 'Hallo. It's turning cold.'

'Yes. Yes, it is.' She smiled at him again before closing the door.

Well, that was heartening—he hadn't seen this one since the night he first came here. Perhaps living with Jimmy had done something for her after all.

When Ma brought his meal up, she seemed in no hurry to return downstairs. 'Did you see their car?' she asked softly.

'No,' he said, 'I didn't.'

'No. Of course; you came in the back way. You'll see it when you go out the front.... It's a beauty. Over a thousand he paid for it. Queenie picked it.... Do you think my Queenie's like me?'

'Yes. Yes, I do.' This was definitely the truth.

Ma tilted her head, as if looking into a mirror. 'Yes, she's like me. I can see myself all over again in her.' She paused in her reminiscences and looked down into the fire.

Rooney looked longingly at his dinner, with the steam spreading away the heat.

'Well'—Ma recalled herself—'we're just as old as we feel, aren't we?' She smiled widely at him, and blinked her eyelids with a coyness that added to her years and made her somehow pathetic.

'Aye, that's true,' he said.

'Now I'll leave you to your dinner. I hope all this noise doesn't disturb you.'

'Not at all,' he said.

'It'll soon be over.' Ma sighed. 'I'll be lonely without Doreen, she's such a comfort.'

Rooney failed to see it, but he replied politely, 'Aye.'

'Now——' Ma looked hastily about her and, as if getting back to business, said, 'You're all right? Everything comfortable? Get on with your dinner then.'

Left to himself, Rooney got on with his dinner, quickly washed and changed, and let himself out of the front door. And yes, he thought, it was a spanking car all right, one of the latest. And it set him thinking that if that pair had so much money why didn't they look after the old girl, so she didn't have to let? But it was generally the way—the more some folks had, the less they did.

There was no one in the M.P.s' corner when Rooney arrived in The Anchor; but Johnny was at the bar.

'Hallo,' he said. 'Squeezed through the mob?'

'Just about,' replied Rooney.

'Full house, the night, eh? Our Queenie and Big Tim there yet?' he asked, mimicking Ma.

'Yes,' said Rooney. 'It seems they've arrived.'

Johnny took a long drink. 'By, she gets me goat, that one. Going to hell with swank. And how that big swab dare come back there I don't know.... But he's soft, soft as clarts. And as miserable as hell. Queenie sees to that. But to my mind he's getting his deserts. I bet he's rued the day he let Nellie go. By lad! I bet he has.'

'Nellie?' Rooney, about to order his drink, paused and turned to Johnny.

'Of course, you wouldn't know nowt about it. Queenie pinched him off Nellie, her and the old girl.'

'That big fellow?'

'Aye, that big fellow. That's part of what done it—him being big and Nellie little. Scoffed the lugs off him, they did ... never let up—all the time. And Queenie buttering him up and slobbering over him on the quiet. And the old girl.... Oh! the old girl—how she worked on that business.'

'But was he engaged or something to the little ... to Nellie?'

'Sort of. He was a traveller what called at Bamford and Brummell's. That's how he met Nellie, just after the war. It appeared they had been going strong for nearly two years afore she let on to Ma. It would have been better if she'd never brought him there at all. Ma had Queenie and him tied up within six months. It was a "give me child a name" job—she had one in the oven.'

Rooney ordered his beer and one for Johnny, paid for them, and sat down. So that was it. But why had she stayed there all these years? Why had she slaved at that machine for them? Why hadn't she stood up to them all and got herself somebody else? There were better blokes, surely, than that big soft goof. Why hadn't she showed them? But she hadn't ... she had, to use Ma's words, let herself go.

The thought came to him from nowhere that Ma hated her, with a deep hatred. Very likely she was a weight on her conscience, the shabby sight of her being a constant reminder of her own connivance in breaking her life.

Rooney had not touched his beer when he asked, 'Why has she stayed there?'

'Beats me really. But I suppose it's the old man ... she was always fond of him, and he dotes on her. Ma would have had him put nicely away behind the iron gates long afore now but for his pension. And without Nellie he'd have been a damn sight better off there. But give old Nellie her due, she's looked after him.'

But the old Nellie was gone ... things had changed since Wednesday. 'Have you been there this week?' Rooney asked.

'No. But Ma came dashing round last night and went on about Nellie something chronic. Says she's going barmy. They'll both go barmy, if you ask me. This wedding's goin' between Ma and her wits. Well, here's one who's not losing half a shift the morrow. Not for Miss Doreen, I'm not. And there won't be a lick of hard, not so much as a smell. Shabby wedding, eh? Ginger beer and buns!'

He threw off the remainder of his beer, and rising, said, 'Well, here I go to be sniffed at. But it doesn't affect me. You know summat?' He leaned towards Rooney. 'I like these Friday nights. Wouldn't miss 'em for the world. I get one or two in on the quiet.... So long. Be seeing you. I suppose it'll be a long session the night.'

'So long,' said Rooney.

Later, when Bill, Fred, and Albert arrived, the conversation swung from the Chief Constable getting the liquor licence stopped at the Christmas British Legion dances to the latest news of the union affairs in the *G.M.W. Journal.* Albert made no contribution to the conversation, not even to comment that all dance halls should be closed; and Rooney, for the most part, sat quiet. For he couldn't get Nellie and the big fellow out of his head. He kept thinking, Poor soul, poor soul. And the more he thought 'Poor soul' the more his dislike of Ma grew.

'Come on, Brother Rooney,' cried Fred; 'snap out of it. The old wife after you now?'

'Oh, be quiet, man,' said Rooney.

'All right, Brother...!'

'Brother!' put in Bill. 'All this brother business. You're talking like the bloody journal. It gets up my nose. It strikes me as if we were a lot of bloody communists.... Comrades and brothers! Brother this, Brother that.'

'Well, they've always done it,' said Fred.

'They've always done lots of things they shouldn't have,' answered Bill. 'When I hears some of them on the platforms calling us Brothers when they want their own way, I think, Brother, me Aunt Fanny! I'm telling you this—the trade unions plus the Labour Party's in a brother of a bloody state, and if one or t'other doesn't soon do something, Brother, we'll be extinct.'

Rooney suddenly laughed. You couldn't help but laugh at Bill. He never stayed on one subject long enough to get anywhere. But as the evening wore on and the conversation jumped from Labour to Tory via the trade union, Rooney found himself possessed of the feeling that could only be termed as boredom. He often had it in a lesser degree when Danny wasn't present in the company. He now found the one-sided talk of Fred and Bill more than a trifle wearing, so nearly half an hour before closing time he rose, saying, 'I'll be off, fellows.'

'What? You going, mate?' Even Albert protested.

86

'I've got a thick head. Cold or something comin', I think.'

'Take a glass back with you,' said Bill, 'and have it hot. That'll sweat it out of you. I thought there was something up with you the night.'

'I've got a drop in,' said Rooney. 'I'll do that ... So long.'

'So long,' they said.

It was a calm night, a bit nippy, with the sky high and star-sprayed, and as he walked through the almost deserted streets —the bars and pictures had not yet turned out—Rooney found, not a little to his surprise, that running through his mind were words that the little one in her misery had spoken.

'Sometimes I wonder what we're here for,' she had said. 'What's it mean ... living?'

His eyes lifted to the sky, far away and impersonal, not understandable.

Aye, what did it mean ... living? For himself, did it mean going on like this, year in, year out, never able to get a house, living in somebody's room, feeling neither particularly happy nor sad, clinging to his bit furniture, evading women, meeting the fellows in The Anchor, going to the Dogs? ... Well, the Dogs hadn't done him badly, had they? ... But that wasn't the point. Well, what was? ... Oh, he didn't know. All he did know at this moment was that he didn't want to go through that blooming room tonight. Nor did he want to encounter Ma, or any of her family.

Because he was so averse to passing through the room, he went to the front door, hoping that he might see someone leaving and so get in that way. But No. 71 was fast closed, and to ring the bell would assuredly bring Ma. So he skirted the terrace, went down the back lane and into the yard.

The buzz of talk reached him even here, and when he opened the kitchen door it flooded on to him. Betty, May, and Pauline were in the kitchen washing up, and their earnest conversation stopped as they greeted him with varied hallos.

'Hallo,' he said. 'Busy?'

'Yes, busy,' answered Betty.

Pauline, with a tea towel in her hand, went into the kitchen, and Rooney heard her say, 'It's ... it's Mr. Smith.'

The buzz of conversation lessened, and Betty asked him, 'Would you like a cup of tea?' But without waiting for his answer, she went on, 'If I know anything, you wouldn't.'

'Surprise you if I said yes, wouldn't it?'

She laughed. 'By, it would.'

'Well, good night.' He nodded to May and her, and together they answered, 'Good night.'

When he went into the room, he saw at once to his dismay that, with the exception of Doreen, all Ma's lot were there, and their men, Johnny, Jimmy, Dennis, and the big fellow, Tim. Queenie was lolling in one armchair and Ma sat opposite her in another. But Ma wasn't lolling, and she didn't entirely look her bright, breezy self.

'You've got back then?' she said.

He did not answer the obvious statement, but returned Jimmy's and Johnny's nods. Dennis did not nod. The big fellow said, 'Hallo.'

Rooney did not answer this greeting; in fact he made a point of ignoring the salute, and the man.

When he was almost at the door, Johnny, as if they had not met earlier, said, 'Had a good night?' And Rooney, looking over his shoulder to give a brief reply, halted both his words and his departure, for the back door had clicked open and a very audible gasp was coming from the kitchen—a gasp which said, 'Nellie!'

What the gasp indicated, Rooney had no idea, except that it concerned the little one. She would soon come into the room and she would have to look at that fellow and his wife and see in her, materially at any rate, all the things she had missed ... and that wasn't counting what she might still feel for the bloke. Even with her new defence she would probably feel it pretty bad. He wondered when she had last seen him—they must have met during the past eight years. And how did the big fellow feel about the shabby little creature she had become?

His hand was on the door knob when Nellie entered the room, and the gasp, like sound carried over a long distance, was repeated.

Rooney's lips parted and his head lifted backwards in surprise. There she stood framed in the doorway. He knew it was her by her eyes, but they were the only instantly recognized thing about her, for she looked, as he phrased it, as near as dammit to the woman in the magazine she had pointed out to him last night. Only the colour of the clothes was different. Her costume was a dull brick colour, and her coat the flecked yellow brown of an autumn leaf, and on the back of her head was fitted a tight velour hat, matching the colour of the costume. And her hair ... her hair made Rooney gape. Gone was the pot-pie-basin cut. He couldn't imagine that there had ever been one, for it now lay in shining careless quiffs on her brow and about her ears. And if this wasn't enough, her face was made up, really made up. And to bemuse him and everyone else further, she appeared taller by an inch or two. Two other things struck him, one pleasurably, the other with dismay. First, he noticed she was wearing the necklace, and secondly, she was drunk. Well, if not drunk, pretty far gone. He was too well versed in seeing a woman in drink to make a mistake. He prided himself he could practically tell how much they were carrying from the film on their eyes. Never before, even remembering the torment caused by his mother, had a woman in drink hurt him as this one was doing. And as Ma gave her usual war-cry of 'Well!' he heard a new and unused voice crying from within him, 'Aw! no, Nellie, you shouldn't have done that. Why had you to go and do that? Aw! Nellie.'

He could have cheered her for slapping them all in the face with her fine get-up. But to get drunk ... she had spoilt it.

'In the name of God!' It was Johnny. 'Why, Nellie! Well, I be damned!' He was on his feet, as was Ma. The others were all sitting upright in their seats, showing different expressions of incredulous amazement; while behind Nellie, in the kitchen doorway, stood Pauline, Betty, and May.

Slowly, Nellie returned their gaze. One after the other, she looked at them ... all except the big fellow. She did not turn her head in his direction although his eyes were fixed upon her. Then with her head cocked to one side, a little smile on her face, and moving circumspectly, she crossed the room. Her intention, Rooney saw, was to pass through without speaking.

But Nellie had counted without Ma, for, like a prancing hippopotamus, Ma bore down on her, and grabbing her by the arm, swung her about.

'You! ... You hussy!'

There was the immediate sound of a ringing slap as Nellie's hand came in sharp contact with Ma's fleshy arm. 'Don't you touch me!' Her voice was thick and uncertain, and it caused Ma to step away from her.

Unlike Rooney, Ma was not versed in the effects of drink, but the combination of Nellie's voice and the smell of her breath was patent proof of the horrifying truth, and that Ma was truly horrified was evident, for she was temporarily derived of her voice. When, with an effort, she regained it, she gasped, in a whisper, 'You're drunk.'

'Not quite.' Nellie's voice was quiet again; there was even a touch of laughter in it. 'No, not quite. He assured me that you couldn't get drunk on four ports and two advocaats. That's all I've had ... four ports and two advocaats. Have you ever had advocaat?' She poked out her head towards Ma. 'It's nice ... thick ... custard with a kick. No, you've never had advocaat.' Her voice rose sharply on a bitter note. 'Vitriol's your drink.'

'It's made your old gig-lamps shine anyway,' put in Johnny quickly. 'Have you won the pools, Nellie?'

'No. No, Johnny, I haven't won the pools.'

'No!' Ma cried, her face almost purple, 'but I'll tell you where ...'

'Be quiet, Ma!' Stepping quickly to her mother's side Pauline took hold of Ma's arm. 'Don't upset yourself. As for you'—she turned to Nellie—'if you had to show off your finery and your emancipation, you could have picked some other time.'

'Why?' It was a blunt if slightly fuddled demand.

'Why? You know why. The wedding and everything.'

'Oh, the wedding!' Nellie's eyebrows moved up and her nose moved down. 'I wasn't asked to the wedding. So ... so I can sleep in the morning. ... I wasn't asked to stay back and look after things in this old mausoleum ... I wasn't even told to do it. ... It was just taken for ... for granted. ... Nellie's there. Nellie's always there. ... Wedding? I've worked for months for that wedding, like I did for all your weddings. I sewed for that young upstart——'

'You dare call——' Ma was prevented from descending on Nellie by both May and Pauline.

'Yes, I dare!' Nellie lessened the distance between them by stepping forward. 'They're all upstarts, every one of them. thanks to you. And thanks to you they've looked upon me as an unpaid servant for years. You've done a lot of harm in your time, Gracie Howlett, but the greatest harm you've done is to them ... what you've turned them into.'

'I hope you're not including me, Nellie?' It was Betty who, although she used a smarmy tone, was, like Johnny, trying to make light of the situation.

'Yes, you an' all. If you're human you've got Johnny to thank. ... And he isn't much cop, when all's said and done.' The last was uttered by way of an afterthought.

'Well, I'll be damned!'

Rooney could have laughed aloud at the sudden change in

Johnny's countenance, but his attention was turned towards Nellie again. She was pointing to Jimmy with an unsteady finger. 'There's the only one among you who's any good ... Jimmy ... him. He's the only decent one among you. The only one who thinks. You think, don't you, Jimmy?'

If this remark had been addressed towards Rooney, however merited, he would have become suffused with embarrassment, and it was with something akin to envy that he saw Jimmy smile and say easily, 'Well, now, Nellie. To the last I'll say, Yes, I try to, although it isn't always easy. And I will return your compliment and say you're looking very nice tonight, Nellie. In fact, you're what they would call a ... smasher.'

Jimmy leant towards her as he said this as if he were addressing a soothing remark to a child, and with almost childlike enjoyment Nellie's face lit up for an instant, and her lips were parted to speak when Ma's voice cut in, not loud this time but weighed down with an emotion that could only be classed as venom.

'Smasher! Whore, more like it. I know where you've got your money. I went to the shop. Miss Tanner knew nothing. But I met old Brummell, and he couldn't look me in the face. None of his business, he said. He's been living with a woman for ten years, and now he goes and leaves her for you! An old man, sixty-seven if he's a day.... You dirty——'

'Ma! Ma! Be quiet.' The request came from several quarters of the room.

'I won't be quiet. Let me be!' She flung off her daughters and faced Nellie.

Nellie did not move, but glared up at Ma, her face drawn and tight, the old Nellie under the make-up. Then, as if something was tickling her from inside, her body slumped, and with a swift movement she turned from Ma and with both hands on the table she leant over it and very gently began to laugh.

It was the most painful sound Rooney had ever heard. It did not touch on mirth, and held neither joy nor gaiety, not even ribaldry; it had an empty, lost sound, that made him want to go to her and lead her from the room.

'Laugh ... That's it, laugh! You! You ...' Ma resorted to her Bible and brought out, 'Harlot!'

The laughter rose, and Rooney, finding it unbearable, was being impelled from within to do something and was actually on the point of moving towards her when Jimmy signalled to his wife, and May, going to the table and gently pressing her mother aside, said, 'Come on, Nellie. Come on up to bed.'

With unnatural suddenness, the laughter stopped, and when Nellie turned and faced the room again it was as if she had laughed herself sober. Hitching her coat up on to her shoulders, and ignoring May's hand, she looked at Ma and said, 'Your detecting got you so far but not far enough. It isn't Mr. Brummell—I turned down that offer a long time ago, for I felt with a little effort I could do much better for myself should I feel so inclined.... What do you say, Tim?'

She had moved her head quickly round, and Rooney, looking at the big fellow, found it in his heart to be sorry for him. His face was a reddy purple, except for his lips, which appeared bloodless and dry. And his tongue began to flick over them as Nellie, moving from the table towards the door, came nearer to him.

The room became quiet; even Ma's spleen was forbidden voice for the moment. Within a foot of him, Nellie stopped. Nor did the big fellow drop his eyes from hers when she said, 'It's eight years gone Wednesday since we last spoke, Tim.... Far too long, isn't it?'

'Really!' Queenie was standing erect and indignant. 'This has gone beyond everything.'

'Oh!' Nellie put up her hand and softly patted the air. It was a pat that ignored Queenie as a whole and pushed her forcibly into her place. 'Don't, as your mother would say, take on, please. Should anybody feel indignant it should be me. What do you say, Tim?' They were still staring at each other. 'Wouldn't you think they would all be rejoicing to see me in the money?' She smiled with one side of her mouth. 'I'm sure you'll be happy, because now I'll be off your conscience, and you have enough to put up with without that.'

'Get her out before I...'

Rooney watched the scuffle to keep Ma in hand. But neither the scuffle nor Ma's voice seemed to have the slightest effect on Nellie. It was as if she heard neither, for looking deep into the shamefaced eyes of the big fellow, she said: 'I've always had one advantage over you, Tim ... I've been a free-lance. Even in my misery I was a free-lance.' On this she turned from him; and Rooney, stepping quickly aside, let her out.

She went past him with her head up, giving him no sign of recognition. And he stood in the doorway watching her mount the stairs while the room to his side became a bedlam.

'By God! Who'd believe it? And to turn on me, and me always sticking up for her.'

'Stop crying, Ma. Look, you'll only be ill. And there's tomorrow, remember.'

'Well, thank God Harry and his people aren't here.'

'I'll throw her out. I will, I will.'

'All right, Ma. All right. Only stop crying.'

' "And the worm when it turned had an elephant's hoof." '

'Oh, for God's sake stop your clever quotations, Jimmy. Just because she said you could think.'

'All right, Queenie. I'm sorry if my quoting upsets you. But it was very nice of her to realize it.... Don't take it so badly, Tim, it's life.'

'He's not taking it badly. And you shut up.'

'Now, Queenie, that doesn't go with all your accoutrements. And what about letting Tim speak for himself?'

'She's nothing but a prostitute! She admitted it, didn't she? And to think, all these years and what I've done for her.'

'There, there, Ma.'

'Where you going?'

The big fellow, his face now devoid of colour, went quickly past Rooney and out of the front door without answering his wife, and Rooney, moving quietly, made for the stairs.

In his room he stood with his cap between his hands looking towards the wall at the head of the bed. The babble of voices coming up to him was not more confused than were his feelings, for only a small part of him was now in sympathy with her. That she had planned her entry he was sure. And he should now be waving a flag for her. But she'd got drunk, or pretty near it. And to him that had taken something out of her act of retaliation. He did not name it dignity. If she had come in, dressed up to the nines as she was, and with a few cool words, as they would have done on the pictures, passed through the room leaving them all flabbergasted, that would have done the trick. Her dressing up and staging her entry had been something like the pictures anyway, but she failed to carry it through. The big fellow had likely deserved all he got. But, by God, he had looked awful. Drunk or sober, she had certainly carried that part out all right—she couldn't have hit him harder or better. Yet somehow or other he now felt sorry for the chap. One part she hadn't done very convincingly. That was about the old fellow. Her laughter had not the effect of denial as she intended it should, but appeared to him a poor cover-up. She had perhaps been taken off her guard by Ma's knowledge.

He threw his cap on to a chair, and having pulled off his clothes got ready for bed. But he did not go to bed. The bed was too near the wall that separated him from Nellie and he did not want to think any more about her or of her business. She had got herself fixed up and his pity would not be called upon in the future.

He sat before the fire, his feet stretched out on the hearth, and as time went on the voices became more subdued, rising only once when he guessed Doreen had come in.

He heard the car starting up outside, which meant the big fellow was back; then voices from the street, one in particular, Dennis's high reedy tone. And he remembered with some surprise that he had been about the only one who hadn't opened his mouth during the do, yet he had looked the most astonished of the lot of them. Of the bunch, it was that bloke Dennis, Rooney thought, he disliked the most.

He was still sitting before the fire when he heard Doreen and Ma coming upstairs, and he put out the light in case Ma, when sanity should return, would mention his extravagance. But he still sat on. The firelight glowed darkly on his dresser, and his pieces of china responded with their usual glints. The glass trinket set from his dressing-table, after trebling itself in the mirrors, sent silver streaks across the lino. The brass knobs of the bed twinkled at him, saying, 'Come on, man, don't be a damn fool.' His bits all spoke to him, bringing their usual comfort, and he rose thinking, Aye, well, I wish her luck. And no doubt she'll need it with an old bloke like him. And I hope she gets some comfort out of her fancy furniture. It did strike him that she was becoming compensated for an antique with more antiques, but he was in no mood for jests.

He made his way to bed, telling himself that he was definitely going to make a move from here, but until he could get away he'd move his bed to the other wall.

5. THE BASHING FEELING

The movement in the house started early—it was the un-usual sound of a fire being raked that woke Rooney, and he looked at his watch—it said ten minutes to five. And try as he might after this he couldn't get to sleep again. The conse-quences were that he lay tossing and turning until, a good half-hour before his usual time, he made himself rise and get ready for work.

He had a thick head, like he sometimes experienced at Christmas when he went over his allowance and took on a drop too much.

For no particular reason, or so he told himself, other than that he had woken too early, he found himself in a devil of a temper. The appearance of the whole room irritated him; the electric light seemed to be starkly glaring, showing up his bits as no light had shown them up before. And it crossed his mind that his bed looked a monstrosity. As he combed his hair be-fore the mirror he was surprised at the sight of himself. His mouth looked set and his eyes dark, and his whole expression vaguely reminded him of Albert.

Downstairs, somewhat to his surprise, it was a subdued Ma he met. She made no comment on his early appearance, but poured him out a cup of tea without a word, and while he was drinking it she went into the kitchen and fried his bacon and eggs. And when she had placed his meal before him she took herself a cup of tea and then sat down at the corner of the table and, staring down into the steam rising from the cup, she asked, 'Well ... now, what do you think?'

He chewed on his food before saying in a voice that sounded to himself almost a growl, 'It's no business of mine.'

Ma nodded at the steam. 'No, I suppose not, but you can't help thinking. Nobody can. An old man, and with a name like he's got. He's been living with this woman up Harton for years. And he has a wife in Harrogate ... I'm so ashamed. Well, she won't stay here ... she'll go.'

As Ma took a quick sip of her tea, Rooney thought, She'll go all right—there wouldn't be much point in the whole business if she didn't.

'The wickedness of her! And to come in like that, drunk, like ... a ... a ...' Ma refrained from repeating last night's denunciation and substituted 'Hussy'. 'And all the upset. She did it on purpose.... Oh, she did it on purpose all right.' Ma shook her head slowly from side to side as she corroborated her own statement. 'Don't you think she did?'

The point-blank question caused him to move uneasily, and without looking up from his plate, he said, 'I'm having nothing to say in the matter.'

'Well, you're right there. But as I said, you can't help thinking. And you thought a bit last night; you were as astonished as any of us.'

That she should have noticed his reaction surprised him. She should, he thought, have had enough to think about without taking in how he looked.

'And to go on to Tim like that. He didn't know where to put himself, did he? She would make anyone believe who didn't know that she had really meant something to him. And she never has; they were only friendly.... Look at the size of him to her. It would have been grotesque. They were like Mutt and Jeff, the long and the short of it.'

She could go on until she was tired here, Rooney thought, and she would never convince him other than what Johnny had told him and what he himself had surmised from the big fellow's face. He had been going to marry her all right, and if the truth were told he was now damn sorry he hadn't.

A movement on the landing caused Ma to get quickly to her feet. She had momentarily forgotten the great day. But the sound of Doreen made her bustle sharply about, saying, 'I don't know where I am this morning. Oh, she's got a lot to answer for, that one. God is slow, but He's sure.' Her voice became ominous. 'As she is sowing so shall she reap. And I'll see her brought to her knees in the gutter yet!'

For the moment it shocked Rooney to realize that she could couple God with her innate desire to see the little one brought low; it seemed to him now that in some odd way she had derived a satisfaction from the drab, colourless creature that Nellie had become, and had experienced some form of pleasure in keeping her like that.

Covertly glancing at her as she darted between the kitchen and the living-room, he came to the conclusion that there were some folks who were past understanding. A man or woman could be jailed for assault, for robbery, for defamation of character, yet a woman like Ma, a regular churchgoer and a woman who, he had to admit, had done all in her means to further the welfare of her family, could slowly and painfully strangle one of her own kind while professing to be doing her nothing but good; but when the victim escaped, as the little one had done, she could become so consumed with the desire to see her brought low that she would stop at nothing to achieve this end.

Rooney's mind up to now had not been used in trying to explain the intricacies of human nature, and he was finding the process rather trying. He could come to no conclusion or cut-and-dried explanation of the social behaviour he was now encountering in this house. All he could say to himself was, Some folks should be fetched up for what they do.

But seeing the cupidity of Ma did not put the little one in better focus. If she had to go on the loose why hadn't she done it years ago? Why had she waited till now? Yet it was undoubtedly the pressure of life in this house of late that had driven her to it.

'I won't see you at dinner-time,' said Ma, as he went out, 'but I'll leave everything ready. Betty's coming round. She'll pop it in the oven.'

'You've no need to bother,' said Rooney; 'I can get my meal out. I should have mentioned it sooner.'

'Well, I won't say that won't be a help. We'll leave it at that then ... you'll have your dinner out. Once this is over we'll be back to our own quiet life again.'

He did not wait to hear more, but saying 'Goodbye', closed the door. Quiet life! Not if he knew it, he wouldn't. There'd be no quiet life for him there. The young one and the little one gone would leave him alone with her. And Ma, he was beginning to feel, was a very uncertain quantity. It could be mothering, marriage, or getting him to God, any one of the three, or all of them ... he wouldn't put anything past her. No, no. He was bolting, and as quick as possible.

Walking through the rows and rows of streets, he thought, Surely there's some place for me where I won't meet with trouble.

These houses were mostly of three rooms on the ground floor and four rooms on the upper, and each floor was classed as a house. And these were the more spacious kind! In Alice Street and thereabouts there were only two rooms on a floor. But each one appeared to him like a palace, and he wished that a miracle would happen and he could get one.

His desire for the accomplishment of this miracle was as fervent as another man's to win the seventy-five thousand pounds' pool; and in the depot, where he met Danny, and with hardly any preliminary, he voiced this to him yet again.

Danny, looking hard at him, said, 'Trouble?'

'No,' said Rooney, 'I just want to get away from there.'

'Who is it, the old one or the...?'

'Neither. I just want to move.'

Although he had already told Danny about the little one, he found he could not pass on the latest developments. He could no more have said 'She's gone on the loose' than he could have talked of his own mother's lapses.

'Why, man, I don't know what to make of you.' Danny rubbed his nose with the side of his finger. 'Well, in any case, whether you stay or go Mrs. D. wants you to come to wor place for Christmas.'

Rooney smiled. 'I'd like that, Danny. Thanks.... Thank her.'

Bill and Fred joined them and, after the usual cursory greetings, they stood together waiting for Albert. And when at last Albert put in an appearance, hurrying across the yard towards them, Danny muttered under his breath, 'Aye, aye! Something's happened here, an' all.' There was a sheepishness about Albert that was unusual, especially since lately his whole attitude had been one of aggression, and Bill, never able to keep his observations to himself, remarked, 'Pinched the cat's milk, Albert?'

'What! No.' Albert lit a cigarette, then looked from one to the other. And after a long, sustained draw he remarked with forced casualness, 'I'd better tell you. I'm ... I'm going to give me notice in.'

They stared at him. A chap didn't give his notice in just like that. It brewed up for a long time. He threatened it, he talked about it. Then one day he did it and no one was really surprised.

'Got another job, Albert?' asked Danny.

'I'm goin' in the pits.'

'The pits! Well, I'll be damned! After the big money?' said Bill.

'Why not?'

'Why not at all,' said Bill. 'But I thought that, like the rest of us, you preferred to meet your number above the gutters.'

'When me time comes I'll go, and not afore.' Albert turned away, and after a quick glance had passed between the others they followed him.

It was not until the middle of the morning, while in the privacy of a long tradesmen's entrance, that Albert, able to contain himself no longer, said, 'She's come back, Rooney.'

Rooney stopped in his tracks and asked slowly, 'You're taking her?'

His eyes following his hand, Albert dusted down his jacket. 'She's turning over a new leaf.'

Albert was now surveying his feet. 'She won't stay in Shields ... we're goin' to Darlington. I've got some relations there; they're letting us have a room until we get settled. I can't tell the others; you could tip them off for me, if you will. They'll say I'm daft, barmy, but it's me own life.'

Side-tracking the main issue, Rooney said, 'But you always hated the pits when you were down as a lad, Albert.'

'I'll get used to 'em again. And me money'll be double what it is now, that's the main thing.' He looked up. 'I'll miss the lot of you. But you more than any of them ... we've been good mates. But'—his mouth and eyes became hard as he turned away—'nothing or nobody matters. I'll work in hell if it's goin' to make things right.'

Rooney walked behind him up the path, through the gate, and out on to the road. What was it that got into a man that would allow him to take back a woman after he knew she had been with other blokes, coloured an' all? What was there to measure the torment of knowing your wife was like that against the torment of wanting her back in spite of it? ... The emotions bred of living were beginning to worry Rooney. If it should happen to him it would drive him mad. But he was consoled that it wouldn't happen ... he would never be eaten up with the passion or whatever it was that drove men to do what Albert was going to do. Again came the consolation that if he had missed any of the transient joys of marriage, he had also missed the more concrete woes.

On top of this came the uneasy thought that things were going to change and change quickly. Albert going, Danny due for his pension next year, and with a new charge-hand they would likely be changed all round. Nothing would be the same. And when he came to consider it, the change had already begun, because nothing had been the same since he went to Filbert Terrace.

At twelve o'clock, after Albert had departed and before they dispersed from the depot, he told the gang the news. Bill swore long and loudly, as Rooney had thought he would. Fred said, 'Well, he'll have no sympathy from me. He deserves all that's coming to him.' Danny, quiet as usual, remarked, 'I guessed it was like that. Mrs. D. won't be surprised either ... she said that's how it would be. Well, it's his life.'

Although it was bitingly cold, the sun was shining as Rooney made his way home, and he was vindictive enough to be thinking it was more than that Madam Doreen deserved, and that it would have served her right if it had snowed and hailed.

Betty was in the kitchen when he went in, and she greeted him affably. 'Oh, hallo,' she said. 'I was hoping you'd be in shortly. Are you going to stay long? I've lit your fire.'

'Well,' he considered, trying to arrange in his mind just how long he could stay in without running into Ma and the party on their return, 'well, I'll be going out about three.'

'Oh, I'll be back before then.... I just wanted to pop home to see to Johnny and if everything's all right. I won't be half an hour. It's only because of Grandpa.... She's in, but I wouldn't ask her anything.'

Rooney was quick to notice this change in Betty's attitude. Nellie had become 'she'—not so much, he considered, if at all, because of her lost virtue but because of her remark last night to Johnny. It was a case of prick a husband and you stab a loving wife.

'I'll just slip my things on. I won't be long. I'll be back before they are anyway. They'll be here shortly after three. They're going to take the wedding presents straight to the flat, then call at Harry's place.'

She had put her coat on and departed before he went upstairs; and as he made his way to his room, he hoped, with a surprising urgency, that he would get there without meeting ... her. Like Betty's his pseudonym for Nellie had changed ... she was no longer the little one, a name that had its birth in pity, but 'her', and he gave no reason to himself for the meaning of the change.

Before going to have a wash he sat down before the fire. It was burning brightly, and the hearth looked neat and tidy and his bits once again looked good to his eye. And he should have felt relaxed and at ease; but he felt neither. He was wishing fervently that he was out of this, yet at the same time he wished that there was not lying before him the search for a new home.

No movement whatever could be heard in the room next door, and he tried to keep his ears from straining to hear some sound by thinking, I have enough on me own plate.

She was likely sleeping off her hangover, and if he knew anything, her head would be feeling as if there was a shipyard riveter inside it ... her not being used to it.

It was after two o'clock when he went across the landing to have his wash. Back in his room, he was fastening the collar on a clean shirt when a tap-tap came on the door. He turned from the mirror and stared towards it for some moments. Then, one hand on the still unfastened collar, he went to the door and opened it.

Nellie was standing there, dressed as she had been last night. He had imagined that when he next came across her he would see her slightly cowed, or at least shamed, but the Nellie before him was in neither of these admonished states; she looked—the only word he could think of was pert.

'Hallo, Rooney.'

He swallowed, brought the other hand to the aid of his collar, then said, 'Hallo.'

'I would like a word with you.'

He blinked at her while trying to push the stud through the hole.

'Are you shocked about last night?' she asked quietly.

He let an end go. 'It's none of my business.'

'Oh!' Her pertness vanished, and she cried with a mixture of irritation and bitterness, 'Don't say it like that, as if I was still of no consequence.'

'Well, it isn't, is it ... no business of mine?'

She looked hard at him, and as she did so she seemed to become deflated, and the old Nellie came back into her look and voice as she said, 'You are shocked because I staged it all, and came in drunk.... I had no intention of coming in like that.... I wasn't really drunk, it was because I'm not used to it. I thought I'd have a glass of wine to ... to give me courage. And then I had another. I didn't think you could get like that on port wine.' She waited a moment and continued to look up at him, and he said lamely, 'Well, yes ... you can ... and badly.'

'I had intended just to walk in and through them and leave them guessing as to where I had got my things.'

To leave them guessing. She was pretty hard-boiled about it. He ignored the thought that she should have intended to do just what he himself had imagined would have been a most effective entry and exit.

'Did I act silly ... talk a lot?'

'Well, you said enough.'

'I feel I did too, although I can't remember everything clearly.' Her eyes dropped. 'Only yelling at Grace, and ... and what I said to Tim. I'm sorry I spoke to him like that. I shouldn't have done it. But it's been burning in me for years. And yet now, today, it seems as if it doesn't matter any more, that it has never mattered. I can forgive Tim, and I'm even sorry for him, but I can't forgive her. What she did was calculated and cruel ... not Queenie, her mother I mean. Queenie just went where she was pushed ... she'd never have carried it off on her own.... Tim and I were to have been married. I suppose you guessed that?'

He did not reply immediately. And when he did it was not to say yes or no. but to ask a straight question. And to his own surprise he asked it angrily. 'Why did you stay on here after, then, if she did all that to you?'

'I stayed because I was afraid to go.' She said this boldly, making of it a statement of fact. 'The only other person in the world I have ever felt belonged to me, other than Tim, was Grandpa.... I needed somebody, I even needed them.' She flung her arms wide, taking in the rooms that had once been full of her relatives. 'I wanted to belong somewhere, to have people to call my own. If I had gone then, I think I would have jumped in the river. We shouldn't be left to face things alone. I didn't feel capable of living without some kind of love.... Grandpa gave that to me, and still does.'

'I'm sorry; I shouldn't have asked.'

'Yes, you should. It's all right.'

'Well, what'll happen to him now, when ... when you go?'

It was a long moment before she said, 'When I go, he'll go, too.' She pulled the strap of a new brown leather bag back and forward through her hands before adding, 'I ... I only came because I ... I felt I owed you some kind of explanation.'

His fingers became agitated on the collar again. 'You owe me nothing. Why should you? You don't need to explain to me, it's none of my business.'

She suddenly brought her eyes up to his, fixing them on him intently, forcing him to look back into them, and as he did so he saw her face change, and she became again, in spite of her fine rig-out and make-up, the old Nellie he had seen on the first Saturday he came here, stiff, buttoned up.

'You ... you believe——' She paused, her hand to her head. 'I've been trying to remember all morning what she said last night about ... about Mr. Brummell. I can only remember——' She paused again, before adding harshly, 'Do you believe that there is something between Mr. Brummell and me?'

What could he say? To say, 'Yes, that's about it. You gave yourself away when you tried to laugh it off,' would be to hit her as hard as Ma had done.

Viciously now, he pulled on his collar, tugging at both ends, his chin stretched up and out. And as he was bringing the ends together her laugh struck him as suddenly as it had done last night. The tightness had vanished, and she looked gay, recklessly gay. 'I don't believe you do ... not really. Stop pulling at that collar for a minute, will you, and listen to me; I want to tell you something. I don't want any misunderstanding with you, Rooney, at least. Here, let me fix it for you and be done with it.'

Before he could step back and ward off her hands, she had reached up and, taking the two ends of the collar from him, was fastening them together with the stud. 'There!' She patted the achievement with two quick gestures similar to those she used after writing Grandpa's notes.

The patting hit his Adam's apple and caused him to swallow. Worse than that, he almost choked, for looking over her head towards the stairs he saw Betty's half-startled, half-shocked face looking at them.

Following his gaze, Nellie swung round, and her colour rose, outdoing the rouge on her cheeks. Then, moving slowly away, she muttered something which sounded to him like 'More evidence'. But still the unexpected sight of Betty did not cower her, for she marched boldly towards the stairs, tucking her bag under her arm to enable her to draw on her gloves as she did so.

Betty had now mounted to the landing, and, looking at Nellie as she passed, she said pointedly, 'You're making up for lost time, aren't you, Nellie?'

Without pausing in her walk, Nellie replied, 'Being your mother's daughter, Betty, it would be unnatural for you to think otherwise.'

Quickly and quietly Rooney closed his door, and standing with his back to it he took in air, filling his chest and expanding his stomach. If that had been Ma, my God!

But no doubt she would get to know, and then . . .

He touched his collar. Never before had a woman fixed his collar. What had made her do it? Trying out her hand? Pert? Yes, that's what she had become. And he didn't like it; he preferred her as she had been, miserable. Yet the little one was still there. But why had she tied his collar? He could feel her fingers on his neck yet. When Ma did get to know. . . . He jerked himself from the door. Blast Ma, and all her works! What had Ma got to do with it, anyway? She was becoming an obsession. What kind of a bloke was he to be frightened of a fat old woman?

He quickly put on his coat, grabbed his cap and mac, and went downstairs. Betty was in the hall. She did not speak, but her eyes spoke for her. And he stared back into them defiantly. He had, he considered, put up with enough; he wasn't going to be cowed by the lot of them and made to feel he was up to something when he wasn't.

He could hear Grandpa's voice coming from the front room, and guessed . . . she was in there. That she might come out and leave the house with him spurted his departure, and he hurried down the street. And not until he was at a safe distance did he slacken his pace. Then a not entirely irrelevant thought struck him. If the man was sixty-five or so, and she took Grandpa with her, it would be like an old-age-pensioners' home. The thought was not funny. A lover of sixty-five and a charge of nearly eighty! . . . No.

He stopped dead in the street. She wouldn't do such a thing. If she was taking the old fellow, then it wasn't Brummell she was going to. Anyway, she had just denied it. But that it was some man he could not doubt; though it must be as she had said last night, that she had done better for herself than Brummell.

She had been about to explain it all to him. She had said she didn't want him to misunderstand, and had seemed anxious that he shouldn't. Yes, when he came to think of it, she had.

He walked on slowly now. If he hadn't left the house like a frightened hare, she might have come out and caught him up.

He was pulled up sharply by his cautious self that had been somewhat neglected of late. What was he thinking now? Did he want to get involved in this business? No, no, of course he didn't. Well then, he'd go for a walk round the market, then to the pictures, and finish up at the Dogs; and keep minding his own business, and let her keep her explanations to herself—he was going to be no recipient of confidences, of how she had got herself a man, one who could rig her out like a fashion-plate at that.

He walked round the market, then went to the pictures. But he didn't go to the Dogs—he went straight to The Anchor. He had considered going to Danny's, but he knew that once he got there and started talking the whole business of ... her might slip out. And more than that might slip out—things inside himself. Oh! he wished to God he had never set foot in Filbert Terrace.

Neither Fred nor Bill was in the M.P.s' corner. He hadn't expected to see Albert there, but before he had been sitting down a few minutes he saw Johnny come into the bar and look straight towards him. But he didn't immediately come over—he ordered his drink first; then slowly crossed to the corner, carrying the pint mug in his hand. And when he reached the table he did a strange thing. Strange for him anyway. He did not greet Rooney right away, but stood looking down at him over the mug of beer.

'Hallo,' said Rooney. 'What's the matter with you?' He did not speak too affably, for he was thinking illogically that if it hadn't been for this fellow he would have known nothing about Filbert Terrace, Ma, her family ... or Nellie.

'Nowt's the matter with me, lad.' Slowly Johnny sat down, put his beer on the table, and with the back of his hand dabbed the point of his nose. It was in no way intended to be a cleansing process, but apparently to engender thought, for Johnny now gazed into the space between Rooney and the bar proper, and became lost for a time in contemplation. When he did return to his surroundings he startled Rooney with a quick demand. 'Well, let's hev it,' he said.

'Have what?'

'Aw! now, look, man ... I'm on your side, even after the way she turned on me last night. She was tight and we all say things when we're tight.' Johnny took a drink from his mug, then looked at Rooney again from beneath his brows, and what he saw made him say, 'Now look, you needn't get on your high horse.'

'Have what?' repeated Rooney again.

Johnny straightened up in his chair, took hold of the sides of the table, and pushed his elbows out. 'It's no business of mine, it's got nothing to do with me, but you must admit I took you there.'

'Damn well I know you did! But what you getting at?'

Johnny's brows drew more closely together and his face took on a surly look. 'Why you trying to come the high hat all of a sudden? Betty saw you.'

'Saw me what?'

'Well, if you must have it in plain words, necking on the landing with Nellie. It didn't strike her till later. And then she put two and two together. She said all along it wasn't old Brummell.'

Rooney had always known just what type of a fellow he himself was ... he was the placid type. His nerves were steady; he did not get het up about the things men usually got het up about, politics, religion, unions, and women; yet he wasn't without his emotions—his two brief love affairs had called up other feelings that could be described as stirrings of the blood. But when the stirrers of his blood had disappointed him his reactions had not driven him to any strong measures; perhaps they had strengthened his affection for his furniture and his own company, but that was all. In his own quiet way he sometimes compared other people's reactions to his own, and found them wanting in control. It was nothing to see two young fellows fighting outside a dance hall over some lass; it was nothing to see two grown men, well in their forties, as he had done a short while ago, come out of the Winter Garden, walk side by side to the nearest back lane, and then proceed to bash each other's brains out. He had walked unsuspectingly behind these two and had been one of the blokes who had helped separate them. As far as he could gather their wives had got mixed up, and he had thought, Fair enough ... have it out. But why had they to make a holy show of themselves in the street? And now, with his hand gripping a large fistful of Johnny's collar and the blood pounding in his head as if he had been standing on it, and a desire to bash this fellow's face in filling every pore of his body, the old placid Rooney was struggling for dear life against this wild animal that was in possession.

'Give over, man! What in the name of God's got into you?' It was Bill pulling at him.

'Leave go! Do you hear me? Leave go!' This was Stoddard,

the manager, at the other side of him. 'Leave go! Come on now, leave go. Whatever it is, talk it out. I want no fighting in here.... You of all people, Rooney! I'll believe anything after this.'

The red mist was clearing and he was seeing Johnny's startled countenance more clearly. He released his grip, and Johnny, although he was standing on his own feet, seemed to drop quite a distance to the floor.

'There, now,' said Stoddard, patting Rooney's arm. 'Sit down. Well, I've seen some things in me time from behind this bar, but nothing that has surprised me more.... There now'— he went on patting—'let up, man ... relax. You want something stiff, eh? What about a whisky?'

Rooney did not reply. But Bill said, 'Let's have three. I think this bloke's more in need of one than anybody.... No, sit down.' He pushed Johnny back into the chair. But Johnny, recovering himself now, shook off Bill's hand and rising on not very steady legs went to the counter without again looking at Rooney.

'You could have knocked me down with a side loader,' said Bill, 'when I come through that door and saw you holding that bloke by the throat. What was it? ... He's the fellow who got you the digs, isn't he?'

Rooney swallowed and blinked. Then taking a deep breath he leant against the back of the chair and closed his eyes. He felt suddenly very tired, as if he had been swimming and gone too far out.

Stoddard came to the table with the drinks, and Rooney took the glass from his hand and drank the whisky in one gulp; then he shuddered, closed his eyes again, and said, 'Give me another.'

It was a full fifteen minutes later when Bill, in some exasperation, exclaimed, 'Well, for the love of Mike! let's have it. What was it all about?'

'If you must know,' said Rooney, staring down into the sovereign gold of yet another whisky, 'he accused me of keeping a woman.'

Bill sat back. 'Keeping a woman? ... You? ... Well, are you? All right! All right! Don't start on me.' He pushed his long arm out, warding off the look that Rooney levelled at him. 'You late starters don't know when to stop. But if you was, it would be the first damn sensible thing you've done in your life.'

'You don't always talk like that.' Rooney did not raise his head, just his eyes. 'You're always growling about being tied.'

'Who's talking about being tied? You can keep her without being married, if that's how you want it. And as for being tied, there's worse states, I'm thinking, for you're never out of trouble, free as you are. I used to envy you, you know, Rooney, but you've run into more bloody hot water through evading women than the lot of us have encountered with all our wives put together, and that, to my mind, includes Albert an' all. Why don't you get hooked? You'd only have one lot of trouble then. And you'd know which street you had it in. So far you've nearly covered the bloody town. It's none of my business, but ...'

Bill left the 'but' in the air, finished his drink, and said, 'What you havin'?'

'The same.'

Bill said nothing but raised his brows as he went to the counter. It was Rooney's fourth and the night was young. He had never known him to take more than two, except on New Year's Eve. In fact, his sticking so rigidly to the rules he had set down for himself had irritated the gang on more than one occasion. That was, all except Danny. But, then, Danny was a bit of an old wife at times....

Rooney drank steadily until ten o'clock, and when he finally got to his feet his legs were afloat. But, he assured himself, he wasn't drunk. No, he wasn't drunk. If he could keep his feet on the floor he'd be all right.

The wooden floor of the bar was kind to him. Possessing some magnetic quality, it attracted his feet from out of the air to it, but once outside, the cold, hard, greasy pavements began to play tricks on him, and nothing would convince him but that some damn fool on the road gang had set the paving stones at different levels. Leaning on Bill's shoulder, he endeavoured to explain the situation, yet he knew this to be a waste of words, for Bill was drunk and he was taking Bill home.

Tentatively he stepped out, hanging on to Bill, and when he tried to speak he again came to the conclusion that somebody had been up to something, for all the words in his head were tied into knots. There were lots of things he wanted to talk about. About life and marriage and women. It was all in his head—he had never imagined he could think such things. Gradually the cold night air undid the knots, and the words began to flow in long, quick-moving lines through his brain. He could see the sense of them as they passed, although many of them were strange, highfalutin words which he had only read and never spoken and which filled his mouth so much when he tried to speak them now that he choked on them and coughed.

At one time during the journey home he could have sworn he was walking down King Street with a lass on his arm and feeling so happy he wanted to sing. Until Bill swore, and he knew it was Bill on his arm and he was taking him home because he was drunk.

'For God's sake if ... not ... not for your own, keep your trap shut else the old girl'll not let you in. Come on! Come on!' Bill tugged at him.

He didn't like being tugged ... he resisted.

'I'll leave you here, mind. Here at the gate, mind. I'll ring ... the bell. Look—get this. I ring the bell, she'll open the door and you ... you make a clean crack for the stairs. Get me? Come on.'

'Gracie, Gracie, gie me your answer, do....'

'For God's sake, man, don't start singing now. Where's the bloody bell?'

Rooney heard Bill say 'Evenin'.'

He heard himself say 'Evenin' '; then lifting his foot over the step, which had risen higher than any paving stone he had yet encountered, he stumbled past Ma and into the hall, shouting '... 'Night, Bill.'

The door banged, cutting off Bill's final farewell.

Rooney was too far gone to appreciate the look on Ma's face, but he saw her skip ... like ... like—his mind told him what she skipped like—like a water buffalo to the room door and close it.

'You're like a ... a water...'

'Go on! Up those stairs.' Ma's voice came in a sibilant whisper from the depths of her stomach. 'How dare you come into my house in this condition!'

He looked at the line of words passing through his mind and discarded buffalo for hog. 'Hog,' he said, 'wa ... ter hog!'

'Get upstairs this minute ... or get out!' It was a petrifying hiss, but it slid off Rooney.

'Out? ... Me furniture.'

Suddenly he was seized by what appeared to be a herd of water hogs and propelled bodily to the stairs and up them.

The hazardous climb was over in a twinkling—it seemed as if he had flown. He was on the landing ... there was his door. But he was going to it himself—no woman was going to push him about. With a jerk he threw off Ma's hands and made a straight line for his room. But through no fault of his the line swerved and he banged into Nellie's door, and as Ma pulled him back the door opened and through a veil of mist he saw the little one.

Ah, there she was ... she was the cause of all this. She had put her hands on him. Pert, that's what she was.

'You!' he began. 'You ...' He was jerked away and Nellie left his vision, and the next second he was in his room, lying back in his chair with Ma standing over him.

'You move out of here again tonight and I'll have you thrown into the street. Do you hear me? ... Mind, I'm warning you ... you move.'

Silently Rooney stared back at her, until her face disappeared. The door closed and he turned his head towards it. His nose twitched like a rabbit's and his face became contorted as he grabbed at words now moving much more sluggishly through his mind.

'Bossy bitch! Who ... she ... talking to? Walrus face! Not move ... out of here? I'll show the fat old dyed ... dust-bin.' He reached the door and pulled it open. His mouth too was open, ready to shout.

'Go on, get in. Get in now.'

He was back in the room and in his chair again, and Nellie was by his side. 'Don't talk,' she said softly. 'Don't, Rooney, that's a good fellow, don't talk.'

She seemed to be pleading with him, and he, not unchivalrous even in his drink, whispered back, 'No ... all right. She's an old cow.'

'Yes. Be quiet now. Let me get your collar off.'

'No, no, you're not. Don't you touch me collar.'

'Please,' she entreated. 'Lie back and don't talk. There now'—she pulled his hands away from his neck—'you'll feel better with it off.'

He did feel better with it off. 'Nellie ... tell me sumthin'.... Will you tell me sumthin'?'

'Yes.'

'Leave me shoes alone'—he tried to stay her hands—'I wan' you ... tell me sumthin'.'

'Be quiet ... don't talk now.'

'Aye, now. Yes, now.'

'In the morning.'

'Albert's wife ... Albert's wife went ... went off with a nigger, an' ... an' he ... he took her back.... You went off with.... No! No! Get by. Leave me coat alone.... No!'

'Sit up till I get it off.'

He pressed harder back against the chair.

'Rooney, listen to me.' Her hands were holding his face. 'Listen to me, will you?'

Her hands felt nice. He tried to look up at her, but he couldn't see her face clearly any longer, for it kept coming and going, coming and going. When for a brief second he did see it, it brought the queerest feeling to him, the queerest feeling ... he wanted to kiss it as he did that lass's hand in his dream. It was funny ... funny. He began to laugh, a deep, low, rumbling sound. The laughter rolled about inside him.

'Sh! Rooney, please. Please listen. Listen to me. I spoilt things for them downstairs last night—please don't you do it tonight. Try to understand.'

It was something in her voice like the sound of crying that got through to him, and he whispered, 'All right. All right.... Let me be. Go on.' The lines of words were becoming more difficult to see and grasp and he could hold on to none of them. He wanted to sleep. He lay back but was pulled upright again.

'Come on, get on to the bed; you can't lie there all night. Come on ... up! Up!'

He was on his feet, rolling like a top-heavy ship.

'Take your coat off. There ... that's it.'

With an effort he reached the bed, and with a heavy relaxed flop fell into its billows.

Her hands were on him, covering him up. She touched his face again, bringing words back into his mind.

'Nellie....'

'Yes?'

'Nellie....'

'Yes. Go to sleep now.'

'I'll be like Albert. It woon't ... it woon't matter what...'

'All right. Go to sleep.'

'Nellie.... Nellie, in the morning ... I want to talk ... to ...'

'Sh! Sh! Go to sleep now,' she whispered; and he went to sleep.

6. AND WHATSOEVER THINGS ARE PURE

In the deep dark of the night that had pressed its blackness into his head Rooney woke feeling past description. For some time he did not realize where he was, and to find himself in bed, still in his trousers, added to his confusion. In a thick daze he got up, supporting his head the while, took off his clothes, had a long drink of water, then flung himself back into the bed again. Thought was painful, so with his face half buried in the pillow he went to sleep again.

The room was in dim light when he finally awoke, but the sun was shining outside, for a bright golden strip from the side of the curtain lay across the dressing-table. Thinking was still painful, but he made an attempt at it. What had happened last night? He could remember seeing Ma in the hall, but from then his doings remained blank.

He looked at his watch, It was half-past ten. He wanted a drink ... a strong cup of tea. The desire for a strong cup of tea got him out of the bed.

He held his head in his hands. God, but he felt awful. Why had he got like this? He had been tight before but never with this after-effect. It wasn't worth it; it wasn't worth the candle; all the drink on earth wasn't worth feeling like this. He'd give it up ... he could if he liked, he only drank for company.... God in heaven! his head was going to burst.

He dragged on his dressing-gown and switched on the light, but the glare hit his eyeballs like a spray of acid, and he switched it off again. He'd have a wash ... a bath. He'd have to before he went down, for if he looked anything like he felt, he looked pretty awful.

He was going round in circles trying to find his towel and soap when a tap came on the door ... Ma ... my God in heaven! couldn't she wait until he could think?

He let her knock again before going to the door and pulling it open. Nellie stood there with a tray in her hands, and she was smiling with a sort of mischievous smile that did nothing but irritate him in this moment.

'I thought you might like a strong cup of tea ... I had to wait till she went to church. Feeling awful?'

'A bit,' he said. 'Thanks.' Then, 'Oh, thanks. I've been praying for this.' He took the tray from her, but to his concern she did not turn away but, putting out her hand, switched on the light and walked into the room saying, 'I'll light your fire.... I'd have a bath if I were you.'

He looked at her already kneeling on the mat. The tray was still in his hands. Funny how she repeated his thoughts.

He poured himself out a cup of tea, and then another, before asking the question that was foremost in his mind. 'What happened last night? Did I...?' He paused, not being able to name whatever type of rumpus he had caused.

She looked up at him over her shoulder, her eyes still merry. 'You did. It's becoming a habit, me one night, you the next.'

'I kicked up a row?'

'No, not really.'

'How did I get upstairs? I can never manage stairs when I'm...'

'She pushed you up, or dragged you or something. Anyway, she got you up.'

His face began to burn. 'Did ... did she come in here?'

'Just to see you were safely in.'

He let out a long-drawn breath, then said, 'In any case I'll be for it.'

'You're not afraid of her?' Nellie's brows drew together.

'No, no.' He didn't know whether he was lying or not. 'But I don't want any trouble with her.'

Nellie rose from her knees, the pan of ashes in her hand. 'I don't think you need worry. She'll likely forgive you and read you a lecture ... she won't miss the chance to try and reform you.'

He gave a weak smile. 'That'll be as bad.'

They looked at each other, like conspirators against a common enemy. Then they laughed.

They were still looking at each other when she asked, 'Who is Albert?'

'Albert? Did I talk about him?'

'Yes. And his wife.'

'Oh.'

'She went off with a Negro.'

'I told you that?'

She nodded, smiling tenderly at him.

'When you're drunk you can't mind your own business ... I'll have to watch out. It's a fool's game anyway.' He wanted to

113

add, 'And don't forget that.' But what he said was, 'What else did I say?' But having said it he found himself suddenly afraid of knowing, so added quickly, 'I'd better have a wash. Thanks for the tea; it ... it saved me life.'

The ash-pan in one hand, the tray in the other, she went out. But he did not go immediately to the bathroom. What had he said last night? And how did she know what he had said, if it was Ma who had brought him upstairs and pushed him in here? He looked slowly around the room, and his eyes came to rest on the dressing-table. On it lay his collar and tie. The tie was folded in four, and reposing on the top of it were his studs. He had never folded a tie in his life.

At the foot of the bed stood his shoes, side by side, unfamiliar in their military position. His coat was not over the back of a chair but on a hanger on the back of the door.

The heat from his face spread over his body. She must have ... put him to bed.

Clamping down on further thought, he went to the bathroom.

Nellie was proved right about Ma's attitude, for when Rooney put in an appearance downstairs, round about one o'clock, she did not go for him but with a pained expression she surveyed him across the length of the room. Then, as if she were admonishing a favourite child, she said, 'Rooney, I'm surprised at you.'

He moved uneasily and strained his neck out of his collar.

'I'm surprised at meself.... I'm sorry for coming in like that.'

'Well, I hope it's not going to happen again, Rooney.'

'No,' he said, 'it won't.' He did not add, 'If it does, you won't see it.'

He wished now that she had gone for him and given him notice; it would have saved him a lot of trouble in the long run.

'Well?' her bust rose with a great intake of breath. 'We'll say no more about it then. I hope things are going to settle down ... everyone seems to have gone mad at once. Come and have your dinner so that I can get cleared away. That one hasn't done a hand's turn ... I came back to find everything just as I left it. She can afford to eat out now that she's in the money ... on the ill-gotten gains of sin.'

Rooney hadn't heard Nellie go out, and the knowledge that she was gone made the house more alien to him. In direct contradiction to this he was experiencing a mounting feeling of irritation towards her.... She had been going to explain things to him yesterday. Why hadn't she? And then this morning, when she'd had the chance, she had said nothing, nothing that threw any light on the subject anyway. But hadn't he made up his mind that he didn't want to know? Oh, blast everything!

'There.' Ma put his meal on the table. 'I've had mine. But I'll sit down a minute, because I feel there's a need to talk to you.' She lowered herself slowly into the chair. 'You know, Rooney, you're like my own son and I don't want to see you...'

No; he just couldn't stand this, not at the present moment he couldn't. So he didn't sit down, but with forced courage faced her, saying, 'If you don't mind I'll ... I'll take it upstairs. Me head's splitting, and I'm no company to meself or anybody else.'

Ma's surprised look also held a touch of indignation. Her lips pursed and her whole face tightened, bringing a group of lines from her nose that made her mouth appear corrugated.

'Well! if that's how we feel, very well. But we must have a talk, and soon. And we'll both feel better for it.'

This was no request but an order.

He escaped with his dinner. But in the privacy of his room he found what little appetite he'd had for it had vanished, and he sat before the fire smoking, his mind not on Ma now but on Nellie again, out eating with the fellow.

About four o'clock he heard some members of the family arrive for tea, and this gave him the needed impetus to get ready and go out. Fifteen minutes later he reached the hall, when, as if he had been awaiting him, Grandpa's door opened.

'Hallo, there,' said the old man. His eyes were twinkling, and his whole manner jovial.

'Hallo,' said Rooney.

'Going out?'

'Aye.' Rooney nodded.

'So am I ... the morrer. Nellie's getting a taxi and taking me out. All round the places I know. Cleadon, Frenchman's Bay, right to Sunderland.... Have you seen Nellie?' This was a whisper.

Again Rooney nodded.

'Ain't she bonnie? Just like when she was a lass. Come into some money, Nellie has ... Has she told you? She's had some money left her.'

Rooney shook his head.

'She will. She's happy now. Doesn't she look grand?'

The room door opened and Pauline came out into the hall, where, ignoring Rooney, she said briskly, 'Come along, Grandpa, come along.'

'Now you leave me alone, madam. I'm just havin' a word ...'

Rooney made his escape, but he could still hear Grandpa's protests after he had closed the iron gate behind him.

What, he wondered as he walked along the streets which Sunday seemed to strip of people and make desolate, would the old fellow's reactions be when Ma informed him just how Nellie was getting her money? He'd likely hit her, as he himself had been going to hit Johnny when he suggested it was he who was supplying it. ...

He had reached Fowler Street when this thought came to him, and although it did not stop him in his tracks, he turned aside and stood looking into the window of a sweet shop piled high with Christmas attractions. That had been the start of it, he could remember it all now ... Johnny coming across to him and saying ... What had he said? That he had been keeping Nellie.

A faint echo of his rage returned. He had wanted to strangle Johnny. But why had he felt like that, like ... like this ... this churned-up feeling inside, wanting to bash somebody? He was as bad as Albert. But it was Albert's wife that had made him like that—he himself had no wife to get worked up over.

He looked at his reflection in the shiny cover of a box, expecting to be confronted by a different being, but he looked the same as ever. Yet he wasn't the same, and he knew it. He'd have to pull himself together and get away from that house as soon as possible, and in the meantime keep clear of the little one, and let her keep all the explanations to herself. It was none of his business, anyway.

He was turning briskly from the window when he thought of Ma and the element of forgiveness in her attitude; and his decisiveness vanished and worry settled on him again, for knowing Ma, he knew that there would have been no touch of forgiveness for him had she been made aware of the tie incident and his resulting handling of Johnny. That retribution was something surely still to come.

Groaning audibly, he went to the pictures, and there, watching the effects of a sizzling sky on a stretch of yellow sand and a pair of uninhibited lovers, he wished he could have gone back a month, for then, in comparison, life had been an easy uncomplicated affair. There might have been Kate Sparks and others like her, but they had aroused no battling tendencies; their impact had not touched his character or his heart. As his mind spoke this word, the sizzling lady on the screen suddenly burst into song. 'Climb up the Garden Wall,' she sang to an opposite number who, apparently, had been getting along quite well without having to attempt this Herculean feat.

Tripe! Rooney stood up, pushed through a row of glue-eyed, hypnotized Sunday escapists, and came out into the dark streets again. But he did not make his way to The Anchor. Instead, hoping to evade an encounter with Ma, he returned home, for he judged that she would still be at church. Arriving in the yard and seeing no light in the kitchen or the living-room, he felt he was in luck. But between closing the door and groping for the switch he was thrown into a state almost of agitation by the sound of Ma's voice coming either from the hall or from Grandpa's room. That Grandpa was also in the thick of it he soon knew, for the old man's treble was at its highest.

'Tell her to get out, would you! You can tell nobody to get out of here. The house is in my name, on the rent book. You're the one that'll get out.... And me furniture ... don't think you'll get that. Or me insurance policy either—it's hers. Ah! I've put a sneck on your neb, me lady. You wait and see.'

'You old devil!'

'Old devil, am I? I can hear you, I'm not so deaf.'

'Be quiet! Go on in.... Yes, yes, go on now. I'll be there in a minute.'

Rooney was surprised to hear Nellie's voice—he could just hear it and that was all, it was so quiet and level.

There was the sound of a door closing, then Ma saying, 'You little liar! You've tried to hoodwink him, telling him you've had money left you. Who have you got that I don't know of who would leave you money? Nobody.... Well, I told him ...'

'Yes, you would. You told him it was old Brummell, didn't you? But let me inform you, Grace, you are mistaken.'

'I'm not mistaken. Don't think you can pull the wool over my eyes—I saw his face when I asked him where you were. And you seem to forget you told me yourself he'd tried his hand.'

'I know I did, but that was years ago. But I tell you again, it isn't him ... Brummell! I wouldn't let that man within a mile of me.'

For no accountable reason Rooney felt his spirits rising, for the words, so quietly and softly spoken, held the quality of truth, and that this had got over, even to Ma, was revealed in her next question.

'Are you denying it's a man?'

During the long pause that followed, Rooney's spirits remained stationary; then, as Nellie's voice, still quiet, came to him, they took a rapid downward descent.

'It would be stupid to deny anything, for you would believe what you want to believe. Yes, there's a man. Are you satisfied? I'm in love with a man. Now that will give you something to rake over in your twisted mind! I'm in love. A state you've never been in in your life, Grace. That's why you could never bear to see me happy. The happiest time in your life was when I was in the depths, when nobody noticed me, only as an object of pity. Oh, I've known almost your every thought and mood for years. You hated my mother because she got the man you wanted. You didn't love him, but you thought he had money. What you did to me through Tim was in your estimation, rough justice, and you would never have taken me into this house in the first place had it not been for the few pounds that went with me and which you claimed in lieu of my keep. But what does it matter now? ... Yes, there is a man. I'm in love, I have money, and there IS A MAN!'

The silence descended again, and Rooney had a picture of them facing each other, their minds fighting without words through their feelings. Then Nellie's voice again, a little louder now, saying, ' "Think on these things." Saint Paul to the Philippians, chapter four, verse eight. I remember you stopping me going with the rest to the sands because I couldn't repeat that verse, word for word. It's ironical when you think of it, you of all people to make me learn that. "Finally, brethren, whatsoever things are true, whatsoever things are honest, whatsoever things are just, whatsoever things are pure, whatsoever things are lovely, whatsoever things are of good report; if there be any virtue, and if there ..." '

He heard her step on the stairs and her voice getting fainter....

As he let himself quickly and quietly out again, a laugh followed him like a husky echo, but full of composure, so full of composure that it transcended Ma's loud howl of raging words. But Ma, nor nobody else, could rattle her any more, for, as she had said, she was in love, she had money, and a man.

Feeling more depressed than he had ever felt in his life, he went to The Anchor.

7. THE LETTERS

It was on Monday evening that Ma showed Rooney the flowers.

'Look,' she said, before he'd hardly got in the door. She was pointing to a large cellophane-wrapped bunch of tousled-headed chrysanthemums lying on top of the machine. 'They came for her this afternoon. "Does Miss Nellie Atkinson live here?" the boy said ... Miss Nellie Atkinson!' Ma's chest expanded. 'Look, a card on them, too. And a letter.' She jerked her thumb towards the mantelpiece. 'That came at dinner-time. . . . Do you want any more evidence?'

Rooney's eyebrows seemed to spring apart. 'Me want evidence? I don't want evidence—its nothing to do with me.'

'But you don't believe she's up to anything, do you? Oh, I know. I wasn't born yesterday, nor the day before that. I know all about it; she played on your feelings and she told you such a tale. . . .'

'She did no such thing. And look here, Mrs. Howlett. This is none of my business, it's no concern of mine, and I don't want to have any say in the matter. And what's more, I don't want to hear anything more about it. . . .'

'You needn't shout, Rooney.' Ma sounded distinctly hurt.

'I'm sorry, I'm forgetting meself. But once and for all, I want nothing to do or say in ... the little ... in her affairs.'

'Very well.' Ma's head wagged. 'I was only pointing out to you for your own good. I know you, and you could be taken. . . .'

'Damn it all!'

'Mr. Smith!'

He was past being affected by her indignation; he was disturbed, upset, all to pot. As he put it, he didn't know where he was, except that he was in this damned house.

He went upstairs, changed, and went out without his tea.

The following morning, Ma brought another letter in from the hall and placed it conspicuously against the clock. But she needn't have done that; he knew who it was for, although he did not look towards it.

The same thing happened on Wednesday. But on Thursday morning Ma threw the letter on to the table, almost to the side of his plate, and he had to check himself from exclaiming, 'Now, look here!' But he and Ma were barely speaking, and he was beginning to wonder which was causing the greater strain, listening to her or not listening to her. As for Nellie, almost the same situation existed there. On Tuesday evening she had come out of her door just as he was coming out of his. She was wearing a different hat and coat and her face was done up. She had said 'Hallo', and he had answered briefly, 'Hallo.' Then she had stood before him, saying, 'Grandpa's had a wonderful day. You know where we've been?' She had not finished, but looking into his face she had smiled, a funny little smile, and added, 'Oh, is that how it is? I'm in your bad books now.'

'Why do you say that? Why should you be, it's got nothing to do with me?'

'I know, I know ... it's got nothing to do with you. Nothing's got anything to do with you. Look, Rooney.' She had strained her face up to his and whispered, 'I'd like to talk to you.'

As he looked down on her, he could hear her voice coming through the days and nights as it had been doing since Sunday, saying, 'I'm in love, I have money and a man.' And to her request, he replied briskly, 'I'm busy, I'm seeing a pal.'

She had let him pass and precede her downstairs, and in the street he had protested volubly to himself. It wasn't fair, her being able to put him in the wrong like that. Looking as if he'd hit her. What did she want? She'd got everything now, she'd said so herself. And then those letters and flowers. The bloke must be an unusual type to send her flowers, either old, like Brummell, or ... a foreigner. There were dozens of white women married to Arabs an' such. God in heaven! what was he thinking about? And anyway, what did it matter to him what she did? Or how many letters or flowers she received.

Now the letter was lying by his elbow, and his eyes slid sideways to it. The writing, like everything about this affair of hers, was odd. It was like script: Miss Nellie Atkinson. . 71 Filbert Terrace. . South Shields. .

Why is it that out of the morass of mannerisms peculiar to an individual one scarcely perceivable motion should impinge itself on the eye of the onlooker and from its small unconnected self create its creator?

Rooney sat staring, fascinated at the envelope, and slowly he was telling himself that if what he was thinking was right there was something fishy here. What did it mean? What could it mean. He threw his mind back to the first time he had seen Nellie take a pencil and a pad from her pocket and write 'Lodger' and go da-da with the pencil, making two dots after the word. He could remember thinking along the lines that it looked a very precise and definite action from such a nondescript person. And there staring at him from the envelope were two dots after Atkinson, two after Terrace, and two after Shields. He knew there was a correct way of addressing an envelope. There was a comma at the end of each line, and at the finish you put a full stop. There might be two people who would put two full stops at the end, but would they do so at the end of each line?

He left a good part of his breakfast uneaten, and in a bewildered state went out to work. It just didn't make sense. Why should she write letters to herself? Yet why not, if it was going to make Ma wild and give her something to think about? ... But there were the flowers. Well, if she had sent the letters, she could have sent them an' all.... But what about the fellow?

During the following hours he had to stand a lot of chaff from Bill because of his more than usual silence. Bill had already made the events of Saturday night into an epic; the whole depot knew that Rooney, that quiet-looking chap with the sandy hair, had nearly killed a bloke in The Anchor because the bloke had asked him the ordinary conversationary question, Was he keeping a woman? And the journey home through the streets Bill had turned into a rip-roaring pantomime in which Rooney had become a cross between a ballet dancer and a mountain goat.

But, make what effort Bill might, the pantomime stopped at the door of '71', for Rooney refused to be drawn as to what he could remember once he had got inside the house.

All this had happened six days ago, but Bill was still playing on it, and by five o'clock Rooney was hating the sound and sight of him. For not even under Danny's cautionary admonition of 'Let up now' had he ceased to tease and mickey him. He had teased and mickied him before, but with no adverse effect; in fact he had enjoyed it, for better than most he could stand a laugh against himself. But the subject of Saturday night, like a constantly scratched pin-prick, was turning into a sore, and it was all he could do not to round on Bill and cry, 'Shut your mouth else I'll shut it for you!' So by five o'clock he was glad to escape from the depot, in case he should create another epic.

He was walking out of the gate with Albert, and Albert was confirming his own views by saying, 'You stand too much. It's your own business, I know, but if he doesn't let up you want to let him have it,' when a voice to the side of them said, 'Hallo.'

'Oh, hallo.' With some surprise Rooney looked at Jimmy.

'Just finished?'

'Aye. Yes.'

'I'm going your way.'

'Oh ... well. ... This is me pal, Albert Morton. This is ... I don't know your name, just Jimmy.'

'Fairbairn.'

The men nodded, and a few yards farther along the road Albert cut off from them saying, 'So long. I'll be seeing you.'

'So long,' they both answered. And then continued in silence for some way, until Jimmy, turning to Rooney, said, 'I don't know what you're thinking but I'm not here by chance, Rooney.'

'No?' It was a question.

'No. I want to ask a favour of you. ... It's about Nellie.'

My God! Rooney did not voice this expression, but waited. 'I suppose it's none of my business and I should let things slide, but I just can't. The fact is they are determined to get to the bottom of this affair of hers. I won't say I'm not intrigued myself, but there's a great difference in that to spying. The fact is they're having her followed.'

'Followed? Who by?' Rooney's step had slowed.

'Oh, the great moralizer, Dennis. Also Ma is determined to get into her room. Nellie has kept it locked since this business started. There's been a great rake round for keys. Oddly enough Nellie's is the only bedroom door that's got one. ...

You'll be wanting to know what all this has got to do with you.'

Rooney pushed his hair under his cap. 'Yes, I am a bit.'

'Well, it's just this! I want you to tip her off. It's impossible for me to catch her, but you're on the spot. . . . Would you?'

After a moment's pause he said, 'Yes . . . aye, I'll put her wise.' There was no need here for him to debate about this. The thought of that long, slimy bloke spying on her brought on him the urge to hit out again. 'What'll I tell her . . . just what you said?'

'Yes. You can't do anything else. And tell her to burn anything of importance.'

Aye, thought Rooney, that would be the main thing. It wouldn't matter if they found out if there was a fellow and who he was, but it would matter if they found out that the letters didn't come from a fellow at all . . . that's if they didn't. . . . Oh, he didn't know what to think.

'I've always been fond of Nellie, and she's had a hard time of it. I don't need to improve your knowledge of Ma, do I? It's been pretty grim watching Nellie going downhill these past few years, especially when one remembers what she used to be like . . . in spite of Ma. But now she's taken on a new lease of life.' Jimmy gave a deep chesty chuckle. 'Sin, to use Ma's term, can be very rejuvenating, don't you think?'

Rooney did not offer his opinion on this but asked, 'When does he intend to follow her?'

'That I don't really know. It could be tonight or any time. It was May, my wife, who told me about it at lunch-time. They've decided it isn't Brummell. All I know is that Dennis has appointed himself Ma's lieutenant and proposes to go there straight from the office and follow Nellie when she leaves the house. Apparently she goes out between half-past five and seven. It's a dirty business and it's got my back up. If she doesn't want to say who the man is that's her affair, and under the circumstances I shouldn't imagine she'll want to divulge who he is, for he's almost sure to be an old fellow or somebody married who will be as anxious as she is to keep the thing dark.' Jimmy paused. 'It puzzles me though how she has met either type with enough money to float her in the style she's adopting, for she wouldn't open her mouth to a man, not even those in the Literary Society. It was myself who got her to join that, unknown to Ma, of course. I happened to go in one evening and she was reading, for a change, and we got talking, and I told her I thought she'd find it interesting. At least she'd find some companionship there. I used to be in it before I joined the Archaeological Society. I know all the members there and not one of them fits the picture.'

Rooney liked this fellow. Like Nellie, he felt he was the best of the bunch, but it perturbed him to find that even he was creating, to a certain extent, the ... the bashing feeling within him. Discussion in any form of Nellie's morals was erupting a new and decidedly disturbing side of himself which he did not want or like but could not disregard.

'You don't mind me asking this of you?'

'No. No, not at all.'

'I'm glad.... Do you think they're a queer lot ... Ma and them?'

'I do, damn queer.' This was said so quickly and definitely as to cause Jimmy to laugh outright.

'After thirteen years, you've either had to get used to them or do a bunk. I myself don't happen to be one of Ma's favourites. One thing of deep regret to my mother in-law is that I've given her no grandchildren.' He inclined his head towards Rooney confidentially. 'Believe me, I've purposely refrained from this indulgence, fearing that heredity would out and I'd be confronted with miniature Ma's for the next twenty years or so. My sense of humour, which I've had to cultivate assiduously as a shield against Ma, could not have stood up to it.'

Rooney laughed. This Jimmy, he could see, was a fellow who could talk, and liked it, but he was a decent bloke all the same.

'I'll leave you here.' Jimmy stopped before they reached the main thoroughfare. 'If you can't find the opportunity to have a word with her perhaps you would pop a note under her door. Would you?'

'Yes, I suppose that would be the best thing,' said Rooney, 'for there's not much chance of conversation there.'

'All right then, I'll leave it to you. And thank you ... it's good of you to bother.'

'It's no bother. So long.'

'So long,' said Jimmy.

Although she couldn't hope to go on indefinitely keeping everything up her sleeve, the thought that the truth might be brought to light by that individual, Dennis, maddened Rooney. Not that it was any business of his, it wasn't, but the least he could do was to put her on her guard. His step quickened, as much he told himself from a desire to keep warm as to get home, for it was beginning to freeze hard.

His approach to Filbert Terrace was from what he called the bottom end, and to get to the back lane he had to pass the front street. The terrace was no better lighted than any of the surrounding streets, and figures walking twenty yards away were hardly discernible, but he checked his step and peered through the dim light when, from half-way along the terrace, he heard a gate shut and saw a slight figure merging into the distance. He stood peering up the street. Was it her? Well, if it was, he should catch her up; there mightn't be an opportunity like this again.

He went up the street, hurrying now. But he still couldn't be sure if it was Nellie, for the figure ahead was hurrying too.

There was a bicycle leaning against the railings of seventy-one and he had gone but a few yards farther on when he heard the door open. He did not turn to see who was coming out, but pulling up the collar of his mac and tugging his cap farther on to his head he cut across the road. The figure ahead was now walking into Deans Road, and as she passed a lamp post he saw that it was Nellie all right. He did not look behind him until he was about to turn the corner of the terrace, when a quick glance told him what he already suspected. The tall hurrying figure was Dennis and he was pushing the bike.

Nellie was almost opposite him now on the other side of the road. Rooney watched her pause at a bus stop and look back up the street, before moving on again. Then quickly, as if changing her mind, she recrossed the road and was walking within a few feet of him. He slowed his pace, for he was now in a quandary. If he were to speak to her here Dennis would imagine he had solved the problem—it would all tie up very convincingly with Betty's story. He didn't want that. But what, he wondered, would be Dennis's next move if she got on a bus. Follow it until she got off, he supposed. That was what the bike was for. Without implicating himself he could not see what his own next move should be. . . . She must not get on a bus, for he too would have to get on it, and he would not escape Dennis's eye. An idea came to him. Waiting until he came to a quiet stretch of the road, he self-consciously moved nearer to Nellie, but still keeping behind her he said softly, but definitely, 'Nellie . . . don't turn round. It's me, Rooney.

Dennis is behind us; he's following you.'

She had given a start and had almost stopped at the first sound of his voice; but after a moment her step quickened.

Passing her without turning his head, he murmured, 'Make for the park, round the bottom, into Stanhope Road.' Then he hurried on briskly ahead. And as he heard the sound of her heels tap-tapping behind him, he thought, I'm daft. What's it go to do with me? It would come out sooner or later, anyway. But the thought of Dennis slinking behind made him add, Well, not this way, if I can help it.

Coming out into Stanhope Road he was confronted with the question, Where next? Automatically he turned right, making for the direction of Tyne Dock. But as he neared the top of Stanhope Road, he thought, This could go on for ever. He had constituted himself leader of this evasive action, and he wasn't, he knew, cut out for a leader. No brilliant escape tactics filled his mind. Nor were there any byways around here where a man with a bike could not follow. He had already made sure that Dennis was still following. He went on, down the slope past St. Peter and Paul's church to the foot of the Tyne Dock station bank, and it was here there occurred to him an idea that might be classed as strategic. Farther on was a very steep incline; it branched off the pavement and doubled back towards the station, and at the top was a piece of open ground connecting with Hudson Street and another entrance to the station. If Nellie were to go up the station bank, under the arch, and up the steps to Hudson Street, there would be nothing to stop Dennis humping his bike that way and keeping her in view. But if she went past the station bank up the incline and on to the dimly-lit land she could, if she were quick, turn either right and go down the station steps, or left and into the Crown Picture House. And Dennis would be unable to tell which way she had gone.

When he neared the station bank he stopped and fumbled in his pocket, pretending to feel for a cigarette, and as he came abreast of him he said, 'Go farther on, up the incline, and run. Go into the Crown.'

She did not pause now, and when a little way along the street she reached the opening off the pavement she turned sharply, and like a puff of wind went up the slope.

Rooney walked steadily on past the incline. But in order to see what Dennis was up to now he looked from side to side under the pretext of crossing the road and he saw Dennis's long legs carrying him and the bike up the slope at a surprising pace. And he estimated that if Nellie was to cross that patch of land and get down the street to the Crown, then she'd have to be going some.

He himself was almost running when he came out into the bottom end of Hudson Street and made his way back to the picture house. There was no sign of Dennis, but there was the sound of a train leaving the station, and he wondered if Dennis was watching it and thinking Nellie was on it.

At the door of the Crown he paused. He had often come here when he lived in this neighbourhood, for he had felt more at home here than in the flashier places in Shields. Upstairs was comfortable, and he had been on speaking terms with the manager. He looked down at himself. He couldn't go in like this. But there was nothing for it, he'd have to if she was in there waiting for him.

Feeling hot now for a number of reasons, he walked into the little lobby, and there she was, standing well back from the door. She was looking now neither amused nor pert, but her face showed deep concern and a touch of the old sadness. He went slowly over to her and when they confronted each other neither of them seemed to have anything to say. When Nellie did speak, it sounded to him a silly thing to say at the end of a chase.

'You've never had your tea yet, have you?'

'That's all right'—he rasped his prickly chin with his hand—'I've a better appetite for it now.'

'It was good of you, but how did you know?'

'Jimmy met me coming out of work and asked me to give you the tip off what Dennis was up to. I saw you leaving and made to catch you up when that . . . he came out of the house, with pretty much the same idea.'

She linked her fingers together, then pulled at them as if straining to get them apart. 'I wouldn't have believed Dennis would do such a thing.'

'Well,' he went on, still rasping his chin, 'I suppose they're all curious.'

She looked quickly about the little hall. A few people were at the box office, but they hadn't reached there without having eyed them first.

'Do you think we could go outside now?'

'I wouldn't risk it if I were you, not for a bit anyway. I'd go in and see the picture, or some of it.'

'I want some place to talk to you.'

He remained silent.

Her voice was scarcely audible when, looking intently up into his face, she asked, 'Do you believe I'm living with a man ... Brummell or any man?'

His eyes fell from hers to his boots. She was placing him on a spot. He felt a quick rising irritation and he wanted to say, 'I'd rather have you say you were outright than have you standing there lying to me.'

'I'm not, Rooney. Won't you believe me?'

'Look,' he lifted his head again, 'I didn't do it intentionally, but I heard what you said to Ma last Sunday night.'

Her eyes screwed up and she repeated, 'What I said?'

'Aye. Yes. You don't want me to tell you, do you?'

The colour mounted to her face and her head drooped.

'Yes, I remember. And it's quite true, all of it ... but I'm not living with him. Rooney, it's difficult for me to make you understand.' She raised her eyes suddenly to his face. 'Look, meet me tomorrow night and I'll give you proof, will you? I can show you the proof. You remember that first letter I got?'

Letters. That was another thing. And then trying to open her door.... Lord, why had he got himself into this? How could he put it without hurting her? How could he say, 'Stop writing letters to yourself?'

'Letters,' he cut in. 'That reminds me. Jimmy says that Ma means to get into your room. She's been raking round for keys.'

He had to turn his eyes away from her face. Her hand was on her lips, patting them like a child in distress. 'Could they find anything?' he asked lamely.

'Yes ... No. Not unless they've got a key to the drawers ... I'd better get back. I've been silly ... foolish.' She drew in her breath and tried to recover herself; then added, 'But what can she find? Nothing. Only ... Oh!' She joined her hands together again, and he said, 'If I was you I'd not send ... well, what I mean is I'd get the fellow to stop...'

'There's no fellow,' she said quickly almost harshly; 'haven't I told you! And don't look like that as if I was the world's worst liar. Anyway, he didn't send me the letters. Oh, dear God!' She moved her head from side to side, then patted her mouth again. 'If you weren't you, I could tell you everything. But I can't, I can't bring myself to.'

He could not understand what she was really driving at, but

he could believe her when she said the letters hadn't come from a fellow. He could believe that all right, and he said so. 'Don't worry yourself about that, only don't keep it up ... the writing, I mean.'

He knew before her eyes began to widen that he had said the wrong thing.

'I mean ... well, what I mean is ...'

'You mean,' she whispered, 'you know that ... I ... I ...' Her humiliation filled the vestibule. She seemed to become smaller with it; and her clothes lost their touch of class as her body slumped within them.

'It's all right, don't take on like that.' He was talking to her bent head, and he watched her shiver as she whispered, 'But how ... how did you know? How could you?'

'Watching you write notes to the old fellow. You always made two dabs with your pencil at the end of a line. I saw them on the envelope. I'm no detective, but it just struck me, that's all. One of those things. It seemed, well, sort of part of you when you did it. I didn't think I had noticed it until I saw the dots.'

'O ... o ... oh!' She was groaning audibly. 'I was mad, but I wanted to give her something to think about ... I ...'

'Look. Come on. Aw! don't cry ... not in here.'

'You must think I'm not all there ... insane.'

'Don't be daft. Now look, don't give way like that. Go on in and see the picture, that's your best plan.'

'No, no.' Discreetly she wiped her eyes. 'I must go back, just in case.... I never dreamed they'd try and get into my room.'

She turned her back on a group of people entering the door, then very softly she asked, 'Will you meet me tomorrow night?'

It was a long moment before he answered, 'Yes, all right. Where?'

She seemed to consider, then said, 'I don't know. Here, at the bottom of this street. At ... at seven o'clock.'

'All right.' He nodded. 'At seven. Go on now, and I'll let you get in first. I'll say I've been doing overtime.'

She looked up at him, not only into his eyes, but at his hair, which was as usual, he knew, sticking out from beneath his cap; at his collar, and lastly his rough, red, blunt hands. Then without saying a word of farewell she turned abruptly away and walked into the street, leaving him very conscious of himself and the eye of the cashier on him.

What should he do now? He'd have to pretend he was waiting for her coming back, then slip out.

This is what he did do. And once in the street, he began to retrace his steps the way he had come, but leisurely now, giving her time to get well in. Outside the back door of seventy-one he hesitated long enough to rehearse his piece.

'Sorry I'm late,' he'd say. 'Had to do a spot of overtime. If ... if you don't mind I'll take me tea up; I'm in a bit of a hurry the night to get out.' And he would be too, for the less he saw of Ma from now on the better.

There was no one in the kitchen, or in the living-room, but when he reached the hall Ma came hurrying out of Grandpa's room. She looked agitated, and exclaimed, 'Oh! I thought it was Dennis.'

She took her apron and wiped the sweat from her face. 'He had a seizure ... upstairs. I was all on my own till Dennis came in. He's gone for the doctor.'

She made no reference to Nellie, but he could hear a movement in the room, and knew she was in there. He could also hear the sound of the old man's laboured breathing.

Ma made no mention of his lateness but went into the kitchen, and he went slowly up the stairs. And as he washed and changed he wondered what had brought Grandpa upstairs. He would know Nellie was out, for she always went into him before leaving the house. Yet it wasn't likely he could have heard Ma at Nellie's door, for he was as deaf as a stone. Or was he? Perhaps he wasn't as deaf as he made out.

Rooney returned to the living-room, and, as Ma set his meal before him, Nellie came from the kitchen carrying a kettle of hot water. Her face under the make-up looked bleached. She did not look towards him, but he knew she was aware of him.

The door had hardly closed behind her when Ma exclaimed, 'Brazen piece! Gallivantin', that's all she does. She's brought this on, telling him she was going to take him away with her! Took him out in a taxi, weather like this an' all. She's got a lot to answer for.... Is your steak all right?'

'Yes, thanks.'

'You were late.'

'Yes, I had to work overtime.'

The back door opened and Ma got to her feet. 'That'll be Dennis,' she said.

She went into the kitchen, and Rooney, reluctantly leaving the last piece of a very tender and well-cooked steak, went quickly out of the room and upstairs again, for it wouldn't do, he told himself, to meet that bloke face to face the night.

A little while later a ring at the door bell and the subsequent bustle spoke of the doctor's arrival. After ten minutes the front door closed again and the house became quiet.

As he sat before his fire drawing quick puffs on his cigarette he found he was anxious to know just how bad the old man was. But he refrained from going downstairs until he felt absolutely sure he would not meet up with Dennis. So when he again entered the living-room it was to find Ma preparing to go up to bed.

She looked him up and down as he stood in the doorway.

'I just wanted to know how he was,' he said.

'Oh! The doctor says he could last weeks ... it's his heart. You never know.... She's making herself a martyr, sitting up in there.' Ma bounced her head towards the wall. 'That won't do much good now. She's to blame ... she should never have taken him out.'

'Perhaps it was him climbing the stairs.'

'The stairs! What do you mean?'

'Well, you said he had the seizure upstairs.'

'I said no such thing, you must have been dreaming!' Ma's face showed a purple tinge. 'It was in the hall he had it.' She turned her back on him and gathered up a small clock from the mantelpiece, a glass of water from the table, and her glasses and prayer book from the sideboard, and saying stiffly through pursed lips, 'Good night,' she left him.

If anything could have proved that she had said the old man had had the seizure upstairs, this, Rooney thought, was it: to leave himself downstairs with Nellie, the dangerous woman.

Having waited a while to make sure that Ma was well in her room, he tip-toed to the front-room door and gave the gentlest of taps.

After a moment it was opened by Nellie, and he saw that she was no longer the Nellie of Friday night, nor yet the one of tonight, nor any Nellie he had seen, for her face was twisted and drawn with anxiety.

'How is he?' he whispered.

She shook her head. 'Very ill.'

'He'll likely get over it?'

She shook her head again. 'No, not this time ... he's going.'

131

She seemed to find talking difficult, and he stood at a loss what to say. But as he looked at her he knew he couldn't leave her here alone all night, with no one to turn to should anything happen.

'Look,' he whispered, 'I'll be next door. I can sleep just as easily in a chair. Just give me a tap if you want me.'

She did not refuse this offer, but murmured, 'Thanks, I'd be grateful.'

Using some duplicity he went upstairs, none too quietly. Then after waiting a while he descended again in his stockinged feet, carrying two blankets and a book, and having settled himself in the armchair he proceeded to read to keep himself awake.

He had no idea at what time he had dropped off to sleep, but when he felt the tapping on his arm he woke, feeling cold and cramped.

'Will you come in? I ... I think he's going ... I can't hold him up.'

He was on his feet in a moment, and still only half awake he followed her into the room.

If he had never before seen a man die he would have known that Grandpa was coming quickly to the end of his time. Following Nellie's directions, he put his arm under the old man's shoulders and raised him up on to the pillows.

Grandpa's cheeks were hollowed and moving like bellows as he fought for breath. His eyes were fixed on Nellie, and between his gasping he made several efforts to speak.

'What is it, dear? What is it?' She hovered over him tenderly.

Again he made an effort, and his mouth formed a word, but no sound came. Then lifting one trembling hand he motioned with it towards a chair.

Nellie turned her head and said, 'Your coat? All right, I'll get it.'

She left his side and brought the coat to him. And when she laid it on top of the bedcover his hand fell on it and rested there for a moment. Then with an effort he pulled at one side of it and exposed the lining.

'Something in your pocket?' Nellie took a number of small pieces of paper and a calendar from the pocket and spread them on the bed, but the old man did not look at them. He waited a moment, and then put his hand into the pocket again and his trembling fingers pulled back the torn lining, and as he did so his eyes looked into Nellie's. And she, following his hand with hers, put it down the lining and pulled out a letter.

As if at the end of some great physical achievement, the old man sank into his pillows and rested now. Rooney looked at the letter lying in Nellie's hands. It bore her name in large scrawling letters on the envelope: 'For Nellie Atkinson.' And as she went to put it into her pocket the old man's hand moved again, and she said, 'You want me to read it now?'

Struggling for breath, he brought out 'Aye.' And Rooney, from the other side of the bed, watched her slit open the envelope and take out two sheets of paper, and, holding them in one hand while with the other she held the old man's hand, she began to read.

She must have covered half the page when he saw her eyes lift. They were wide and staring. He watched her mouth fall slack as if in amazement. She sat on staring ahead at the row of furniture against the opposite wall. The old man's hand moved in hers, and she brought her gaze slowly to the letter again. And as she came to the end of it Rooney watched her head droop lower, and still lower. Then with a choking cry she was on her knees by the side of the bed, her head buried in the coverlet, her arms across the old man.

'Oh, Grandpa! Grandpa!'

His hands moved on her head and he spoke her name. 'Nellie.'

She raised her anxious face, and as the old man touched it Rooney felt he could not bear to witness any more, for never in his life, not even when his father died, had he felt like this.

Quietly he went out and into the living-room, and for something to do he put the kettle on, and stood over it, waiting for it to boil. When the tea was made he poured out a cup and took it into her. She was sitting on a chair now, her face buried in the pillow beside that of the old man. And Rooney saw that he was dead.

Putting down the tea he went to her and, placing his hands beneath her arms, took her from the bed saying, 'There now. Come into the other room. Come on now.'

Her body hung limp in his hands. Her back was to him, and she swayed as she looked down on the old man. Then turning swiftly about she stood with her face buried in her hands, her sobs shaking her body.

It was the most natural thing in the world for him to put his hands on her shoulders and bring her to rest against him, and as he stood in the furniture-cluttered room and looked over her head to the slumped form of the dead old man on the bed he knew that he was experiencing the strangest moment of his life, for in him was a tenderness, such a tenderness that softened the whole of life, the whole world even.

When she drew herself away his being became empty, and as she dried her face he asked, 'Will I go and get her up?'

She shook her head, then said brokenly, 'I'll lay him out myself.'

'You can't do that.' His tone was shocked.

'Yes. Yes, I can. He wouldn't want her to touch him.' She looked up at him through swollen eyes. 'Would you give me a hand?'

'Yes.' He did not hesitate in complying with her request, but nevertheless he did not relish the task, and as the business proceeded he relished it less. But overweighing this was his admiration for the capability, the deftness, and, overall, the patient love which she brought to this last rite.

Grandpa had died at five minutes to three, and at half-past four he lay dressed for his last journey in the long shirt and stockings he had kept by him for years for this purpose. The room was left as tidy as it could be made, and on the bedside table Nellie had placed the flowers that had arrived in cellophane, and she had lit one ordinary candle. And when the electric light had been switched off Grandpa's face took on a happiness that the gentle glimmer of the candle seemed to draw from within him. And Nellie, after standing looking down on him for a moment, closed the door and went out with Rooney into the living-room.

As if now at a loss what to do, she sat on the edge of the chair and looked at the low embers of the fire. Her face was composed, but her eyes held so much sadness that he found it almost painful to look at her. He stood on the hearthrug, seemingly at a loss, too; then feeling that he must say something he brought up the topic of common irritation.

'She's going to get a surprise,' he said. 'It's a wonder she hasn't been down afore now.'.

Nellie did not immediately answer, until the movement of his feet seemed to attract her attention, and then she said, 'She sleeps heavily. And her surprise will be in more ways than one.... Would you read that?' She withdrew from her pocket the letter she had taken from Grandpa's coat.

He hesitated. 'You want me to?'

'Yes.'

He took the letter from her and having unfolded it slowly began to read.

'Nellie,

'I never was much of a hand at letter writing, but I want you to know one or two things. First, I want you to know that apart from my Elsie you've been the best person on earth to me. And if I'd been left to that 'un's mercy I'd have been dead years since. I hate her, Nellie, I've always hated her, and I've died hating her. Its always been my great fear that she'd get a penny of mine. If she had thought I had anything she'd have had it out of me years ago. You didn't think I had anything either, did you, Nellie? It's twenty-five years ago since I got the compen. for losing my two toes and the shock that knocked me deaf. That one thought we had gone through it. Both Elsie and me made her think that. But we hadn't. We spent a bit, but we put the rest by. We didn't believe in banks, so we kept it hid in a box screwed to the bottom shelf underneath the chest of drawers. You would have had to turn the whole thing upside down afore you could see anything was there. And it's been there for years. All the hundred and eighty-four pounds. And lately it got to worrying me, for although I'd left a letter saying you was to have it I got frightened of that 'un claiming her lot to be next of kin and doing you out of it. I had thought of giving it to you. But knowing you, you would have spent the lot on me, and I didn't want that, as I'm past enjoying anything but a good fire ... and I can't get that.

'Well, Nellie, I thought and thought, and then I got an idea. I took the money and went out one day and went to Mr. Pomphrey, the solicitor who fought my case years ago, and told him what I wanted. I wanted you to have the money, anonymous like, and for him to say you were to spend it and have a good time. But there was one condition: you had got to leave that shop. And he was to send you the letter on your birthday. And I asked him to get in touch with the insurance company and for them to pay you me insurance. There was a big snag here, as I wanted no letters sent, and I had to go back and sign a form for the insurance. I didn't feel too good that second time going out, and I got a taxi back. And Nellie, it did me heart good to see her face when she seen I'd been out again, and to make her pay for that taxi. Well, Nellie, you got the money, and it's made you young again, and the fun and enjoyment it's given me watching you will last me the remainder of me time.

'I'll be gone when you read this, Nellie, and there'll be nothing to keep you here any longer. Get away, away from her, Nellie. And you're to have me furniture, the solicitor knows. I told her you were going to take me away, but I knew I would never leave this house again, not alive anyway. Now, Nellie, you're not to worry. Take care of yourself and know that you were the only bright spot in my weary days since I lost Elsie.

'God bless you, lass, and send you happiness, for you deserve it.

'Grandpa.'

Rooney sat down. He was bemazed. It was incredible. All this business about a man keeping her. Even when he knew the fellow hadn't sent the letters he himself had still thought there was one. Talk about circumstantial evidence, and giving a dog a bad name. Well, this would just show you.

He sat on, looking at her, the letter still in his hand, and pondering; and it came as something of a shock to him that even now when he knew where the money had come from it made no real difference to the state of affairs, for hadn't she admitted herself that there was a fellow. By! the old man had started something when he played Fairy Godmother to her Cinderella, and not only to her but to himself, for he doubted if the tight-compressed little one could have brought him, even with his pity for her, to the state of unrest the present Nellie, the outcome of Grandpa's strategy, was doing. But there was one thing sure: she was going to miss the old fellow more now than she might have done had she not known of his kindness.

'Well, now you know.' She was still staring into the fire, and she spoke without turning her head.

He could find nothing to say.

'And me thinking the money came from Mr. Bamford.' She shook her head derisively at herself.

'Bamford?' he repeated.

'Yes, Bamford, the other partner in the shop. He's older than Brummell. He used to manage the Wallsend one. They've got

136

six shops altogether, and years ago when I was going to leave he came over himself and asked me to stay on. He gave me five shillings rise and told me if I kept things going he would not forget me. A year ago Brummell and he dissolved partnership. I ... I thought because of the conditions that I should leave the shop that it was he who had arranged for me to have the money to spite Brummell. And I wasn't averse to spiting Brummell myself, because he's a pig of a man.' She made a derogatory sound in her throat and her lip curled slightly. 'What a gullible fool I've been! Just as if a close-fisted devil like him would give me anything. I don't suppose for a moment I ever crossed his mind again, only when I wrote, as I frequently did, to say yet again that the assistant had left.... No one in their right senses would have stayed there all those years. As Grace so often has kindly inferred, I'm not all there, I'm odd. And I must be, stupidly odd.'

'You're no such thing.'

'Well, looking back now, I don't see myself as possessed of any powers of reasoning at all, for, lonely or not, I should have broken away. At least I should have got a new job. I could have done that.... Well, now I've got to get one.'

Yes, he thought, a hundred and eighty-four pounds at the rate she had been spending this past week wouldn't last for very long.

'What are you going to do?' he asked.

She rocked herself slightly. 'I don't really know. I've been looking round. There's plenty of work in factories and ... and the big shops, but'—she put her hands between her knees—'I've worked practically on my own for so long I'm scared of going among crowds. And I wouldn't like factory work anyway. I'll get a sewing job of some kind.... Oh, I'll get a job.'

'You're leaving here, then?'

'Yes, that's one thing I am doing, as soon as Grandpa's gone.'

'Nellie,' he leant towards her, 'if there's anything I can do to help you, I'll do it....'

'Thanks, Rooney.' She glanced up at him. 'You don't know how much you've done already. If it hadn't been for you ... well'—she moved her head—'I don't know what I would have done.'

'I've done nothing yet. Look, Nellie.' He bent still nearer. 'I would like to ask you something just to get things clear.'

'Yes, Rooney?'

'Well, it's like this....' He was stuck. Her eyes were on him, waiting, but he couldn't say, 'Is there another fellow as you said, or have you just been making him up an' all.' This wasn't the time or place to ask a thing like that. It would really be indecent, and the old man lying dead next door and her in the state she was. He straightened up. 'It'll keep. I'll talk about it later.' He stood up and her eyes followed him, and at this moment there came the sound of a door opening overhead.

'Here she comes,' he said.

Nellie rose slowly and faced the door, and Rooney, who was only a foot away from her, did not lengthen the distance between them but waited, as she was doing, for Ma to enter.

They heard her step on the stairs; then the front-room door opening; and still they waited. Fully two minutes passed before she appeared in the living-room doorway, and that she had received a shock was evident.

Rooney had a swift and laugh-inspiring picture of the old man standing outside himself with his thumb to his nose as she looked down on his recumbent remains.

'You think you're clever, don't you?'

Nellie made no reply; and Ma turning her glare on Rooney demanded, 'And what are you doing down here?'

'I've been here all night,' said Rooney quietly.

'What!' This bold answer evidently took Ma further aback. 'You've what? Well, there'll be a stop put to this, and I'm telling you.' She bustled past them. 'I'd thank you, Mr. Smith, to keep out of the household concerns.'

'I asked him to stay with me.'

'Oh, you did, did you?' Ma turned with her usual agility. 'Whose house is this anyway?'

'It was Grandpa's, and, if I choose, it is mine now, furniture, insurance policy, and the rent book. He has left all he had to me. You can contact Mr. Pomphrey, the solicitor. He will tell you everything you want to know.'

If Ma had had a seizure there and then Rooney would not have been surprised. He saw that she was finding breathing difficult, and no words would come to relieve her congested feelings. Although he could not rake up a spark of pity for her, yet he could no longer stay and witness her discomfort, so, with a small nod to Nellie, he went out and up the stairs to his room.

8. THE EFFECTS OF LOVE

The first thing Danny said to Rooney on his arrival at the depot was, 'You look under the weather. You all right?'

'Yes, I'm all right,' said Rooney. 'A bit tired ... been up all night ... The old man died.'

'Oh. Sorry to hear that,' said Danny. 'Sudden?'

'Yes, a bit.'

'I always think death around Christmas time seems worse somehow, puts the damper on things. And have you noticed that all the accidents seem to gather around this time an' all?'

'Cheerful Charlie Chester,' said Bill, mounting the cab. 'Come on, man, and let's gang and meet an accident, it's never been my policy to wait for things to come to me.'

This quip brought a smile even from Albert, and Rooney, pulling himself up beside him into the loaders' cab, thought, Funny, he's happy again.

Rooney found himself watching Albert covertly most of the morning, for he was intrigued by the air of suppressed excitement about him. Today was Albert's last day on the job and tomorrow he was leaving the town. Perhaps it was the prospect of a new start, or ... having her back again. Well, whatever it was it was making him easy to work with, just like it used to be.

But that wasn't much good, seeing it was his last day.

The loader had stopped opposite Honeycroft, and Rooney asked, 'You going to pay your last respects to old Double-Barrelled, Albert?'

'Not likely,' said Albert. 'I want to finish quiet.'

'Go on, man,' said Fred. 'She might give you a Christmas box if she knows you're leaving.'

'You talking of Christmas boxes?' said Bill, coming up with a bin on his shoulder. 'Wait a minute ... I bet you don't cap this one.' He tipped the contents of the bin into the loader. 'She——' He nodded towards a house hidden by a tall hedge, and mimicking what was to his mind a superior tone said, '"There you are," she said, "and will you be good enough to remove the rubbish near the gate?" ... You know what she offered me? Threepence!'

'No!'

'Aye, she did.'

'What did you say?'

'What did I say? I said, "Thank you, missus, but you'll be needin' that afore me, and we can't take on all that junk, we're nearly full, there's other folk's dustbins to be emptied.'

They all laughed, and Danny said, 'Well, you know, Bill, if everybody you met the day gave you threepence you'd have a bit. You must admit some of them won't even give you a kind word.'

'Aye,' said Bill. 'Well, she can keep her bloody threepence, and I can tell her what to do with it. Great big hoose like that an' all. Why, they never offer you threepence in Dock Street.'

'No, that's why they're still living in Dock Street,' put in Fred.

They dispersed laughing, and as Rooney went down the sidewalk of Honeycroft he thought he would have had to take the threepence rather than hurt the woman's feelings. Yet the act of receiving any kind of present always put him on edge, for he had never been able to accept a gift gracefully ... he liked giving, but hated receiving. Why, he had never worked out.

When he reached the yard he was surprised to find not the old woman at the kitchen door but a man, a round tubby individual with a pointed beard and almost bald head, which brought back to his mind Danny's description of the son who lived in France. This fellow looked French all right, and when he spoke the impression was confirmed, for his English had just a trace of something different about it. His tone was polite, even chummy, not a bit like the old girl's.

'Hallo,' he said. 'I wonder if you'd mind taking this stuff?' He pointed to a pile of cardboard boxes and old clothes lying under the covered way.

Rooney looked at the salvage. It would mean holding up the loader until he came back and collected it, and some oaths from Bill for getting behind, but it was dry stuff, and the fellow was a nice civil bloke.

'I'll be back for it,' he said.

'Is he going to take it?'

The door the tubby fellow had pulled to behind him was jerked out of his hand, and there stood the old lady.

'Oh, that one will take it,' she said; 'he's all right ... it's the other one. If you had been here and heard him you would ...'

'You go in, Mama, it's too cold out here.'

The little fellow's voice was coaxing, and to Rooney it sounded funny to hear a grown man calling his mother Mama.

When he returned and was gathering up the stuff the man came to the door again and extended his hand towards him palm downwards.

'Oh, that's all right, sir.'

'Good lord!' The ejaculation was full of surprise, and the only reason for it that Rooney could see was that he had hesitated in putting out his hand. The man stood looking at him as he rammed the rags into the boxes.

'Cold job?'

'Yes, a bit, sir.'

'Perhaps you could help me about getting rid of some stuff. I'm clearing out the top rooms. There's two brass and iron beds and two mattresses dropping to bits with moth, and a stack of other stuff. It's no use to anyone; would your people take it?'

'Yes. Yes, they'll send a lorry to collect it for you. All you need do is to phone the cleansing superintendent. The only thing is you'll have to get it down and stacked, say in the yard here.'

'Oh, I'll manage that. Thanks, I'll do that. They'd come within a few days, would they?'

'Yes. You tell them you're in a hurry to get cleared, and they'll meet you, I'm sure.'

'Lance!' The door was jerked again, but this time the little fellow held on to the knob.

'Lance, I forbid you to dismantle those rooms.'

The little man pulled a face and winked, and Rooney, laden with the boxes, went across the yard smiling to himself as he heard the fellow say, 'Now, Mama.'

Mama. It was laughable, but he seemed a nice bloke. He didn't envy him his job with the old girl, though, yet somehow he thought he'd be able to manage her all right.... Mama's attacks were likely to bounce off that round, stolid body of her son.

It was when they were having their break at the end of the road that he showed them the half-crown, and he did it more to cause a bit of fun than in any form of show-off, for it was agreed among them that what they received they stuck to. Pooling tips had years ago brought up some dissatisfaction, as it had been suspected that all donations had not found their way into the common purse. No one had been accused, but four of them had felt that it was odd how Fred was always unlucky.

Albert was the first to comment, he having been at grips with the old lady. 'Well, I'm damned!' he said. 'She gave you that?'

Rooney nodded—it was more of a joke when it was supposed to have come from the old girl.

'It's that bloody soft-soap look he wears,' said Bill. 'Makes all the old wives go for him. From Monday I'm partnering you, lad. Round Christmas, anyway. I'll rattle the bin lids and you stick near the back doors and smile at the dames. If you do your stuff properly we'll get enough to get a television.'

'Who'll get the television?'

'Me,' said Bill.

'I thought you would,' laughed Rooney.

'Take some smiles to draw out half-crowns,' said Danny. 'Yet the old girl used to be pretty open-handed at one time, but she's had to draw in her horns these last years.... Well, come on, let's get going ... this won't get you your television, Bill. It's a watch I'm wanting meself.'

With back-chat and laughter they spread themselves out again, and for the rest of the day they were all merry, seeming to make an effort to send Albert off with pleasant memories. And at four-thirty, when Albert shook hands all round, he looked as if he were genuinely sorry to be leaving them. And to Rooney as they walked together out of the gates for the last time, he repeated what he had said earlier, 'I'll miss you, man.' And he added, 'There aren't many blokes like you about, you know ... easy to get along with.'

Alone and walking homewards, his head down against the cutting wind that spoke of snow. Rooney was finding that his liking for Albert went much deeper than he had imagined. Perhaps it was because Albert had shown his own liking for him. There might be something in that. Yet he hadn't imagined that Albert, or any other fellow for that matter, considered him other than an ordinary bloke. And anyway, that's all he was, and he knew it. But it gave a chap a bit of a lift inside to hear something like that. That's how Nellie must have felt when she thought her boss had remembered her services—sent her all gay and carefree....

His mind was back on Nellie; it really hadn't been off her all day, but he had made his work keep it layered down. But now he'd have to think of her ... he wanted to think of her and what he was going to say to her. But—he pulled himself up—what he had to say must wait till after the funeral; he couldn't talk about such things until this business was over. And anyway, what he'd better set his mind to during the next couple of days was to find some place to live, and quick.

Before he entered the back door he knew there was company, for the buzz of conversation reached the yard. Committee, he thought, to debate Nellie getting the policy, and whether a rent book could really be left to anybody. And they certainly were going at it, he considered when he entered the kitchen. The door leading to the living-room was closed, but he could distinctly make out Dennis's high-pitched voice and that of his wife's, but as he changed his shoes he was a little surprised to hear Jimmy's deep tone, too, and the broad twang of Johnny. They hadn't lost much time ... must have come straight from work, the lot of them.

His opening of the door seemed to cut off their voices, for no one spoke as he entered the room. Then Ma, from her position in front of her daughter and the three men, turned and confronted him, saying, 'Well!'

It was no new addition to her vocabulary, and it left Rooney thinking, Aye, well, what's it about this time?

'You've got an eye-opener coming to you.' Ma's voice seemed to be dragged from the depths of her chest, and each word was ominous.

Oh my Lord! was she going to start on him in front of all these?

'You took her side, didn't you? I always knew you were gullible. But I warned you.'

'How was he to know,' said Jimmy, 'any more than the rest of us?'

'What should I have known?' asked Rooney quietly.

Ma's head came forward like a charging bull about to gore its victim. 'That she was a thief!'

Rooney said nothing to this but stared back into Ma's infuriated face.

'She's one of a gang ... she's a thief.'

'Nellie?' Rooney felt his nose expanding as his lips stretched, allowing for the incredulity in his voice.

'Yes, Nellie! She was in on the robbery at the house in Westoe, the Bailey-Crawfords' house.'

Rooney looked towards Jimmy, and he nodded sadly and said, 'Yes, it's hard to believe, but they've been here and taken her.'

'Taken Nellie?'

'Taken Nellie,' mimicked Ma.

'What did I tell you?' said Johnny, turning and spitting into the fire.

Rooney looked sharply at him. It was evident that Johnny had it in for him and that he had spilled the beans to the old girl, and Ma's next words left no doubt in his mind.

'I'm giving you notice, Mr. Smith, I'm having no improper carry-on in my house.'

'Don't worry,' said Rooney quickly, 'I'm going. I was going to give it to you. And as regards improper carrying-on, I'd better warn you to be careful what you say.'

'Warn me! I've got proof. And you're welcome to her when she comes out of jail. I always said it would be either jail or the asylum. Sending flowers to herself! Did you ever!'

'She never sent flowers to herself.'

'She did.' It was May speaking, and Rooney turned sharply and confronted her.

'How do you know?'

'I happen to have been told by the proprietor of Portal's when I went in to order our wreath. I gave her this address, and she said she knew it as the boy had brought some flowers here during the week, and she described who had bought them.'

'After you asked her.'

May's face tightened. 'This matter concerns our family.'

'She likely wrote the letters to herself as well, for there's nothing in her room, only this, and she had no time to clear anything up today.' Ma snatched up a piece of paper from the table, and with her lip curled back read:

'You taught me things I never knew;
 The fascination of your sandy mane,
 Spun from the sun itself into golden strands,
 A lair for my hands,
 Your hair.

Your neck,
 Tight, firm, forcing its strength against your collar in corded
  bands....

'Licentious twaddle! Did you ever!'

Slowly Rooney's skin began to burn as the five pairs of eyes were levelled at him, and only in time did he stop his hand from going up to his head. Their eyes were moving from his hair to his neck, but he could see that Ma was only now approaching the conclusion that the others had already arrived at, and as he watched the purple tinge creep into her face Jimmy began to laugh, a deep rumbling sound as usual, and it distracted attention from Rooney for a moment.

May said tartly, 'It's neither the time nor the place, Jimmy, to practise your sense of humour.'

Jimmy sat down. 'I can't help it. He knows what I'm laughing at, don't you?' He nodded towards Rooney.

Rooney did not answer. Jimmy was likely thinking of his request asking him to put Nellie on her guard, and he was no doubt now thinking that it was he, Rooney, who had written Nellie the letters. Over a thing like that you would either have to laugh or get blazing mad. He was blazing mad himself; he was filled with such an anger that he was shaking with it. And it wasn't only against this lot, but again Nellie ... pinching, stealing! My God! Jewellery an' all. That's where she had got her money.... What was he thinking? What about Grandpa's letter? Yes. Aye, there was that. But what was a hundred and eighty-four pounds these days, especially the way she had been spending; and out of a job and looking up swell furniture.

'You've been taken for a ride.' It was Johnny's voice, thick with satisfaction.

'Well, mind you're not taken for one, and in an ambulance.'

The aggressivensss inside himself startled him. For two pins he would have laid Johnny on his back.

Sensing this, Johnny retreated behind the armchair, and now Dennis's voice took up where Johnny had left off.

'You won't be able to afford her ruby necklaces unless you find another appointment.' Each precise word carried a sneer.

Rooney had always wanted to hit this bloke—it had dated from that first meeting—but in the act of swinging about he stayed his hand. 'What did you say?'

'You heard; I have no need to repeat it.'

Rooney advanced a step. 'Say it again. What did you say about a necklace?'

Dennis stretched his neck out of his white collar. 'I said that you won't be able to buy her one, not like the one she was wearing.'

'What kind of a necklace?'

'A ruby one. I've told you.'

'Yes. And the brazen piece has been sporting it for days,' cried Ma. 'Daring to wear it ... the nerve! If that Mr. Crawford hadn't seen her in King Street and recognized it and followed her here, she would have got off with it. Likely gone on.'

'Six beads hanging from fil ... from a sort of tin affair?' cut in Rooney, still staring at Dennis.

'For your knowledge, the tin, as you call it, was old silver.'

'But they couldn't take her for that.'

'Why not? It was part of the stuff they're looking for.'

'It wasn't! It isn't!' He swung about, looking rapidly from one face to the other, 'I gave it to her.'

'You?'

'Aye, me.'

'You gave it to her? Where did you get it?' This came from all quarters at once.

'Never you mind; I gave it to her.'

'You're lying.'

Dennis delivered this flatly and with authority. 'She's one of a gang. I know, for I trailed her.'

'Yes, you trailed her. And you trailed me an' all. All through the park, up Stanhope Road, and she dodged you up the bank, near the station, didn't she?'

Dennis's face was a study. He looked comical with surprise.

'You sneaking rat, you!' Rooney moved nearer.

'What! How dare you! How dare you speak to me like that! You forget yourself. All I can add is that Nellie's let herself down much further than I'd imagined ... an ashbinner!'

As Rooney's fist crashed into his chin, Dennis's feet shot up as if he were demonstrating a backward dive. He fell straight across Jimmy's 'nees; and in a moment the room was filled with a bedlam of cries and exclamations of horror.

'My God!'

'You beast, you!'

'What did I tell you?'

'You've killed him!' cried May.

Rooney, rubbing his fist up and down the front of his waistcoat, cried back to this, 'It would be a damn good job, too.'

He knew that he would never have spoken like that to a woman if he had been possessed, but he knew he wasn't himself—far from it, for he was possessed by a pulsing life that was speeding up his thinking and his actions and loosening his tongue. He could have set about the lot of them in this moment, Ma an' all. Oh yes, Ma ... he'd love to land one at Ma.

He pulled himself together. He must be going barmy ... he'd better get out.

The same thought was in Ma's mind. 'Leave my house,' she cried, 'before I call the police.'

'I'm leaving your house, don't worry,' he barked back at her. 'But I'll be back for me things the morrow.'

'You'll find them on the street.'

'You do, if you dare!'

He seemed to be towering over her. 'You touch one piece of my furniture and I'll have you up. I will, mind, if it's the last thing I do. It's about time somebody told you just how far you can go. Mind, I'm warning you.' He pointed at the astonished and seemingly paralysed Ma.

He moved away towards the door, past Johnny and Jimmy as they assisted the groaning and bemused Dennis on to a chair.

May, turning from her husband's side, like an angry vixen, cried at him, 'This is what comes of taking a ... a scavenger'— she used the old disparaging title—'into the house! You're a low, common ...'

'Aye, all that,' he cut in sharply, 'an' more. But there's one thing I'll tell you: I'll have to drop a bit to come down to this family's level.'

He went into the kitchen, banging the door behind him, and there, rapidly changing into his coat and shoes again and stuffing his old slippers into his pocket, he left the house. But once outside, in the dark of the back lane, he paused and wiped the sweat from his forehead. What had come over him? He had never had a row like that in his life. He'd never knocked a man down before; nor had he ever felt the blood racing through his brain as it was now, nor had his thinking been so keen. ... Nellie ... they'd taken Nellie because of the necklace. But how? Why? Why hadn't she told them where she had got it?

He didn't have far to go for that answer. She thought he had pinched it and was shielding him.... Oh, Nellie!

What was he to do? He asked this of himself as he stood in the main road. He could go to the police and say he gave it to her, and that he'd got it out of the bin. But would they believe him? Wouldn't it be better if he went and saw the son and explained to him what he thought had happened—that the old girl, his mother, must have thrown the necklace away that day with all the rubbish, and when her jewellery and stuff was stolen she had imagined it had been taken then. It must have come out of that box with the bairns' toys.... The toys! That was an idea.... Bill's bairns might still have the toys. If Bill came along with him and said he'd picked up the toys for the bairns at the same time as he himself had taken the beads, then they would be more likely to believe him—or should he go by himself?

He stood pondering beside a lamp-post. My God! Just what should he do? If Bill came with him and became implicated, it might mean them both getting the sack for helping themselves. And Bill couldn't afford the sack. Every now and again somebody had to be a guinea pig and provide a test-case, and like as not they'd make this one, for there had been one or two rumpuses lately over totting.... But there was still Danny: he'd go to Danny; Danny would know what to do.

9. THE CHAMPION

When Mrs. D. opened the door, he almost pushed past her, saying, 'I'm sorry for disturbing you, but I've got to see Danny.'

'Yes. Well, come in,' said Mrs. D., laughing now at his back as he went along the passage. 'Is something wrong?'

Danny turned from the table, with his fork holding a melting-looking piece of buttered finnan haddock paused half-way to his mouth. The fork went to his plate again, and he asked, 'What's up, man?'

'Everything, I think,' said Rooney.

'Nothing that a cup of tea won't better,' said Mrs. D., going to the hob for the teapot.

'You know Nellie, the one at the house? She's been l...l... locked up,' he stammered in his agitation.

'Locked up!'

'Aye. They think she took the necklace—a ruby necklace.'

'A ruby necklace! What necklace?' Danny pushed back his chair.

'Here, drink this up,' said Mrs. D.

Rooney took the tea without the usual acknowledgements. 'What was stolen from the Bailey-Crawfords' place. But I gave it to her.'

'Look,' said Danny, 'drink that tea and then start at the beginning.'

Rooney took only a short sip from the cup, then put it down and rubbed his hand tightly over his mouth.

'It's like this. Some weeks since, I was pushing the muck back when I saw a box full of bairns' toys and beads. Bill took these for the bairns, and I saw a necklace affair and pocketed it, meaning to pass it on to Bill later. You see'—Rooney's eyes flicked downwards—'you came on the scene. And then it slipped me mind. And after I'd cleaned it up, it didn't look a bairn's piece, so ... so I give it to her ... Nellie. Well, when I got in the night, the house is up in arms. They'd been and taken her ... the polis. If she'd said where she'd got it, they would have been an' collared me afore now, but she must have kept mute, thinking I'd pinched the thing.'

'Well, I'll be damned!' Danny leant back in his chair and shook his head. 'I've told you, this is what comes of totting. I've told the lot of you time and time again.' He stood up and reached for his pipe off the mantelpiece. 'Now we're in a hell of a fix. You and Bill'll be for it in some way. As for me, who's supposed to be in charge of the damn lot of you, I'll be up on the carpet.'

'But they were only bairns' pieces, man.'

'Bairns' pieces,' said Danny. 'Bairns' pieces be damned! Ruby necklaces!'

'Aye. But don't you see, she must have thrown it away with the old toys.'

'The only thing I can see,' said Danny, 'is that this is going to cause a bit of a stink, whichever way it goes. What do you propose doing now?'

Rooney had come here to Danny thinking that he might supply a solution, but now, to his own surprise, he laid out the plan of action that he had himself thought of earlier. 'I was for going to Bill's to see if there's owt left of the bairns' toys, and taking them to the fellow ... the son, and asking him if he recognized them, and telling him how I came across the neck-lace.'

'Yes,' said Danny, 'you could do that.' And taking the action further, he went on, 'You could say that you took the bairns' toys an' all; that would cut Bill out, for you never know where this might end. He's got six bairns where you've only got your-self.'

'Yes, that's true,' said Rooney. 'Yes, I've been thinking about that. I'll say I picked up the lot.'

'Where's me coat?' said Danny.

'Where you going?' asked Mrs. D.

'To Bill's.'

'But your tea, Danny.'

'That can wait.... Come on.'

'I'm sorry, Mrs. D.,' said Rooney.

'That's all right,' she said. Then laughing, she added, 'Oh, Rooney, you do get into fixes. Never mind'—she patted his shoulder—'I'll come and visit you in jail. And look ... leave those slippers here.'

He handed her the slippers as he smiled weakly. 'There's many a true word spoken in a joke, Mrs. D.'

With the exception of Nancy, the eldest child, who let them in, Bill and his entire family were seated around the small table in the living-room. Bill rose, wiping his mouth, asking, 'What's up? Don't tell me it's Albert again, and the black fellow's back.'

'No, it's not him,' said Danny. 'Can we have a word with you?'

'Aye.' Bill looked at his brood. 'Come on. Get that stuff golloped up and get outside with you.'

Five pairs of eyes fixed themselves, first on Danny, then on Rooney, but there was no sign of golloping.

Bill signalled to his wife, who, with utter complacency, was eating a meat pie. 'Get them moving.'

'They've just started,' she said. 'Can't you go into the other room?'

Bill's face took on a slight tinge of colour as he retorted, 'No, we can't.'

'Here a minute.' Danny, taking Bill by the arm, moved to-wards the front door, and there, in a low voice, he roughly explained the situation.

But if Danny saw reason to keep the matter from the chil-dren, Bill did not, for coming back to the centre of the room, he cried, 'Now look, Danny, it's a sore point with me. I've said afore and I say again, what's chucked away belongs to nobody.'

Oh, my God! thought Rooney. He's not going to start on those lines now.

'That's all very well,' said Danny, 'but a woman's been pinched.'

'That's too bad, and it should never have happened, because stuff that's been classed as abandoned material——'

'Look, Bill.' Rooney quickly forestalled a debate on Bill's ideas of the moral rights of refuse. 'All I came for is to see if you've got any of the bits left, to help me prove they were picked up altogether.'

Bill turned to his wife. 'Those blocks and beads and things I brought for the bairns, where are they?'

'Oh'—she rose leisurely—'what's left of them should be in the bottom of the cupboard. Get down, Nancy, and look.'

Nancy got down. 'The monkey's broke,' she said, 'but the blocks are here.'

'There were beads . . . lots of beads,' said Bill.

Nancy stood up, saying nothing, but her hand went protectingly to her none-too-clean neck, where hung an assortment of different-coloured and -shaped beads.

'Look,' said Rooney, 'I'll buy you a fine strap for Christmas . . . pearls.'

'Will you?'

'Yes, I will, honest.'

Slowly, Nancy pulled the beads over her head and handed them to Rooney. Then going down on her knees again, she gathered up the bricks and the monkey.

'I'll say I picked the lot up together and later passed them on to you,' said Rooney to Bill.

'You'll say nowt of the sort; I'll stand by what I did, and I'll maintain what I said. . . . Once in the dustbin——'

'Aye, we know all about that, man,' impatiently put in Danny. 'But what about the court that recently took the view that the blokes on that particular corporation were stealing 'cause they picked out some lead from the loader?'

'I know all about that,' said Bill, 'but that was different . . . it was in the depot. And once it's in the shed it's Corporation property, but not afore.'

'You're splitting hairs, Bill. You take my advice and let Rooney do as he wants.'

'No bloody fear!'

'Be nice if you lost your job.'

Bill turned on his wife, growling, 'Damned good thing if I did! It'd make you go out and get some of that lazy fat off you.'

Mrs. Stubbly seemed in no way put out, but Rooney thought, This is marriage: and his mind made to leap away from the subject. But he stayed it. There were other marriages —Danny's, for instance, and many more like it.

'Well, what do you propose doing?' Bill turned to Rooney.

'I'm going to take these things up to the house and show them to the son. He seems a decent bloke.... I saw him this morning. And perhaps the old woman will remember that the necklace wasn't with the other jewellery. Perhaps she'll remember...'

'Aye, it is perhaps. Sounds a daft scheme to me. And that old girl always struck me as being up the pole a bit. She'll not be able to remember what she did or when she did it.'

'Not a bit of it,' put in Danny. 'She's all there.'

'Well, have your own way about her,' said Bill, 'but if you take my advice'—he had turned to Rooney—'you won't go near the house. Go to the polis station right away. If you go and see this fellow first, you could be brought up for intimidating witnesses or something.'

'Intimidating me grannie's aunt!' said Danny shortly. 'There's been no case yet. Look, Rooney, it's up to you. How do you feel about going to the station?'

How did he feel about it ... and everything else? He felt terrible.

'If you go to the fellow you'll still have to come back to the station,' warned Bill, ''cause remember, it's in the polis's hands now.'

Yes, he thought, there was that in it: he'd still have to face the police.

'Well, what's it to be?' asked Danny.

'I'll do as Bill says, I'll go to the station. But you needn't come, or Bill.'

'Go on, get moving.' Danny gave him a shove. 'Come on, Bill.'

'You won't forget me pearls, Mr. Rooney?' called Nancy as they went out.

'No,' said Rooney, 'I won't forget your pearls.'

'For a bloke who has nowt to do with women,' said Bill as they hurried down the street, 'you manage pretty well ... you get into more scrapes than a Hollywood film star.'

'Never mind talking of women,' said Danny. 'What we've got to make up our minds about is what Rooney's going to say.'

'That's simple,' put in Rooney. 'I'll just say I picked the stuff out of the loader and gave it to Bill's bairns later.'

'You know you'll likely be in for it from Bannister, and maybe the office?'

'Aye, I know all about that. But there are plenty of other jobs. I won't starve. Anyway, a change will do me good. Best thing that could happen, I think.'

Both Danny and Bill looked at him. But he did not answer their looks, for he was at the moment concerned with himself. Aye, perhaps it would be the best thing that could happen. What did it matter if the Corporation did give him the push? There were the shipyards, the mines, the factories. He'd get a better job, and, like Albert, make more money ... and for almost the same reason.

'What says you get ten years?' said Bill, as they entered the police station.

'Don't joke, man,' said Danny.

Rooney said nothing, until they were in the main office, and there it was he who answered the duty officer's enquiry as to what their business was.

'I'd like to see the inspector, please. It's ... it's about a woman you locked up the day. She was wearing a necklace, a ruby one ... I know where it came from.'

The policeman looked from one to the other, then said, 'Take a seat, will you?'

They did not sit down but watched him go out. And when he did not return for some minutes Bill, looking about him at the various notices on the walls, said, 'Gives you the willies, don't it? I'd swear me mother's life away to get out of here.'

Again Danny cautioned him: 'Be quiet, man!'

The policeman returned, and with him a sergeant and another man in plain clothes. The sergeant looked hard at Danny and said, 'Macallistair, isn't it?'

'Yes, sergeant.'

'Well now'—he looked at Bill and Rooney—'what can I do for you?'

'It concerns me,' said Rooney.

'Yes?'

'You took Nellie, Miss Atkinson, up because she was wearing

a necklace the day. She never stole it, I gave it to her.'

After a long stare at Rooney, the sergeant said, 'What's your name?'

'Joseph Rooney Smith.'

'Just a moment.' The sergeant walked to a door, knocked, then entered the room.

The policeman at the counter was now dealing with a man wanting to know whether a fountain pen he had brought in two months previously had yet been claimed. The plainclothes man was casually examining articles in various cubby holes, and Danny, Bill, and Rooney stood stock still waiting.

The door at the far end of the room opened again, and the sergeant appeared in the doorway, saying, 'Come in here, will you?'

One after the other, they went into the room, and the inspector sitting at the desk looked up at them.

'Which of you is Joseph Rooney Smith?'

'I am.'

'You want to make a statement?'

'Yes, sir. I want to tell you how Miss Atkinson got the necklace, and where I got it.'

'Go on.'

Rooney went on, surprising himself with his lucidity. But when he had finished, the inspector did not seem at all impressed, or convinced. He looked across at an officer sitting writing at a table at the opposite side of the room; he looked at Bill, then Danny; he looked at the beads, blocks, and the broken monkey reposing on his desk; and finally he looked at Rooney.

'You say you took these things out of the lorry. Have you any proof of this?'

'Yes.... No.'

'No? ... No proof?'

Rooney stopped himself from glancing towards Bill. He hadn't thought about proof. In a few words these blokes could twist you about till you didn't know which end of you was up or what you had said.

'That's a pity.'

Bill shuffled from one foot to the other.

'Mrs. Bailey Crawford, she would recognize them, and remember when she threw them away,' said Rooney. 'They're likely the son's toys. He might remember them, an' all.'

The inspector stared at him, then said slowly, 'Yes, you

might have something there. But it would have been better if you had...'

'He has got proof.' All eyes were now on Bill. 'He never took them things, I took them for me bairns. And Danny here'—Bill's head jerked sideways—'Danny's our overman, he was coming to the loader and he's dead nuts on us touching stuff, so I stuffed the bits in me pocket, and Rooney, seeing the red beads, pocketed them an' all. He meant to hand them over to me for the bairns, but he saw they wasn't a bairn's piece, that's about it.'

The inspector again said nothing for a moment. Then he asked, 'Why didn't you say this at first?'

Rooney cut in just as Bill was about to speak. 'Because he's got a big family, sir, and we'll likely get pulled over the coals and I didn't want him to get into trouble or anything. If it hadn't been for me taking the necklace there'd have been none of this. These'—he pointed to the table—'are only bairns' bits and no use to anybody. You can see that, sir.'

The inspector moved the blocks about with the point of his finger, and without raising his eyes said, 'You know there was quite a lot of plate and jewellery taken from the Bailey-Crawford residence?'

'Yes, I knew there had been a burglary.'

'When did you pick up the necklace?'

'Oh, it was afore that.'

'How long before?'

With the eyes of the others upon him, Rooney stood considering. 'It was on a Monday. I moved to my digs on a Saturday. Yes, it was on a Monday. It would be November ... November the twenty-first.'

'Are you sure of this?'

'Yes, sir; I'm sure.'

'Well, we'll be able to check this with Mrs. Bailey-Crawford. She'll remember when she threw the stuff away.'

'Let's hope so.' Bill's forefinger travelled the length of his nose.

'What?' The inspector's mild blue eyes were on Bill. 'Why do you say that?'

Bill moved his feet, then his shoulders, and then his head. 'Well, it appears to me the old girl's a bit 'centric. If you're to go by what she stuffs in her bin she must brew about six pounds of tea a week. Her bin's always full of wet tea-leaves. She lives on tea.'

The inspector's eyes lingered on Bill for some moments. Then without making any comment on this information he addressed Rooney. 'You know, of course, we'll have to go into all this?'

'Yes, sir.'

'Have you anything further to tell me?'

'No, sir, nothing. I've told you everything, and the truth. . . . Sir?'

'Yes.'

'Will you be able to let Miss Atkinson out now?'

'Well, we can't do that at the moment, Mr. Smith.'

Rooney's heart took a painful plunge downwards. 'But, sir, I . . . I swear it was me that gave it to her.'

'Why do you think she didn't say so when she was questioned?'

'Because . . . because, sir, she must have thought I'd pinched it, and . . . and . . .' The words, 'and she was shielding me', seemed to assume an almost sacredness, and he found it impossible to utter them. He knew that were he to speak them, the meaning that he dared not allow himself to recognize would fill the room and would be reflected from the five pairs of eyes as knowledge to be laughed at.

Yet without him going further there came an amused light into the eyes of the inspector, and a quirk to his lips as he asked, 'You know Miss Atkinson well?'

'No . . . that's . . . well, only six weeks.'

Bill coughed, and Rooney, without looking at him, thought, If he makes any funny cracks I'll hit him.

'Well, Mr. Smith, we'll have to contact Mrs. Bailey-Crawford.'

'Yes, sir.'

'And I don't think there's any need for you two to stay.' The inspector was now looking at Danny and Bill. And it was with something akin to disappointment in his voice that Bill said, 'But it was me what took the bits.'

'Well, that's a matter for the Corporation. We'll contact you if we need you. Leave your names and addresses in the office.'

Both Bill and Danny turned and looked at Rooney as the inspector continued, 'But we would like you to remain for a short while, Mr. Smith.'

'Yes, sir.' Rooney now sounded distinctly nervous, and Bill, unable to suppress a wisecrack even within the portals of the police station and the inner sanctuary itself, said, 'Well, so long, mate; see you in Durham.'

'Will you come along to us when you come out?' asked Danny, when they were once again in the outer office.

'That's heartening,' laughed Bill. 'When he comes out!'

'For God's sake shut up, Bill!' Danny turned away, saying, 'We'll expect you, lad.'

Rooney nodded, and when he saw them pass through the doorway a tiny feeling of panic assailed him.

'Take a seat,' said the policeman from behind the counter.

Rooney took a seat, and as he did so he glanced at the clock, and was amazed to see it was only a quarter to seven. He had seemed to have done so much and experienced so many different emotions since leaving work that he could not credit that it had all happened in under two hours.

The pendulum of the wall clock swung slower than that of any clock he had ever seen, and its hand took much longer to move from minute to minute. This was borne out when, after listening to the policeman answering the telephone numerous times, dealing with the report of a lost child, a purse theft, and an almost tearful boy giving notification of a stolen bicycle, the clock struck seven.

It was almost on its last stroke that the door opened and Mr. Bailey-Crawford entered. At the sight of him, Rooney half rose from his seat, then sat down again. The little man looked towards him, but without recognition, then went straight to the counter where he gave his name. A few seconds after the policeman had spoken into the phone, the office door opened and the sergeant came out, and when Rooney saw him take Mr. Bailey-Crawford in, he felt as if he was witnessing the retirement of the jury and that their verdict of guilty was a foregone conclusion. He had thought old Double-Barrelled's son a nice bloke, but no bloke appeared nice inside here if he was on the other side of you, so to speak. He could understand now Bill's saying that a fellow could be made to half swear his life away.... And Nellie; what in the name of God had she felt like when they brought her in? And what was she feeling like now? She was somewhere in here, likely in a cell. God in heaven! He got to his feet, and as he did so the policeman glanced up, and he went over to him.

'Miss Atkinson—you know, she's small ... slight, the one they brought in the day—where will she be? Is she in a cell?'

The policeman looked down at the counter and wrote something on a pad before saying, 'She's all right.'

'But is she in a cell?'

'They're not so bad as you think.' The policeman smiled.

Rooney rubbed his mouth, then turned his back on the counter and the policeman. This fellow was likely a Shields bloke, they were all likely Shields blokes, but they were all as foreign as men from another planet. He'd go barmy if this went on much longer. He could understand now why fellows made jail breaks ... there was something constricting even in the look of this policeman, although he seemed civil enough.

'Will you come in here a moment?'

'What? ... Oh.' Rubbing his lips, one over the other, he went once again into the inspector's office. And now Mr. Bailey-Crawford did recognize him, and his friendly tone when he said, 'Oh, it's you,' somehow lightened Rooney's burden.

'Yes, sir.'

'Well, we didn't expect to meet here, did we?' His manner was light, almost jovial.

'No, sir.'

'Mr. Bailey-Crawford recognizes these toys, Mr. Smith,' said the inspector.

Rooney's muscles relaxed and the tightness left his jaws.

'But we haven't as yet ascertained when they were thrown away.'

'Oh.'

The little man's head went back and his beard wagged. 'My mother will undoubtedly remember that. In fact, I could almost name the day myself. It would be when she received my letter saying that I was positively not coming to England again until she had made up her mind finally to leave the house and go into a flat, or home or something. Last year she had me over here five times on stupid pretexts ... maids leaving, the odd-job man dismantling the greenhouse and making off with it.'

The inspector checked the jovial flow with a laugh. 'I remember that. But now, if we may see her, and the date tallies with that given by Mr. Smith, we can then dispense with him.' The inspector looked at Rooney.

'Thank you, sir.'

'Can we see her tonight?'

'Yes, yes, of course. And I can well believe now that the necklace was thrown out with these things—she has never valued it. It belonged to my grandmother, and it was because I had seen her wearing it so often that I recognized it when I saw ... the person wearing it. That's a point.' Mr. Bailey-Crawford turned to Rooney. 'Why didn't she say you had given it to her?'

'We have been into that, Mr. Crawford,' said the inspector quietly, rising.

'Oh.' The little man's eyebrows moved upwards.

'Sir.'

'Yes?' The inspector's mild eyes appeared kindly as they rested on Rooney. 'About Miss Atkinson. If the dates tally, can she come out?'

'Yes, if the dates tally.'

There seemed to be still some doubt in the inspector's mind, and his mild tone brought a sickness into the pit of Rooney's stomach, as he went on, 'There is a point that needs clearing. Perhaps, you being a friend of hers, can throw some light on it. Miss Atkinson has recently been spending quite a bit of money. She has no known income and she has left her employment, so her aunt, Mrs. Howlett, tells me. When Miss Atkinson was asked where she got the money, all the information she would proffer was that it had been left to her.'

'Yes. Yes, it had.'

'Oh.'

'By her grandfather. Well, not her real grandfather ... Mrs. Howlett's father-in-law.... He thought the world of her, and she him. I read the letter meself.'

'Well, why didn't she say this?'

'She wouldn't want Ma, that's Mrs. Howlett, to know. They never hit it off. But you can easily tell if she's speaking the truth there by the solicitors who did the job for the old man. Before he died he went to them and got them to send her all he had.'

'Who was the solicitor?'

'Pomphrey & Mears ... Mr. Pomphrey.'

'Oh well, we can easily check on that in the morning.'

'In the morning!' Rooney both sounded and looked aghast. 'Do you mean you're going to keep her all night?'

'Now, now,. Mr. Smith, this isn't the Dark Ages.'

'No. No, I know, sir, but if you knew what she's gone through all these years living with Ma ... Mrs. Howlett. I've only been there six weeks, and it's nearly turned me white. Nellie's good, she's a good woman, she's——'

'All right, Mr. Smith. Now don't you worry. Would you like

to come along with us now?'

'Yes, sir.'

'Come on then.'

Outside, Rooney got into the back of the police car with the sergeant, while the inspector sat next to the driver. Mr. Bailey-Crawford had driven off in his own car, and within five minutes they were on the drive of Honeycroft, and, as he stepped in through the front door, Rooney could not help but ponder on the strangeness of life, for who would have thought this morning when he moved the bin that this evening he would be going in by the front door with the police?

'Come in here,' said Mr. Bailey-Crawford, ushering them into a large room that reminded Rooney of Grandpa's, so crammed was it with furniture.

'We would like to see your mother alone for a moment,' said the inspector.

'Yes, yes, of course.'

Left alone in the room, Rooney stood by a massive, deeply carved table, and glanced about him. It was evident that the whole place was in need of a duster, yet it looked lived in, for a large coal fire was blazing in the grate and a small table holding a tray with a tarnished silver coffee jug and two cups on it stood by a much-worn leather chair. At another time the furniture would have caught his interest, but now it brought up no comment in his mind other than that it might be grand stuff but it was much too big. How long, he wondered, would it take the old girl to remember? What if she couldn't remember, or if she swore she hadn't thrown it away?

There was a commotion in the hall, and the door was thrust open.

'All this fuss about nothing! Why couldn't you come to me at first?'

'Now, Mama.'

'Be quiet! You treat me like a half-wit.... Why couldn't you find the people who stole my Sevres and my Georgian silver?'

As the old lady stamped across the room, Rooney thought that she looked a bit different from when he had seen her last, for her hair was not hanging about her face but was now in looped strands, neatly coiled on her head, and she was dressed in blue velvet. It looked an old-fashioned dress, the skirt trailing on the ground, but she no longer looked the poor old wife he had felt sorry for, but a noble old woman, and much more awe-inspiring.

She stopped for a moment at the sight of him, and, as her son had done earlier, she exclaimed, 'Oh! it's you.'

'Yes, mam.'

'And it was you who picked up the necklace from out of the dustbin?'

'Yes, mam.'

'You were a fool. That necklace has caused more trouble in this family than enough. It belonged to my husband's mother —she was a hateful old harridan. That's all she left me, and she put a curse on it.'

'Mama!'

'Be quiet!' She rounded on her son. 'She did. Doesn't this prove it, getting this man into trouble and locking up a woman? I did not throw it away by mistake, I threw it away to get rid of it ... as I threw away all your things that I'd cherished for years, because you don't know your duty as a son. Sit down!' This was to Rooney.

Slowly, and with his eye on the inspector who was standing in the doorway, Rooney slid into a chair.

'And don't stand in that door. Come in or go out, I hate draughts!'

Much to Rooney's amazement, the inspector did as he was ordered, and was followed by the sergeant, who closed the door gently after him. The old lady seated herself by the fire. Then after allowing a pause, she looked straight at the inspector and said, 'Now that this stupid mistake has been rectified I feel that there is an apology owing to this man.' With a somewhat theatrical gesture, she indicated Rooney with a sweep of her arm.

Rooney, not daring to look at any one of them, said, 'That's all right, mam.'

'It isn't all right. Hasn't this woman, this friend of yours, been put in jail? It's Freda they should have put in jail. But you can't find Freda, can you?'

When the inspector did not answer, she went on, 'Freda was too clever for you ... she planned her work. She must have had every piece in this house worth anything checked. And now she's most probably in somebody else's house, busily checking there. All she had to do was to dye her hair again.'

'Mama, be quiet.'

Rooney glanced covertly at the inspector. He was smiling; he even seemed to be enjoying the old girl. But when he spoke, there was no trace of amusement in his voice, only a certain deference. 'You're likely right, mam, but we do our poor best.'

'That's a very good word for it.'

The inspector cleared his throat. 'We must go now. Good night, mam. Are you coming, Mr. Smith?'

'Yes. Yes, sir.' He rose hastily, then turning to the old lady, said, 'Good night, mam.'

'Good night, and don't let them frighten you.'

'No, mam. Good night.'

In the porch and out of hearing of his mother, and between a laugh and a sigh, Mr. Bailey-Crawford said, 'I wish I was back in France.'

The inspector smiled. 'I can see you've got your work cut out. When are you returning?'

'As soon as I can find somebody to look after her. She just flatly refused to leave this house, and I can't get anyone to live in. I've even offered the old coachman's house rent free with added baits in return for some small services for her. But can I get a couple? No. They all want the rooms, in fact offer rent for them, but as for doing anything in the way of domestic help, it seems to horrify most of them.'

'Yes, it is a problem. But at least we've solved one tonight. Yours, Mr. Smith.'

The inspector had a way of turning a conversation, and Rooney was brought back from a startling prospect that had suddenly been conjured up in his mind by Mr. Bailey-Crawford's remarks.

'Yes, sir. Is everything all right now?'

'Well, we'll go back to the station and then we'll be able to tell you. Good night, sir. I'm sorry we've put you to so much trouble.'

'Oh that's all right. I'm glad it's been cleared up. Well, good night.... Good night, Smith. Sorry about everything.'

'Good night, sir.'

In the car once more, the inspector began to laugh, and to no one in particular he said, 'I bet that old girl leads him a life. His garret in Paris must appear like paradise after a week-end at home.'

'He's a painter, sir, isn't he?' said the sergeant.

'Yes. Becoming quite well known too, in more ways than one ... divorced three times.'

'Oh yes? Well.' They both laughed. And Rooney thought, That's it. I couldn't place him, with him being so free and easy, and chatty. But if he's an artist...

Once more they went through the main room and into the inspector's office. And there the officer behind the desk rose and handed the inspector a typewritten paper.

Rooney watched him as he read. He watched the slow movement of his hands as he folded the sheet in two and put it on his desk, saying, 'There, then, that's that.'

Rooney waited.

The inspector sat down and joined his hands, resting them on the desk.

'Well, everything seems in order now, Mr. Smith. Mr. Pomphrey has vouched for Miss Atkinson as to where she got her money. I may want her to meet Mr. Pomphrey tomorrow, just a matter of mutual recognition, but I think we can safely say that everything is all right. I'll just have a word with her before she goes.'

Relief made Rooney giddy. 'Thank you, sir.'

'Go with the sergeant now and you'll see Miss Atkinson in a minute. And if I may advise you, close your eyes when you see a ruby necklace in future.'

Rooney smiled sheepishly. 'You bet, sir. If I see the Crown Jewels in a bin, I'll cover them up. Good night, sir.'

'Good night, Mr. Smith.'

He felt almost gay as he went into the main office, but as the sergeant left him with, 'I won't keep you a minute, a wave of shyness filled him with painful confusion. What would he say to her? How could he thank her for trying to shield him? Would she feel bitter?

But whatever her reactions would be, there was one thing he knew for certain: for him, life was changed, nothing would ever be on the old humdrum level again after all this set-to. Sitting before strange fireplaces, surrounded by his bits was going to be devoid of even comfort now, for his furniture had suddenly become meaningless. It was most disturbing, but he really didn't care if he never saw it again, unless...

There she was, looking more like a child than ever against the blue largeness of the sergeant. Her face was white like it had been when he first saw her, and although her expression was strained her eyes held no bitterness. He moved slowly towards her.

'Hallo, Nellie.'

'Hallo.'

He could hardly hear her voice.

The inspector appeared behind her in the doorway. He looked jovial; the sergeant looked jovial; the policeman behind the counter looked jovial; the man and woman standing before the counter looked interested. Rooney buttoned up his coat, stretched his neck out of his collar, and said, 'We'd better be getting along.'

Nellie's eyes drooped as she moved from the shelter of the sergeant to his side.

'Good night.' It was Rooney's final word.

'Good night,' they all said together.

He opened the door, and Nellie passed out before him into the corridor. In the lobby there was a maze of doors and corridors, but without hesitation or touching her he led her to the main entrance. Only let them get outside of here and they would talk . . . he would talk. Never before could he remember such an overwhelming desire to talk.

He opened the outer door, and there, at the foot of the steps, was the street. And for a moment it looked wonderful, until from out of the shadow of the lamp-post moved two figures, Danny and Bill.

Swearing had never been a form of expression with Rooney —he had always told himself he left that to Bill—but now he was in a good way to outdoing even Bill. Why had they to be here at this particular moment? This was the time for him to say what he had to say: he was full of words and his mouth appeared oiled for their flow.

'By, mate, we thought they'd pushed you along the line. Evening, Miss.' This from Bill.

'We had to come back, lad. Just a bit worried. How do you do?' Danny inclined his head towards Nellie. 'You've had a bit of a nasty do, Miss.'

'It was an experience.' There was a little smile in Nellie's eyes.

'I'd say,' said Bill. 'And how did you come off?' he asked of Rooney.

And Rooney, feeling all churned up inside and wishing Bill in the warmest region he knew of, answered, 'Oh, it's a long story. And . . . and she's tired, she wants to get home.'

Nellie looked up at him. And in her eyes he saw a touch of the anxiety that had once been their permanent expression. 'I can't go back there tonight . . . I couldn't face them tonight. Tomorrow I'll have to go and see to Grandpa, but tonight I'll get a room somewhere.'

Rooney looked down into her face. 'Come back to Danny's place with us. She can, can't she, Danny?'

'Yes. Aye, the wife's expectin' us.'

As if Danny and Bill were not there, Rooney held her eyes and entreated softly, 'Mrs. D.'s nice, you'll like her.'

'It's kind of you.' She meant this for Danny, but her eyes stayed on Rooney's until she turned and moved away.

Rooney walked by her side, with Danny and Bill behind, and without further words they cut up a side-street and into the market place, and from there took a tram. And when they alighted in Eldon Street, Rooney did something that surprised himself still further. Pulling Bill to one side, he said, 'Will you mind, man, not coming along with us now? She's gone through a bit the day, you understand?'

Bill's look did not convey his understanding, but it showed how deeply he was offended. 'Well, if that's how you feel. I only came because I didn't want to see you in a mess.'

'Yes, I know, man. And it was good of you, and I'll not forget it, and I'll tell you about things the morrow.'

'To hell with the morrow!'

'Good night, Danny.' It was Bill's only salute, and showed the extent of his pique.

Blast! thought Rooney, as Bill marched off. Yet it was far better that he should take the pip than be given the chance to start his wisecracking in front of her the night. Somehow it had become a matter of importance that the folks she met who were connected with him should be nice, and a bit refined like: and, to his mind, there was nobody further removed from this description than Bill, or better fitted for it than Mrs. D. But, had he been allowed to get going, Bill's patter would have swamped Mrs. D.'s refinement.

Mrs. D. greeted Nellie as if she were an old friend, and straight away offered her her solace for all ills, a cup of tea. And although she talked as she trotted back and forth, setting the table for a meal, her patter did not seem to put Nellie at her ease. There she sat, in the armchair at one side of the fireplace, relieved of her hat and coat and looking, to Rooney's eyes, more lost than ever. Guilt weighed heavily upon him. It was being shut up in that place that had done this ... pushed her back to where she was before she had got the money.

Alone with her, Danny having gone into the back-yard to get some coal and Mrs. D. being occupied in the scullery, he smiled at her, and said, 'They're nice, aren't they? I've known them most of me life. They're the best friends I've got.'

'Yes.' To him the syllable had a funny cracked sound, his smile faded. She continued to look at him, then, to his utter consternation, she began to cry. In almost as much distress as herself, he watched her gripping her throat as if to cut off the sound trying to escape, and he rose hastily, exclaiming in a helpless fashion, 'Don't, Nellie, don't!' His hand went out to her shoulder, but instead of a tentative touch quietening her distress, it acted as a spring for its release. Her face now buried in her hands, the sound of her sobbing filled the house and brought Mrs. D. from the scullery.

'There, there, that's the best thing you could do. Just you cry it out, hinny. And you know what I think?' Mrs. D. was holding Nellie to her now. 'Bed. Bed'll be the best place. And in the morning you'll feel a new woman. There now, there now.'

'I'm ... I'm so sorry.'

'There's nothing to be sorry for, lass. Have another cup of tea. Pour one out, Rooney.'

As Rooney hastily did as he was bidden, Nellie said between gasps, 'It's ... it's the kindness. You're ... all so kind.'

'Kind? We've done nothing yet. Here now, drink this.' Mrs. D. took the cup from Rooney and continued, 'I'll fix the couch in the front room for you. It's fitted Rooney, so it'll fit you all right. There now, that's better.' She stood back from Nellie as she drank the tea, and turning to Danny, who had come back into the kitchen, she said, 'Give me a hand, will you?'

'Aye. I'll just wash me hands.'

Two minutes later Danny followed his wife out of the room, and Rooney slowly and deliberately pulled up a chair to face Nellie. He took a deep breath, pulled at his collar, and opened his mouth. But to his utter consternation the oiled words filling his brain refused to flow. He knew now what he wanted to say—aye, he knew all right—but there they were, sticking in his throat. He could have said them pat at the police station, for the glow of high adventure was still on him then, and Nellie had just been snatched, as it were, from danger. But now things had simmered down and the words just would not come.

'I'm sorry I went on like that,' Nellie said softly.

'That's all right.'

'I suddenly felt'—she handed him the cup, then clasped her

hands tightly in her lap before adding—'so lost ... of not belonging anywhere. That awful feeling of aloneness. You know?'

This was a good enough cue, but he couldn't take it, for he suddenly thought of Mrs. D. and Danny next door ... what if they should come in in the middle of what he had to say. That'd be worse than never starting at all.

'It's ... it's the loss of Grandpa,' he said, 'making you feel like this.'

'Yes, that's it, I suppose.'

'And ... and being in that place all day. Were they awful?'

'Oh no, they were rather kind. But the place was awful. Something about it.'

'Why ... why did you do it, Nellie?' He leaned slightly forward. And she looked down at her hands, and her voice was small as she said, 'You had been kind to me, it ... it was nice to be able to do something for you. At least I thought I was doing something. But it's like Grace says, I'm a fool.'

'You're not.... Her!' At the sound of Ma's name, his new self erupted to the surface again, making him feel as he had done earlier in the evening, capable of conquering the world ... if it was only with his fists.

'By!' he said, 'it's a wonder I didn't hit her an' all the night.'

Nellie's head came up. 'You hit someone?'

'Dennis.' There was a quirk to his lips and a sly smile in his eyes. 'It was a nice feel.'

'Oh, Rooney.'

The gentle chiding made him lower his head.

'He went out like a light.' His eyes lifted and met hers, and their glances held and mingled as he went on sheepishly, 'I'm a bit scared of going back; I might be tempted to try it on again ... with Ma.'

'Oh, Rooney.' The little smile broadened; then suddenly died away, and making a small movement with her head she said, 'I'll have to go back; I'll have to get my things. I saw the undertaker about Grandpa this morning. They're burying him on Tuesday. I must get my things away before then.... I couldn't go back after he's gone.'

'What are you going to do, I mean, after?'

'I'll get a job.'

'Nellie....' He moved on to the edge of his chair. 'Nellie, would you mind doing a job like ... like service, looking after someone?'

She was staring at him, her face soft now and full of a shy youthfulness. Gently she answered, 'No, I wouldn't mind, Rooney.'

He watched her lips as they rounded his name. He had never heard that daft name sound so sweet. He swallowed and moved restlessly. 'Well ... you know the ... the old lady who owns the necklace, Mrs. Bailey-Crawford ... well, her son wants somebody just to keep an eye on her. And they can have the coachman's house. The son was telling the inspector the night. Would ... would you take it?'

He watched the brightness fade from her eyes, and when she said, 'Yes,' her voice was flat and heavy with weariness.

'I just thought,' he said lamely, 'it might suit you.'

'Yes; yes, it would. Oh yes, I'm sure it would.'

He saw that she was making an effort. She was tired out; he couldn't expect her to appear over the moon about anything the night, anyway.

'I'll have to find some place meself, an' all. Later on, I'm going along to the chap who usually moves me. I'm putting me things in store with him until I look round.'

There fell a silence between them, and he was almost glad when Danny and Mrs. D. came out of the front room.

'There then, it's all ready when you are.' Quite abruptly, Mrs. D. took hold of Nellie's arm and raised her to her feet, saying, 'Come along, my dear.'

'Good night,' said Nellie quietly.

'Good night,' said Rooney.

'Good night, Mr. Macallistair, and thank you.'

'Good night, lass. And sleep well.'

Danny watched his wife and Nellie out of the room; then going to the mantelpiece, he took up his pipe, knocked it on the hob, and exclaimed, 'Well, you didn't get it over then?'

'Get what over?'

Danny turned round. 'Rooney, I'm not given to swearing, but I'm going to say now, you're a bloody fool. I thought after you had the spunk to push Bill off ... Oh, what's the use!' He turned to the fireplace again.

The colour mounted to Rooney's hair. They had been in there waiting, listening ... his two friends. He pushed back his shoulders and buttoned up his coat, but all he said was, 'I'm off to the phone.'

Bloody fool, was he? Now, remembering the almost dead look on Nellie's face, he supposed he was. 'Would you like to 'look after someone?' he had asked. But Danny and Mrs. D. listening! He wouldn't have credited it. What if he had asked her? The sweat ran down his face at the thought.

10. AS YOU WERE

At half-past nine the following morning Rooney walked out of Danny's with Nellie, feeling a variety of emotions, not the least among them, irritation. And this against Mrs. D. of all people. She knew he had to be at the Bailey-Crawford's house afore ten, and there she had been, for the past half-hour, with Nellie in the front room. Natter, natter, natter. He had listened to her voice going on and on until he had positively begun to dislike the sound of it. His restless night, spent rolled up in blankets on the mat, had not fortified him for today, and now he was feeling at an acute disadvantage walking under the cold hard sunshine with Nellie, and her got up in her best.

On the other hand, Nellie seemed to be fully recovered. In fact, her whole manner was a trifle disconcerting. She seemed almost like she was when she had first come into the money, except for the pain of Grandpa's loss still in her eyes.

He said, for the second time that morning, 'I feel I should have gone back to seventy-one and changed.'

'Oh, you look quite all right. And I doubt whether you'd have got in. If she guessed it was you she'd have pretended to be asleep.'

'Yes, perhaps you're right.'

They boarded a bus and sat in silence until they came to the Fountain, but when they had alighted Nellie said, 'It'll be odd if I get this place, for I've always had a longing to live in Westoe.'

'You have?'

'Yes.'

He quickened his step, almost causing her to trot alongside him. It would be just like the thing, wouldn't it, if someone had stepped in afore them. But the son had said last night on the phone that he'd be only too pleased to see her, and that if his mother took to her it'd suit everybody.... Still, you never knew.

'There, that's the house ... the top of it, behind yon trees.'

'It's big.'

'Yes, and it's in a mess inside ... I'd better warn you.'

'Oh, that won't matter.'

'Well, here we are.' He rang the bell, not of the back but of the front door, as he spoke; then smiled at her. And she smiled back at him. And somehow he felt better.

'Oh, hallo, Smith. Come in. By!' Mr. Bailey-Crawford stopped Nellie as she passed him, 'you're small, aren't you?'

'Yes, I am rather.'

'Make me feel quite a giant. Look, come into the kitchen, will you? I'll tell my mother in a minute.'

When they were in the kitchen and the door closed, he looked hard at Nellie, saying, 'You're a surprise, you know. I had imagined some great bustling dame'—his eyes slipped to Rooney—'someone who could manage mother. Well, not exactly manage her—no one will do that, I'm afraid—but ...'

'I'm used to looking after people. I've seen to my ... my grandfather for years.'

Mr. Bailey-Crawford laughed. 'He, I feel, wouldn't come up to my mother. I'd better warn you she's rather a tartar; I don't want to give you the wrong impression. Smith here has met her.' He turned to Rooney. 'She's no docile old lady, is she?'

'Well, sir, no.... But I rather took to her.'

'Yes, that's funny, for she likes you too. Well, now, Miss ...?'

'Atkinson.'

'Well, Miss Atkinson, there's not a great deal of money in it—two pounds a week and the coach-house free. It will make a nice flat, but it wants seeing to. But if you shouldn't like sleeping there alone you can sleep in the house....'

'And who, may I ask, is going to sleep in the house? Didn't I tell you to let me know when she arrived?'

The old lady, aided by a silver-topped cane, sailed into the kitchen, immediately filling the room with her presence and bringing on it a silence. She fixed her gimlet eyes on Nellie. And Nellie returned the look quietly but unsmiling.

'You're small ... you look like a child.'

'I'm quite strong, madam.'

'Have you been in service before?'

'No, madam.'

'Then how do you know you can do what is required?'

'I can but try ... I have looked after my grandfather ...'

'I don't want to be looked after.' The old lady glanced fiercely at her son. But what retort she was about to make was checked as a pain attacked her leg, causing her to wince. Whether her son or Rooney would have dared to aid her to a seat cannot be known, but Nellie did. Quietly she put her hand on the back of a dusty wheel-back chair, and turning it about, placed it near the old lady.

Mrs. Bailey-Crawford stared at her for a moment before sitting down. 'How old are you?'

'Thirty-four.'

'You don't look it. What's your name?'

'Nellie. Nellie Atkinson.'

'Hm.... Well, let's get some points clear.' She nodded her white head briskly. 'I'm not in my dotage. Also I might inform you there are no more valuables left in this house to steal. Moreover, no matter how nice you are or what you do, you'll be left nothing in my will, for I have nothing to leave ... but this old house, which will be turned into flats the minute I'm gone.'

Rooney's heart sank; he lowered his eyes away from Nellie ... she'd never stick the old girl.

'What do you consider the most important thing in a house?' The old lady's voice sounded like that of an army commander.

'Warmth.' Nellie's tone was full of deep sincerity as she made this statement, and Rooney glanced up to find her looking at the old woman with the kindly light in her eyes that she had kept for Grandpa, and he thought, with surprise, she likes her.

'What are you two to each other?' The old eyes flicked between them, and as Rooney searched wildly to give an answer, Nellie replied quietly, 'Friends. We're friends.'

'Pity; I'd have liked him round about. It's a nice coach-house; he could have done odd jobs.'

Rooney's colour had reached his hair when the son took pity on him. 'I'll show Miss Atkinson the rooms, Mama, and let her decide.'

'She can't sleep over there all alone, she'll have to sleep in.' There was a command in both voice and eyes.

But Nellie replied quietly, 'I'd prefer a ... a flat, madam, if I may?' The small wrinkled eyes and the large brown ones

171

held. Then the old lady's switched away. 'Very well. Go and see it. You won't like it; the rain comes in, and the fire smokes.... Go on....' She waved them all out.

In the yard Mr. Bailey-Crawford wiped his perspiring brow. 'You see what I mean?' he said.

'No,' said Nellie, with what to Rooney appeared to be alarming frankness. 'I only see that she is old and very lonely, and'—she paused—'so vulnerable.'

The little bearded man stopped and looked at her before saying, with something of a shamefaced look, 'Yes, perhaps you're right. I hope you decide to stay. She took to you, although you mightn't think it. I should stay with her, but I can't, and she won't leave the house.' Quickly he turned away and moved on ahead of them towards the coach-house.

Here he unlocked the door by the side of what appeared to be a converted garage. 'Mind,' he warned, 'the staircase is dark and a bit cobwebby.'

The staircase leading to the rooms above was dark and cobwebby, but when they stepped from the top of the stairs directly into the centre of a large room they both stood and stared about in surprise, for windows on two sides flooded the room with light, and on the side opposite the courtyard they looked directly on to a roof of tangled trees that had once been the orchard.

'This could be your living-room. There are two other rooms, but the unfortunate thing is they all run out of each other. The last is the kitchen ... through here.... This is the bedroom——' He stopped in the second room. 'It has a fine view, that is if you like trees. In the spring it's a picture. And here's the kitchen. It's not bad really, although it doesn't look much at the present moment. The water has been coming in a bit.' He pointed to the corner above the sink. 'It was a stopped gutter, but I cleared it. I think you'll find it all right now.' He addressed his remarks to Nellie, and Rooney stood back from them, looking about the kitchen. There was an open range, besides an electric stove; the sink was good and the floor was covered with red lino. The room only wanted a coat of paint to make it look grand. It was large enough for a couple of easy chairs and a good-sized table ... and a dresser.

'Well, there it is.' Mr. Crawford now looked from one to the other. 'Do you mind if I leave you to have a look around?'

'No, no, not at all,' said Nellie.

'Call in when you're finished.'

'Thank you.'

As they heard his steps going down the stairs they turned to each other, and Rooney was the first to speak. 'It's fine, isn't it?'

'Yes.'

He couldn't make much of her reply. And when, abruptly, she moved out of the kitchen and through the centre room into the big room, he followed her, thinking, She's not taken with it; it's not modern enough for her. And he recalled her enthusiasm for the furniture in the magazine.... He watched her walk to the window and look down into the garden for a moment, before turning to face him. There was almost the width of the room between them now, and suddenly, there was the width of the world, of taste, of temperament.

'It's not very modern,' he said quietly.

'No,' she said, 'it's not.'

There came a dull hurt ache beneath his ribs. He was filled with a sadness that almost made him sick. To him the place was wonderful, like a palace dropped from the sky and come to rest on the treetops, but to her ... it wasn't modern. It just showed how different people could be. The ache became an acute pain. No two people could make a go of it, thinking like that. She was different. Hadn't he known she was. That night in the kitchen with the magazine, he knew then that she aspired to things, things that he would never possess, because he would never want them.

He made himself say, 'Perhaps you could make it do until you look out for something else?' His voice was as cold as his heart now.

'Yes, perhaps I could.... Rooney?'

'Yes?'

'Are you blind?'

'Blind?'

'Yes, blind.... Or don't you want to see? Can't you see I don't want a modern house ... or anything? All I said about modern furniture that night was just talk, don't you know that? I love your brass bed, and your chairs and your dresser, and everything you have, don't you see?...' Her voice dropped to a whisper, but a clear whisper. 'All I want is you, Rooney.'

The floor dragged at him, staying the wild leap of his body to her, but the space between them widened, making room for what he had to say, what he must say. Even in this moment, his cards must be put face up on the table.

'There's one or two things you've got to know, Nellie. I'll never be other than I am. I've had to face it—I've no ambition. All I want is to stay put, in the same job; to know that I'm safe. Yesterday I thought I wouldn't mind changing, but I would. What's more, I'm like all them back in seventy-one ... I'm ignorant. I could never keep up with you, or go to your Literary Societies and things.'

'Oh!' Her voice cracked on the exclamation, cutting off his flow, and her great brown eyes sent the tears flooding over her face. Yet in the same instant she threw back her head and laughed. 'Literary Societies!' Then moving only one step towards him, she whispered across the distance, 'I want you to stay put, never to change ... never ... your outlook, or your furniture, or anything about you, ever.'

For a moment she became lost to his sight.

'Don't you want me, Rooney?'

The last words brought her into focus again. She was only a few steps away from him now. There she stood, like a young girl, her white face even whiter and her eyes even larger. His throat swelling, his heart pounding, he thrust out his arms, and pulled her against him. And as she smothered her crying in his shoulder an uplifting feeling of wonderment filled him, and her words came back to him: 'What are we here for? What does it all mean?' Well, he knew now.

TWO NOVELS BY CATHERINE COOKSON AS CATHERINE MARCHANT

THE FEN TIGER
by CATHERINE MARCHANT

In a lonely mill house deep in the wild fen country, Rosamund Morley lived a cloistered, poverty-stricken existence with her sister Jennifer and her alcoholic father. Rosamund was the prop and stay of the family – and it was she who ran for help the night her father set his bed alight after a drinking bout. That night was to change the course of Rosamund's life – for, fleeing through the woods, she encountered Michael Bradshaw, the long-absent owner of Thornby House. He appeared rude, abrupt, and arrogant, and Rosamund immediately christened him the 'Fen Tiger'.

When she knew more of Michael's past and the fate that had forced him to live in isolation, Rosamund's initial feelings of dislike changed to compassion . . . and then to something deeper . . .

0 552 10074 9   £1.75

HOUSE OF MEN
by CATHERINE MARCHANT

Tor-Fret was a lonely old house high on the Northumberland fells. And when Kate Mitchell applied for a job as part-time secretary there she had no knowledge of the strange household that was comprised only of men . . .

Her employer, Maurice Rossiter, was an embittered victim of polio, subject to fits of temper and depression. Kate could not understand his peculiar hatred of his elder brother, Logan on whose charity he was forced to depend. It wasn't until she accidentally saw Maurice and Logan's fiancée together that she began to realise some of the secrets of Tor-Fret, and suddenly, against her will, she was becoming involved too deeply, with Logan Rossiter and the other inhabitants of this mysterious household . . .

0 552 09796 9   £1.75

A SELECTED LIST OF CATHERINE COOKSON NOVELS IN CORGI

WHILE EVERY EFFORT IS MADE TO KEEP PRICES LOW, IT IS SOMETIMES NECESSARY TO INCREASE PRICES AT SHORT NOTICE. CORGI BOOKS RESERVE THE RIGHT TO SHOW NEW RETAIL PRICES ON COVERS WHICH MAY DIFFER FROM THOSE PREVIOUSLY ADVERTISED IN THE TEXT OR ELSEWHERE.

THE PRICES SHOWN BELOW WERE CORRECT AT THE TIME OF GOING TO PRESS (MARCH '86).

☐	08700 9	THE BLIND MILLER	£1.95
☐	11160 0	THE CINDER PATH	£1.95
☐	08774 2	FANNY McBRIDE	£1.95
☐	09318 1	FEATHERS IN THE FIRE	£1.95
☐	08353 4	FENWICK HOUSES	£1.95
☐	10916 9	THE GIRL	£2.50
☐	08849 8	THE GLASS VIRGIN	£2.50
☐	10267 9	THE INVISIBLE CORD	£2.50
☐	08251 1	KATE HANNIGAN	£1.95
☐	08056 X	KATIE MULHOLLAND	£2.95
☐	09720 9	THE MALLEN STREAK	£2.50
☐	09896 5	THE MALLEN GIRL	£2.50
☐	10151 6	THE MALLEN LITTER	£2.50
☐	11350 6	THE MAN WHO CRIED	£2.50
☐	08653 3	THE MENAGERIE	£1.75
☐	08980 X	THE NICE BLOKE	£1.95
☐	09373 4	OUR KATE (Illustrated)	£1.95
☐	09596 6	PURE AS THE LILY	£2.50
☐	10630 5	THE TIDE OF LIFE	£2.95
☐	11737 4	TILLY TROTTER	£2.50
☐	11960 1	TILLY TROTTER WED	£2.50
☐	12200 9	TILLY TROTTER WIDOWED	£1.95
☐	12368 4	THE WHIP	£2.50
☐	08821 8	A GRAND MAN	£1.50
☐	52141 8	LANKY JONES	85p

Writing as Catherine Marchant

☐	10074 9	THE FEN TIGER	£1.75
☐	10030 7	HERITAGE OF FOLLY	£1.95
☐	09796 9	HOUSE OF MEN	£1.75
☐	10780 8	THE IRON FACADE	£1.75
☐	10321 7	MISS MARTHA MARY CRAWFORD	£1.95
☐	10541 4	THE SLOW AWAKENING	£2.50

All these books are available at your book shop or newsagent, or can be ordered direct from the publisher. Just tick the titles you want and fill in the form below.

CORGI BOOKS, Cash Sales Department, P.O. Box 11, Falmouth, Cornwall.

Please send cheque or postal order, no currency.

Please allow cost of book(s) plus the following for postage and packing:

U.K. Customers—Allow 55p for the first book, 22p for the second book and 14p for each additional book ordered, to a maximum charge of £1.75.

B.F.P.O. and Eire—Allow 55p for the first book, 22p for the second book plus 14p per copy for the next seven books, thereafter 8p per book.

Overseas Customers—Allow £1.00 for the first book and 25p per copy for each additional book.

NAME (Block Letters) ....

ADDRESS ....

....